DRETHI ANIS

LUST

THE SEVEN SINS SERIES

LUST

THE SEVEN SINS SERIES

DRETHI ANIS

COPYRIGHT

OTHER BOOKS IN SERIES

BOOK 1: GREED

BOOK 2: LUST

BOOK 3: ENVY

BOOK 4: GLUTTONY

BOOK 5: WRATH

BOOK 6: SLOTH

BOOK 7: PRIDE

Next book in the Series is Envy follow this Universal Link: https://books2read.com/EnvySevenSins

BLURB

Heavily Inspired by The Book of Tobit

Lace, white, everything frilly and pretty. The theme to Sara's life used to be that of a princess, one she romanticized. But when her previously perfect world turned upside down, Sara became convinced that she was cursed. She hid herself in the shadows to spare others from the agony she brought along.

The only person she could never hide from was her adopted brother.

Tristan Marcolf wasn't the run-of-the-mill rich and successful politician. It was his ethereal good looks that left others bewildered. So much so, they wondered if his looks were a gift from God. Only Tristan suspected that the gift wasn't from God at all, but from the Devil. Because the cursed gift gave him everything he wished for, except for the one thing he truly desired.

His adopted sister, Sara.

With Tristan's unquenchable thirst for Sara spiraling out of control, the Demon of Lust, Asmodeus, rejoiced in the victory, for he loved to play with mortals. He had orchestrated the perfect setting to prove to God that humans would choose pleasures of the flesh and materialistic desires over the simplicity of LOVE. The two souls set out to prove him wrong and humble his vanity, but rarely do demons give in without a fight.

***There are no heroes in this dark PNR series, only villains. It consists of explicit content, dubious, and graphic situations that some readers might find offensive.*

To Brooklyn, Dylan, Marissa, Billie, Talli, and Tara.
It was an honor to write with you all. I'm as humbled as our demons will be by the end of this series. Love you.

Acknowledgments

Thank you to the wonderful Angie Hazen for sweating profusely and having panic attacks on behalf of my procrastinating self.

Thank you, Julia, for hopping on board last minute and staying on top of it.

A special thanks to Alexis & Ashley for your nonstop support of indie authors.

Thank you to my wonderful Beta readers—Alice, Tori, Robin, Erin, Ashley, Lindsey—for making my insane deadlines.

Last but not least, a huge shout out to Maria, Kathy, Crystal, Kelly, Karen, and Jill. All of you have followed me throughout this journey from the very beginning without wavering. You have no idea how much that means to me.

Each and every one of you on this page fills my heart with warmth.

Playlist

Speechless - Dan and Shay

Take Me to Church - by Hozier

Dirty Little Secret - The All-American Rejects

Play with Fire - Sam Tinnesz and Yacht Money

YES MOM - Tessa Violet

"Lips of an Angel" by Hinder

Rewrite the Stars - Zac Efron and Zendaya

Secret - OneRepublic

The Departure - Max Richter and Lang Lang

"Blood was spilled on the holy land for the worst kind of LUST was driven by the desire for God."

CHAPTER 1

Tristan

Karens ignore trigger warnings, only to later complain about said warnings. Don't be a Karen. This book contains somnophilia and a graphic non-consensual sexual scene that made some readers uncomfortable. It also includes unsavory topics such as suicide and abuse. This book is only intended for open-minded readers interested in exploring their fantasies in the realm of fiction while exercising good judgment to differentiate it from real-life situations

"And how does that make you feel?" I rolled my eyes at the most basic question a therapist could ask. For three hundred dollars an hour, I expected something less cliché.

How does that make me feel?

Frustrated that I was having this conversation in the first place.

"You are the expert, so you tell me. How do *you* think it makes me feel?"

Grabbing a water bottle from the mini-refrigerator stationed at the left corner of the plainly decorated room, Michael sat at the edge of his desk. He studied me closely, Nordic blue eyes gleaming with purpose. He knew I was fucking with him but decided to play ball.

"Frustrated," he answered decidedly.

Goddamnit. I hated that he was good at his job and always had a direct line into my thoughts.

He stood to his full six-feet four-inch height and took the seat across from me. Michael didn't look much like a therapist. He was young with shoulder-length honey-blonde hair. None of those traits reflected a sought-after clinician with the ability to change your life.

Yet, here he was, so successful that appointments with him were rare, client list exclusive. Mary pulled a lot of strings for me to be sitting here. Although I resisted the idea of therapy, her insistence wore me down.

And somewhere deep down, I admitted to not having returned to normal even three years after Dad's death. Enough of this grief. Suddenly, the idea of a confidante in an enclosed space wasn't so horrific. After months of dragging my feet, I was now a regular.

For our current session, we were discussing Mary's upcoming nuptials to my soon-to-be stepfather.

"Why do you think I feel frustrated?" I asked curiously for his take on the topic. After all, I didn't have a problem with my mother remarrying. She had suffered for long enough as a widow.

"If I told you, it would defeat the point of charging you three hundred dollars an hour. Don't you think?"

The sly smile on my face was a rare, genuine one. Michael was upfront, the type of honesty that was unmatched in my society.

"Why don't we start with your stepdad? Tell me more about him."

I shrugged. "What's there to tell?"

That was obviously a lie. There were tons to tell about my soon-to-be stepfather, Raguel Nineveh.

He had migrated from Brazil to the United States for college, then met the love of his life, Maya. They married shortly after and settled here in Washington, DC. The vibrant capital was also where they had Sara, their one and only darling daughter. All was well until Maya met her fate during a car accident, leaving Raguel a broken man.

Nonetheless, Raguel's olive skin and distinct gray eyes attracted the attention of tons of other women, my mother amongst them. They recognized the despondency in each other's eyes and decided to be together. They had only been together for six months when Raguel put a ring on it. Their fast-track relationship was supposedly a courtesy to "the kids."

Raguel's daughter, Sara, deviated toward Mary upon their initial meeting, craving the mother's love she lost too early in life. In contrast, I was cold to her. Like every other person in my life, my mother couldn't break through to me anymore. When Dad died, so did my ability to connect with others, landing me at Michael's doorsteps.

Mary's constant efforts to change my outlook were off-putting, whereas Sara was the poster child she craved. She wanted to adopt Sara, which brought on the formality of marriage. Raguel insisted on adopting me in return, which was plain weird.

"From what I understand, you like Raguel. So, why are you opposed to this adoption?"

"It's a little weird to be adopted at my age, don't you think?"

"You are only fifteen—"

"Almost sixteen."

"Nonetheless. You've mentioned struggling with making real connections since your dad passed away. Clearly, you miss familial bonds. This would be a great opportunity to start over. Don't you think?"

I was silent.

Logically, there weren't any good reasons to oppose the idea. Not only was Raguel a good man, but he could also prove beneficial to my future career.

The Marcolfs were a family of politicians with every heir harboring secret dreams of running for Presidency. Due to his untimely death, Dad fell short of becoming a senator. By God, even if it were the last thing I did on earth, I would achieve his failed ambitions.

Raguel could help get me there. Our family's 'white privilege' had long been brought into question. What better way to break the norm than by having a diverse father?

Not to mention, Raguel understood my political dreams and the weight the name Marcolf carried. So much so that he offered to change his and his daughter's last names to match mine.

So, yeah, Raguel was a great man. And there were only upsides to this arrangement.

"I suppose that's true," I conceded.

Michael smiled. "This is great progress, Tristan. On that note, let's finish our conversation from the last session."

Dad. He wanted me to discuss the night of Dad's death.

Michael looked me over with unfathomable eyes. This time he didn't refer to his notes. "Are you still having the same dreams?"

I nodded.

He sat up, elbows leaning against his thighs. "Should we revisit that night?"

I had given Michael tidbits of the first time I had such a dream. It had been years since, yet the nightmares continued to haunt me. It was time to divulge and get to the bottom of this.

"I was a mess on the night of Dad's accident. I had finally forced myself to go to sleep when someone appeared in my dreams with a... premonition?" I contemplated. "No, that's not the right word. It was more like an offer."

Michael watched me under hooded eyes. "What did the manifestation sound like?"

"Manifestation?"

"Our minds can sometimes manipulate our inner thoughts to help us cope," he explained.

"The... manifestation," I said tentatively, "sounded deep... distorted." It was odd not to have a better description for the voice that had frequented my dreams for years.

"What did it say?" he prodded.

"He offered me desirable things if I gave up my heart and soul."

"What kinds of desirable things?" he asked curiously.

I shrugged. "Money, women, power, looks... superficial things, I guess."

I swallowed several times, then looked away. It sounded absurd. Like I had sold my soul to the Devil in exchange for power and women, or something equally ridiculous. Michael was probably seconds away from having me committed.

Nevertheless, it was hard to deny that life had, in fact, improved superficially. Dad's previous investments had brought on significant returns out of the blue. My looks had changed, too. After turning fourteen, my amber-colored eyes had lightened to resemble gold, attracting attention I had never known.

I could make no sense of these fortunes. Instead, I gave into my teenage urges and started having sex. Lots of girls, older ones, threesomes. Everything. My appetite had become insatiable to the point that it scared even me.

"He said I could have everything I desired. My looks will only grow with age. My image and success will be unmatched. More money than

I'll ever need." I looked at Michael and smiled, "And the female interest will never waver."

"In exchange for?"

"Love," I replied simply. "Or anything real for that matter."

"Lust versus love," he rephrased. "Materialistic desires in exchange for love."

"I guess."

Michael didn't speak for several moments. "Do you believe in God, Tristan?" he asked abruptly.

Surprised by the turn of conversation, I frowned. "I suppose."

Michael put his notebook away. "It's popularly believed that God had dismissed seven angels from Heaven for defying him. These fallen angels became the Princes of Hell, carrying out sins God had warned humanity against."

I tried to recall my knowledge of religion. It wasn't extensive. At most, it stemmed from rare church attendance on select occasions.

"One of the Princes of Hell is Asmodeus, the Demon of Lust."

The name was unfamiliar to me, but something in Michael's voice made me believe that he was drawing a parallel between us.

"This Demon, Asmodeus, wasn't like the other princes of hell," Michael continued thoughtfully. "He didn't revel in cruelty and loved music, had a passion for dancing, intoxication, and all types of... fun. He didn't see anything wrong with it and believed it was humans who turned merriment into a sin."

"What does that have to do with me—"

"You see, Asmodeus rarely showed himself in physical form. Instead, he came to men in dreams to lead them astray. Or he whispered in their ears with temptations of things they ought not to desire."

"You're not suggesting that this Asmodeus came to me in my dreams?" I asked incredulously. Surely, Michael wasn't some religious nut. It'd be a huge disappointment were it to be the case.

Catching my drift, Michael quickly added, “It’s just... ironic, I guess. Because you have a new sister named Sara. Asmodeus had a woman named Sarah in his life, too, except his Sarah had an H at the end of her name.” He smiled though it didn’t quite reach his eyes. “And Asmodeus was known for coming to men in their dreams with similar offers. I’m only pointing out that your life has relevancy to his story.”

“Oh, okay,” I said uncertainly.

“Would you like to hear it?”

“Hear what?”

“Asmodeus’ story and how he met Sarah.”

I looked at my phone. “Umm. Our time is up—”

“It’s on me,” he dismissed. “I think you might find it helpful.”

Before I could open my mouth to tell him that I didn’t care, Michael transported me to a different world, his words so eloquent that I could almost see the story unfold in front of my very eyes.

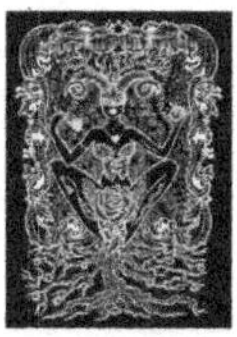

It was a languid afternoon with all the promises of a summer day. Sarah lay on the grassy lawn of her favorite garden, a thick head of mane spread around her, coating her with all the softness of ethereal beauty.

A pauper interrupted her contemplations, begging for money. She didn’t have her coin purse. In its stead, she took off her jewelry and gave the man all she had.

However, a cruel passerby stopped the pauper a mere distance away to taunt him for his gout and accuse him of stealing the lady’s jewelry. Sarah watched the scene unfold. Her beautiful gray eyes twinkled, and when the passerby sat on a bench, she crawled underneath it to tie the man's shoelaces together.

Asmodeus watched her mischief, mesmerized. He could hardly distinguish whether it were Heaven or Hell inside the girl's heart. She was sweet and warm with a tender heart. She was equally wicked and sought out mischief.

She was his perfect match.

Asmodeus had spent eons as a lover rather than a fighter. He indulged in all women, his appetite voracious for the pleasures of the flesh.

In between his pursuits, Asmodeus enticed humanity with temptation because it was dreadfully dull to enjoy merriment by your lonesome self. For the first time in his eternal life, he felt far from weary because Sarah's smiles didn't permit it. Nor was there any place for cold-heartedness because she was warmer than the sun.

There was a feeling stirring inside him, a foreign one he couldn't understand. And for the first time in his wretched life, Asmodeus' needs surpassed the desires of the flesh.

Michael paused just as the story had piqued my interest.

Other than the fact that the lust demon showed himself in dreams and someone named Sara was to join my family, I couldn't draw any other connections. I chalked it off to coincidence, but Michael wanted me to walk away with a lesson.

"I want you to remember this story next time you're at a crossroads."

"Why?"

"Because it's not always about materialistic good. Even Asmodeus, the demon of lust, understood that."

Did it make me worse than a demon that I didn't care how I achieved it, as long as I fulfilled my Dad's lifelong dreams?

Instead of telling Michael so, I gave him my practiced smile. "Will keep that in mind. Hey, man, listen. I have to get going for a family dinner. Uhm, thanks for the extra time and the... story."

I rose to my feet, but Michael stopped me with another question. "In your dream, did you give that voice an answer?"

"Yes."

Michael's head was turned toward the window, his intense gaze staring out as he awaited my response.

The insinuation was clear. Michael told me this story because he didn't want me to be so quick in giving up things that were real. Unfortunately for his efforts, "I chose lust."

Perhaps it was a figment of my imagination, but Michael closed his eyes in a motion that could only be described as... pity.

"Tris!" Mary exclaimed. "You're home."

A suffocating feeling had followed me out of Michael's office and all the way home. I managed a curt nod, not in the mood for chit-chat.

"Right on time. Ragu's making his famous stew, and Sara is in the kitchen being his little helper." She glanced at me nervously. "I hope you remembered about dinner tonight."

I had shown little interest in meeting Raguel's daughter though Mary desperately wanted us to get along. That was the point of tonight's dinner.

With a shoulder lift and a muffled, *yeah*, I followed her to the kitchen. I made a beeline for my usual seat at the table. Except, a four-feet monstrosity already occupied it, and I used that word in kind.

A five-year-old kid in a multicolored tulle dress sat crossed-legged on the cushioned chair.

My cushioned chair.

A halo crown—meant to be part of an angel costume—was stuck on top of the curly mounds of hair on her head. And she wore a heap of makeup that made her look utterly ridiculous.

Did that thing just escape a mental asylum?

"Tristan, you're home." Raguel slapped me on the back. "You finally get to meet my daughter. This is Sara."

The little shit occupying my chair looked up. And I took a sharp inhale at the piercing silver-gray eyes to stare back.

Didn't Michael mention that Asmodeus' Sarah also had gray eyes?

It was eerie. Gray was an uncommon shade of eye color, and hers looked even rarer when contrasting against her beige complexion and shining like crystals in the dim light.

"Sara, come say hi to Tristan," Raguel instructed.

Sara huffed as if uncrossing her legs and descending from the chair required the exertion of all her energy. "Hi!"

I nodded politely in turn.

Raguel appeared apologetic. "Sorry, she dressed herself today, then got into Mary's makeup."

Clearly.

"Mary let me play with her makeup," Sara added, inspecting me as suspiciously as I studied her.

"I see."

"We put makeup on my doll, too." Sara held up a doll that held a striking resemblance to her. "It's an American Girl Doll and looks just like me. See?"

"I had that custom made," Mary chimed in proudly.

Sara pulled the doll to her chest. "Do you like it?"

"Sure."

"What do you like about it?"

"I don't know."

"How come?"

"I just don't."

"Why not?"

This was going to be a long night.

Suppressing the urge to roll my eyes, I took my jacket off, draping it carefully over the back of a bar stool. There was some lint on the sleeve. I tsked and grabbed a lint roller to brush it off.

Sara curiously watched the care I exercised with my favorite piece of clothing item. Putting the roller away, I was once again met with the kid's expectant face. Mary's apprehensive gaze flickered between us. I hadn't been the talkative type since Dad passed away but attempted to converse. The little shit made it difficult with the number of questions she kept firing off without taking a breath.

"What's your favorite color? Mine's green."

"Great."

"We are having beef stew tonight. Do you like stew?"

"Yes."

"Did you know that my new room is supposed to be next to yours?"

I glanced at Mary, perplexed.

"Umm... so that's what we wanted to talk to you about," Mary said, tucking strands of blonde hair behind her ear. "We thought tonight could be a trial run with all four of us staying in the same house. It makes more sense for Ragu and Sara to move in here with us."

Generally, Mary limited her visits to Raguel's condo, which is why I had never met Sara before. If they were getting married, I supposed living together came with the territory, and this mansion made more sense for a family of four.

"Only if you are okay with it," Raguel added while Sara looked quizzically between the three of us.

"It's fine," I said absentmindedly before following up with a question of my own. "You still plan to change your last name to Marcolf, right?"

My dad came from an affluent family. They were adamant about avoiding gold-diggers looking to sink their claws into a Marcolf. So, things like family homes, land, and money were all put into trusts and could only be passed down to an offspring of the same last name, not a spouse.

Though everything was to remain in a trust until I came of age, this house was my property. Raguel's request to move in here only solidified my bargaining chip despite him having previously offered to change his name.

"Of course," he said easily. "I already started on me and Sara's paperwork."

I needed to hear this confirmation because I could concede to him moving into my house, marrying my mother, and even adopting me. But there was no way I'd give up my last name, and I refused to be the only person in this household with a different surname. I couldn't take those feelings of alienation.

"I'm so glad that's settled." Mary clapped her hands, looking relieved to be done with it. "Now, let's eat. Sara, do you want to help me set the table?"

"Yes!"

Sara did the plate setting with great care under Mary's guidance while Raguel finished cooking. I contemplated helping, but the three of them shared such a natural streamline that I didn't dare interrupt. This wholesome experience was entirely foreign to me, and these people might as well be aliens.

Every politician had their strategy; Dad's was to be vocal only during rallies and debates. Otherwise, he was selective with his words so as to give the press less ammunition. He raised me to follow in his footsteps by keeping a neutral front and a reserved personality.

Mary hated it.

Her husband kept her at arm's length during the entirety of their marriage, only for her son to do the same. It bothered her that I was inexpressive of my thoughts and barely laughed or conversed. Even with my closest friends and family, my interactions were aloof at best.

My closed-off nature worsened with Dad's death. Meanwhile, Sara and Raguel were regular chatterboxes and accepted Mary with open arms. I stared at the perfect family with their natural chemistry, and it dawned on me that the dynamic was here to stay.

And just like that, I had become a guest in my own home.

Despite my best efforts to stop that from happening, a name change meant nothing in the grand scheme of things. The theory was proven throughout the awkward dinner. Unable to connect with anyone, I inadvertently shut down. In the interim, Sara spoke nonstop about her damn doll. Mary acted so animated around Sara that I stared at my mother like she was a perfect stranger, and an irritation like I had never known gnawed at me.

"Can I call you mom now that you're marrying my dad?"

My fork halted midair. Sara asked the question so innocently that no one would have assumed it was premeditated.

I didn't turn my head. My ears perked, waiting to hear Mary's response.

"Oh my God." Mary put her hands to her chest. "Of course, sweetheart. I would love that. Ragu, did you hear that?"

"That is so sweet."

"You little angel. What do you say we have dessert now? Ice cream?"

"Yes! Yes!"

I ground my teeth. That little shit knew exactly what she was doing. Mary couldn't see it, but she was being manipulated.

While Ragu and Mary adjourned to the kitchen to fetch bowls, Sara ran her fingers through her doll's hair. "I'm going to name you... Tris." She glanced at me. "After Tristan."

I had no idea what propelled me. Snatching the damn doll out of her hands, I dunked it inside the bowl and into her half-eaten stew.

Big crystal eyes gaped at the brutality suffered by her precious doll. With a smug smile, I waited for the little shit to cry. Or at least scream.

Not a single tearful peep.

"Sara, what did you do?" Raguel yelled as soon as he returned to the table.

"Oh my God." *My* mother gaped at the doll dunked into Sara's bowl. The crime scene appeared intentional rather than an accident, and destroying the expensive toy was an insult to Mary. "Why?" she implored.

I braced myself, expecting Sara to rat me out. But the little shit said nothing, staring back blankly at Ragu and Mary.

"Apologize to Mary. Now!" her father thundered.

"I'm sorry," Sara spoke in a small voice, devoid of earlier enthusiasm.

"Put your bowl away and then march yourself straight to bed," Raguel ordered. "No dessert for you."

Ragu and Mary fussed over the doll, ultimately taking it to the laundry room to salvage it.

Sara's questions had stopped, and I wondered if I had extinguished the light burning inside her. Guilt should have coursed through me, yet I felt nothing. I sat with my elbows on the table, index finger to the forehead. Why didn't she rat me out? Why take the heat on my behalf?

Sara pushed her chair back and picked up her bowl as instructed by her father. Very carefully, she carried it to the sink. En route, she grabbed my jacket draped over the back of a bar stool.

I was too mesmerized—and frankly curious—to question her motives.

Without a second thought, Sara threw my jacket inside the sink and dumped her remaining stew over it.

THAT. LITTLE. SHIT.

She confidently strode out of the kitchen with her head held high.

It was minutes before I realized that the roaring and hackling were coming from me. For the first time in years, I laughed without holding back.

Hours later, I sat in the living room, flickering through the TV channels, when curly mounds of hair came into my vision line. Mary had taken the makeup off Sara's face, though she still wore the angel halo crown.

Haunting grays stared at me meaningfully before handing me the leather jacket she had spoiled earlier tonight. It had been cleaned up.

I glanced at the jacket suspiciously. I had respect for Sara when she ruined it in retaliation for destroying her toy. I hadn't a clue how to feel about her returning it in mint condition.

"Mary helped me clean it. Said it was your dad's jacket," she finally spoke. Toying with the heart necklace around her neck, she pulled it up for my benefit. "This was my mom's."

A small child, who should be clueless about death, somehow understood the meaningfulness of mementos left behind. She commiserated with my loss in the dark, regretful of her actions even though I had deserved it. Then she engulfed me in a hug without warning.

Shocked, I couldn't move for several moments.

No one, not even Mary, was familiar enough with me to show affection. We never built that kind of a rapport, and to try it now would be awkward.

However, nothing about this hug was awkward.

It was... comforting.

I patted her twice on the back. "Thank you, little angel. Go to bed now."

She didn't seem surprised by my term of endearment and broke the hug. After she left the room, I found myself fiddling with my phone. I pulled up the site to American Girl Dolls to order that little shit one more of her damn dolls.

CHAPTER 2

Sara

Fifteen Years Later

"I have rights, you know!" I hollered, poking my face out of the small window with railings to address the cop in the hallway.

"Not the right to assault an officer," the man retorted dryly.

"Allegedly," I sulkily countered and studied the dingy room in the basement. This building was a private shelter for low-income families in need. It consisted of several floors, each with multiple units to house them. The main floor was used for office and administrative purposes, as well as afterschool care for the kids. Meanwhile, the basement was too run down to be occupied. There was rubble on the floor, and the paint on the wall was chipping away. Only one window peeked into the hallway, allowing me access to my jailor—the aforementioned officer.

He was silent, watching me with tired eyes.

A few years ago, my family took over the upkeep of this shelter and regularly hosted charity events to raise money for it. Per my brother's orders, I wasn't allowed to have a job other than my charity work. So, I became involved in the organization's plight that was focused on providing a safe space for victims of domestic abuse. This brick-and-mortar building was somewhat of a safe space for me as well. It was ironic to be held captive at the very place I considered a sanctuary.

This building, along with the surrounding ones, had been purchased by developers, some blood-sucking corporation. They built a buzzing plaza, encouraging a bidding war for rental space. They were in the process of relocating this shelter as it didn't fit their agenda for gentrification.

It caused an uproar in the community and a demonstration that I had personally led.

The developers had called upon police officers to cover the perimeters and contain the rally. But the number of attendants had doubled by noon, and the demonstrators were shoved against one another. When someone slammed into me with brutal force, I accidentally bumped into an officer of the law standing behind me. The fierce shove caused him to fall, and as a result, I was restrained for assault.

Un-fucking-believable.

The cops were under strict orders to ensure a nonviolent rally. It would be a PR nightmare for the precinct if anyone were harmed during a peaceful protest. Soon, another officer escorted me inside the building to a room that had been repurposed for violent protesters. All the streets had been blocked off, so they deemed it necessary to detain me here until the protest ended.

"This is ridiculous," I announced. "No one even saw me push that cop."

"If a tree fell in a forest, but no one heard it, did it not make a sound?"

His attempt at a philosophical discussion was unseemly. I hated the superiority act as if he were on the right side of the fight.

"You know, Katniss Everdeen was also persecuted for standing up to the man," I informed with the same sense of morality he seemed to possess.

"Are you really comparing your unsolicited attack on an officer of the law with a fictional character who freed a dystopian society?"

He crossed his arms across his broad chest, which only added to his intimidating aura. Unsure of how to get out of this quandary, I observed my jailor closely for clues to his psyche.

He was handsome with locks of dark hair, golden skin, generous lips, and a six-foot frame. At most, he was in his early twenties, though his body language vibrated with the righteousness of an old soul. Unmistakably, he took his job seriously. He was left to man the depraved souls brought into this room with a current population of one—me—though he'd much rather be in the frontline.

Voila.

"Silly mistake. Anyways, I didn't catch your name," I said brightly, hoping to build rapport.

His skeptical eyes fixated on me as if I were seconds away from prison break. "Tobias," he spoke, his strong jaw clenching with tension.

"Lovely name," I quipped. "Tobias, don't you think it's an utter waste of your talent to babysit me instead of being at the frontline? Why don't you let me go and join your friends in action instead?"

Tobias scoffed at my suggestion. "So you can assault more officers?"

"Again, allegedly," I corrected. My actions were far from an orchestrated attack. "You are holding me here without evidence."

Tobias leveled me with a look that tethered on impatience. I had been yapping away since my arrival, and he was finally worn out.

"Don't you think it's ironic to restrain a woman in a shelter meant to *protect* women?" I resumed my case, though he had long tuned me out. "Just let me go. I work here, so I can go sit in my office until the rally ends."

Tobias ignored me.

"Hello!!" I waved my arms in a crisscross motion. "What you are doing is totally unconstitutional. You can't just lock someone up without following proper protocol. No one even read me the Miranda rights, nor did they declare my right to remain silent."

"Oh, you definitely have the right to remain silent," he warily responded. "Whether you are capable of shutting up is an entirely different issue."

I rolled my eyes. "Can I at least get a phone call?"

"This isn't jail, Princess. Your family knows where you are. They are coming to pick you up."

I frowned. "How did you get their numbers?" I asked after a hesitant pause, unsure if I had given anyone my last name.

"We didn't," he replied airily. "Someone saw you getting into trouble at the rally and let us know they called your family. Apparently, everyone around here knows you guys. I would've thought that would make you behave better, but oh well."

As soon as he spoke, Tobias' phone started ringing. He picked up the call, grunted at the person on the other side, then held open my door.

"He's here."

Tobias patiently marched me out of confinement and down the narrow hallway. Before turning the corner, I heard a set of familiar footsteps. My heart leaped upon realizing who it was. There was only one man who walked like he owned the room.

The noise of the furious shuffling increased, confirming his presence before I saw the hulk of a man, the supersized biceps and broad shoulders fitted perfectly into a black T-shirt and blue jeans.

I was met with Tristan's glowing orbs, though his demeanor was otherwise masterfully camouflaged. He had the acute ability to peruse me like a farm animal, then devalue me without uttering a single word. We had spent our lives pranking and torturing one another but were on the same team at the end of the day. If anyone other than Tris so much as touched a hair on my head, he'd chop their hands off.

My brother was... slightly overprotective.

He was also the talk of the town as the youngest congressman to win his district in Virginia. Following law school, Tristan worked tirelessly to weed his way into becoming a politician. Though most aspiring politicians loved to talk, he was the quiet type. When he first started campaigning, voters were rattled by the unique approach but later loved him for not making false promises.

After turning thirty, Tristan started his campaign to become Virginia's youngest senator. The impossible feat might actually be possible given the female voter turnout at every one of Tris' elections.

Tristan had been gifted with unearthly good looks, and I didn't use the word callously. With jet black hair and the rarest amber-gold eyes, he was known to be angelically beautiful to the point women went mad for him.

However, I didn't have any physical attributes in common with him, including our skin color. While no one contradicted us when we disclosed our relation, their faces often twisted with bafflement. It was one thing for family members to look different but differing in race was a game-changer.

Tobias' bewildered look at our mismatched pairing might be one we were accustomed to, but it was no less hilarious. He frowned, turning to me for clarification. "Dispatch told me your brother was here. I mean, no one else should have access to this part of the building, but... Is this him?"

I shrugged. "I've never seen that man in my life."

Tobias was instinctively alarmed by my declaration. An outstretched arm went up protectively to act as my human shield. "Sara, stay behind me. This man could be anyone and quite possibly armed."

Though I was touched by his concern, my personal warden had a flair for theatrics. I held up both hands in surrender. "Just kidding. I know him. I saw him near the rally earlier today. He was driving around in a white van and handing out free candy to kids."

Tristan's dry eyes landed on me, unamused.

Whatever.

I was pissed at him for the prank he pulled earlier this week. That jerk spent a large sum of his money (and time) purchasing identical replicas of all my clothes, then swapped them out with a smaller size. It took me days to figure out what he did. Days I spent crying, convinced that I had gotten fat.

Oh, that Tris could be so cruel at times.

But when Tobias reached for his walkie-talkie, ready to call for backup, I conceded. "Okay. Okay. He is my brother."

Tobias' hand slackened, though his eyes remained distrustful. Tristan appeared equally apprehensive. He closely watched Tobias' arm, which lightly grazed the front of my body.

"Tristan Marcolf," he said tersely in a deep voice.

"Tobias DeSilva," my warden countered.

"Well, Toby," Tristan drawled, intentionally reducing the name. "Do tell me why you detained my sister without cause."

"It wasn't without cause. Your sister was caught assaulting an officer of the law."

Tristan looked me up and down, pointing at me with an index finger. "How could that scrawny-looking thing possibly take down a grown man?"

"Hey!" I indignantly objected.

Tristan strode closer, ignoring me. "She obviously didn't do it, but you still held her without cause. If I find out that you so much as laid one finger on my sister, I'll make every last person in your precinct pay the price." He looked me up and down, then added an insult in case his words made the mistake of touching my heart. "She already looks like a little boy. And I highly doubt it will bode well for your budding career if word gets out that you're in the business of kidnapping little boys."

"We didn't kidnap a little boy; we only detained—"

"I'm not a little boy," I mumbled, looking down at my slightly flat chest.

Tobias caught his next words, uncomfortable at the direction of this conversation. He cleared his throat to regain professionalism.

"Your sister physically harmed an officer," he repeated. "We were happy to let you pick her up as a courtesy, but if you like, I can take her down to the station instead, and you can post her bail."

Though Tobias was threatening my arrest, I glanced at him with admiration, impressed with his ability to challenge my brother. For the first time, I pegged Tobias as not only an attractive man but a man I was attracted to. In fact, I was suddenly really attracted to him.

Sadly, our meet-cute had come to an abrupt end.

Tristan's eyes swept over us. A glint of anger flickered through them, and he yanked at my arm to drag me away, staring down the man who had spoken out so bravely against him.

"Whatever. We are leaving."

"Don't get into any more trouble," my former jailor called after me. He wasn't sneering; instead, his voice was filled with sincerity.

I only had enough time to put up a three-finger salute, imitating Katniss Everdeen from The Hunger Games. "May the odds be ever in my favor."

Perhaps it was my imagination, but I could have sworn his lips twitched to something resembling a smile.

CHAPTER 3

Sara

Our mansion-like home stood tall over the other houses in Georgetown, the heart of Washington DC. I walked past the front door on heavy legs. A crystal chandelier dropped down from above the foyer, the reflection visible on the tiled marble floors. Tris loved the latest fashion, the most expensive brands, and lavish showpieces. Our house was reflective of his taste.

Unlike the grandness of our home, the mood was solemn in the dining room. Dad paced restlessly while Mom poured herself, what I presumed, was a second glass of wine. Tristan's posture was unruffled, hands stuffed inside his pant pockets.

Might as well get this over with.

"It wasn't my fault," I phrased the poorly prepared statement.

I should have mentally prepared during the car ride, but it was hard to concentrate with Tristan's snippy mood. The disdain in his face had coiled around my spine like a slimy snake.

He had been angrier than usual after we left the shelter and only uttered one sentence to me during the drive. *"I don't want you to be seen with any more cops, Sara; it's not good for publicity."*

Distracted, I hadn't prepped for the forlorn look on Dad's face. "I thought it stopped." He pinched the bridge of his nose. Anger would have been better. The sadness behind his eyes twisted a knife into my heart.

"Dad, I swear. I didn't do anything."

He nodded, a small smile on his face. "I know, sweetheart."

Dad wasn't referring to my detainment at a rally. Young people taking an interest in politics was the driving force behind Tristan's campaign, and activism was considered fluff for a political family like ours. This emergency family meeting had been called to discuss my other fuck-up.

I was cursed, you see.

It sounded like an excuse, but for me, it was the greatest truth of my life. Anyone who got too close was burnt down to a cinder, hit with catastrophic misfortunes. And for the last few years, my loving step-mother had struggled with the misfortunes I had brought into her life.

Mary was a Southern belle. True to her roots, she sent me to etiquette school so that I could be formally presented in society at a Debutante ball. She even hand-selected my escort—her best friend's son, Noah.

Under her watchful eyes, Noah and I tirelessly practiced our cotil-lion dance, though we never had the opportunity to perform it. The young boy was poisoned the very night of the party, landing him in the hospital. And I happened to be the last person to see him before the impromptu hospital visit.

It was the first of many unfortunate accidents surrounding me. To be precise, seven similar incidents occurred in my presence. Every time another boy was hurt, I was the last person to be seen with them.

Our circle in the DC area noticed the trend. Word got out that associating with me led to the demise of young men. People eventually moved on from superstitious theories to suspecting me of attempted murder, and I became a social pariah. The gossip became endless, prompting me to apply out of state for college.

Unfortunately, Tris put a stop to it, suggesting that I attend Georgetown University instead. It was close-by enough in case they needed to sweep more dirt under the rug. I couldn't deny the logic behind it. Tris was at the cusp of achieving a senate seat, and I had been implicating his wholesome platform with my scandals.

I had been a cautious recluse due to my unexplainable phenomenon. I never engaged in romantic entanglements, nor did I let anyone get close. My lonely heart was tired of the solitude, but at least no one else had been hurt.

That was until two girls from my past started spreading the old rumors that Tristan had paid good money to bury. They taunted me all semester. I ignored their jabs and was relieved that today was the last day of classes. I had already moved home for the summer and returned to my dorm to sign off with the Resident Assistant when I halted mid-step upon hearing their voices.

"Do you remember what happened to the last guy she went out with?"

"She must have a magic pussy if men are willing to die for it." The second girl laughed, a crowd forming around her.

"I wished it was her instead of him."

"If I were her, I'd just kill myself to suppress the urge to hurt anyone else. God, I don't even want her in this dorm. I'm seriously scared for our safety—" the second girl stopped speaking because I had come into their line of vision.

I had pretended not to care, but their words cut me deep. The sad truth was that I agreed.

I wished it were me instead.

An hour later, both of the girls fell down a flight of stairs. Apparently, both negative and positive feelings toward me rendered a target on people's backs. Several students were aware of the transaction between us. It was too far-fetched that the girls were severely injured shortly after I overheard their vulgar comments.

It was one thing to be treated as an outcast, entirely another to have accusatory eyes question your hand in attempted murder. There was nothing I could say to convince people of my innocence. I had become an unwelcome perpetrator and, according to society, potentially dangerous.

This insanity started during my high school years, and my family was determined not to allow for a repeat.

"Honey," Mom placed her wine glass on the dining table made of ornate wood. "It's okay."

My back stiffened at the choked-up emotions in her voice. We might not share the same blood, but she was my soft spot. Mom was the only person who believed me.

Unfortunately, Dad didn't feel the same. "No one can blame you for feeling angry toward those girls—"

I closed my eyes. "Dad, I swear. I didn't hurt them."

"We believe you," Mom said quickly, while Dad stared at his interlaced hands. *Dad believed that I believed it.* He knew that I didn't lie or believe in violence. So, he suspected me of suffering a mental illness where I had convinced myself of my innocence.

"I don't know why these things keep happening around me," I whispered.

Dad sighed. "It's okay, sweetheart. We'll take care of it."

I bit my bottom lip. *Take care of it because he thinks I did it.*

"We just need to get ahead of this thing before word gets out. We are all going to the fundraiser tonight, so let's start there. Sara, I want you to show everyone how wonderful and kind you are. Lead the first dance, be polite, charming, talk about your charities."

How difficult could it be to give out the vibes of '*not a sociopathic killer'* to a room full of conservatives?

"Once everyone sees that you are a perfectly respectable young lady, no one will dare throw accusations your way." Dad didn't sound angry, merely exasperated. "There is no reason for this thing to escalate."

I lowered my eyes to the ground. "Yes, Dad."

"Angel," Tris called me by the childhood name he had dubbed for me. "I don't think you should live on campus next semester. It'll be best if Mom and Dad can keep an eye on you from now on."

My chest constricted.

It sounded like Tristan didn't believe me either, and somehow that hurt much worse than anything else. Of all people, Tris knew that I hated violence just as much as I hated deceit. I stupidly thought he wouldn't think so lowly of me despite our differences.

Was that the reason he was so angry with me in the car?

"He is right," Dad chimed in. "If today's mishap ended up in the paper, it could have implicated Tristan's campaign. We need to be able to get ahead of these things in the future. Honey, for tonight, focus on being on your best behavior and show everyone how well you fit into this family."

My heart twisted at the thought because I didn't fit into this family.

My father was Brazilian of European descent, and my biological mother was Black. Other than our distinct gray eyes, I didn't share any other physical traits with Dad, Tristan, or Mary.

The three looked like a picturesque suburban family, while I stood out in every family photo. Though I'd never say the words out loud, I didn't belong with them. Physically, I didn't look like them, and emotionally, I brought them distress.

The knowledge made me feel lonely.

Sadness bubbled up in my heart, but I stomped over it.

They were right. A troubled sister with sociopathic tendencies didn't bode well for the polls, and I refused to cost Tris his lifelong dreams with one more of my implicating stories.

"I'm sorry," I whispered to the room in general. Although I didn't hurt those girls, I felt responsible, nonetheless. "I won't let it happen again. And I'll be on my best behavior tonight."

CHAPTER 4

Sara

The fundraiser tonight was a Victorian-themed ball hosted at some grand mansion in Northern Virginia. The venue had a large foyer with an overabundance of appetizer stations and spreads, and a spacious ballroom was visible through the crevice of the foyer door.

True to my promise, I took the time to present myself impeccably. My hair had been relaxed, then curled into waves. I put on soft makeup and even bought a new creamy tulle dress to go with my kitten heels. The feminine dress provided me the modest disguise of the old Sara, the one from before the torrid rumors.

I suspected my efforts would still be in vain if the news had already spread about the two girls writhing in pain at the hospital. Unlike Tristan, I couldn't trick people with a pretty face. As he often pointed out, our family had one good-looking offspring, and it sure as hell wasn't me. Even this afternoon, he made sure to get in one last snide.

"I have to attend a meeting before the fundraiser, so I'll meet you guys there. Wear something presentable that makes you look less ugly."

Ugh. He was such an ass.

But I had to put a pin on our sibling rivalry for the night. With a deep breath, I focused on the game plan instead—to show off angelic Sara.

"Mom!" I found my parents near the entrance to the grand ballroom. We drove separately because Mom was the head organizer for this event and had to arrive early. She loved antiquated parties and was no doubt in her element.

"Sara." Mom smiled brightly. "You look beautiful."

We had barely exchanged any pleasantries when my parents were pulled away by a vital donor likely to contribute to Tristan's campaign.

"Sweetheart, we have to speak with Mr. Reynolds for a minute." Dad leaned in to whisper, "Remember our discussion. No mistakes tonight."

I nodded at his ominous mien.

"Oh, stop it, Ragu." Mom dismissed Dad with a carefree wave. "Don't listen to him, honey. Just go have fun," she threw over her shoulders as they walked away. "By the way, we have a surprise waiting for you in the ballroom."

Before I could press for answers, they had both disappeared.

Closing my eyes, I braced myself as I entered the grand ballroom. The past rumors about me had been subdued, and hopefully, the new rumors hadn't reached these people.

The soiree was in full swing inside. High heels clicked against the marble floor, and designer dresses glided gracefully across the room. Scanning the area for potential photographers, I strolled to the bar.

"Vodka-soda, please," I requested.

"Make that just soda," a voice behind me contradicted. "She is nineteen."

I turned around at lightning speed. My mouth dropped, eyes widening in surprise. "Jailor?" I shook my head. "I mean... T-Tobias!"

What the hell is the hot cop doing here?

Green eyes gleamed at my stuttering, forcing my heart to skip a beat. Fuck, he was tall. Incredibly good-looking, too, might I add. Slacks and a crisp white shirt hugged his body, while his brown hair was an unruly mess.

I drew in a breath which sounded ragged even to my own ears.

"Hi, Princess. I didn't think you had it in you to be rendered speechless."

Yes, I was speechless, a trait I had never been accused of possessing. It was impossible not to be at the sight of the last man I expected to see.

"I-I am just surprised," I managed. "Are you here with someone?" It was unlikely he'd attend such an event otherwise. My heart sank at the thought.

Tobias smiled, displaying a full set of white teeth. He had a dimple on his left side. It dipped to make such a perfect dent that I nearly reached out to touch it. "Actually, yes. I'm here with you."

"W-what... h-how?" I stammered. "I don't understand."

He laughed at my furrowed brows. "I'll explain later," he gently appeased my bewilderment. "For now, I'm under strict orders to ensure we lead the first dance."

But Tris and I always led the first dance; the words remained at the tip of my tongue. It was traditional for someone to lead the first dance at Mom's events. She always bestowed that honor upon Tristan and me.

Did she orchestrate this? Was Tobias my surprise? How did she even come to know of the handsome cop?

Tobias reached out, slowly entwining our fingers. My mind was riddled with confusion as I followed him blindly, the warm palm heating my cold hand.

He tilted his head to the side. "By the way, you look beautiful."

"Thank you," I murmured, trying to steady my racing heart.

"In fact, you are the most beautiful girl here tonight."

"I bet you say that to all the girls."

"But I only mean it with you," he retorted.

"I'm flattered," I said dryly. "Should I swoon now?"

"I'll be here to catch you if you do."

Christ. Tobias was the kind of man that could ruin a girl. "Did my parents put you up to this?"

"Maybe," he drawled mysteriously. "Are you excited to lead the first dance?"

I shrugged. "I'm under strict guidance not to make any mistakes."

Tobias laughed. It was all warm and kind and infectious. "I didn't take you for one to follow the rules."

Assembling the last morsel of residual indifference, I countered, "And I didn't take you for one to encourage others to break the rules."

Tobias leaned in, lips grazing my ear. "Only if the outcome is worth it."

I wondered if my heart would burst into pieces at the rate it was beating. Undoubtedly, a mistake had been made if a man like *that* was whispering suggestive words to me.

The overpowering trance remained in place as the DJ announced the first dance. Tobias led us to the middle of the floor. It was a hazy blur as he moved—no—as he *glided* gracefully, forcing me to follow his lead. He spun me in place, moving me naturally into the choreography. The expert skills were a testament that he was from a similar background where boys were expected to learn proper dancing.

Other couples joined us on the floor, but I hadn't the slightest clue of my surroundings. Tobias pulled me close, one hand resting on my waist. His soft breaths, the rhythmic movements, it was all a dream. The ground could have opened up to swallow me whole, and I'd have been none the wiser.

I did my best to remain composed, but my poise was overruled. A waft of his musky smell drifted into my lungs. It was so intoxicating that I unintentionally leaned in.

Dance must be the way to a woman's heart. By the time the music stopped, I was positive I had fallen in love with the beautiful stranger.

Yes, it was absurd to be enamored after one dance. This strong of a reaction to a man I had known less than twenty-four hours was nonsense.

This was happening because I craved physical intimacy. Yearned for it. Practically salivated over it. I had fantasized about sex nonstop since the thought had first crossed my mind. The fact that I hadn't touched a man in years only increased my budding need. My first intimate physical contact in years was muddling my emotions. Plus, he was so fucking hot that any girl would fall in love after one dance.

"You knew all the moves," I said breathlessly.

Tobias smiled mysteriously, his dimple digging in deeper. "This isn't my first rodeo."

"Slut," I teased.

Tobias chuckled warmly. I studied every line on his face but demanded no more explanations over his presence. I didn't care anymore why he was here, as long as he stayed by my side.

"How about I get you a drink while you think more about why I'm here?" Tobias asked before quickly adding, "A non-alcoholic drink."

Smiling shyly, I stepped away from the dance floor. "Coke, please."

Tobias left, my lust-induced haze following closely behind. My blatant gawping was interrupted when the room suddenly fell quiet. I redirected my attention to a specific corner of the ballroom where the silence was stretching.

My brother—surrounded by a herd of women—had arrived.

Every pair of eyes were focused on Tristan's entrance. It's as if the room had been doused in an overindulging orgasm. He walked in, and a harem of women followed in his wake, transfixed.

Tris' effect on the female demographic was nothing short of a phenomenon. It couldn't be explained, only experienced. Women acted mad around him, fools ready to kill one another in the quest for his approval. Over the years, he has had multiple stalkers, women pledging their virginities to him, vowing their everlasting love, anything to make him notice.

Tristan appeared detached per usual and was dressed immaculately, as expected. While in public, he didn't tolerate anything less than perfection. Not one strand of his inky black hair was out of place. The tux was pressed and tailored to fit his broad chest, and his muscular build towered over, radiating with the hidden connotation of his powers.

We were at odds with one another. Surprise, surprise. He had been angry with me all day, and my resentment stemmed from his belief that I hurt those two girls. At most, I played pranks on people, namely Tristan. I would never so much as hurt a fly. It hurt a lot that he'd think otherwise.

"Did you miss me?" Tobias passed me a coke, interrupting my thoughts.

"Huh?"

"Didn't you notice that I've been gone for five minutes?"

I gave him a blank stare because I hadn't, too preoccupied with Tristan. "No," I responded truthfully. Ugh. I needed to snap out of it and focus on this handsome man instead. What was his purpose here anyway?

Tobias didn't appear affronted by my answer. "I like your honesty."

"It's my greatest flaw. I can't lie."

He laughed softly. "How about one more dance, and we can brainstorm ways of turning you dishonest?"

I smiled, never wanting this night to end.

Tobias grabbed both of our glasses and settled them on a nearby high-top table. "Let's go." he dragged me back to the dance floor.

I laughed, trotting happily. Most of the guests had joined the dance floor for an upbeat song. Nonetheless, Tobias hugged me close to recreate our previous embrace, holding each other like two star-crossed lovers. His arms wrapped around my waist while my breasts pressed against his warm body.

Only a loud laugh snapped me out of the moment. My eyes opened to make contact with Lilith. It was the first time I had seen her tonight.

Lilith was one of Tristan's oldest friends/on-and-off hook up. She was the perfect candidate to be a senator's wife—well-bred, polite, and most importantly, no history of scandal.

But Lilith was mildly racist. She wasn't discriminatory in the acute sense of the word, nor did she use bigoted slurs. The DC area was much too politically correct to tolerate outright prejudice. Around here, racism was only fashionable if expressed through microaggressions.

For example, *I'm surprised at how articulate you are.*

And my personal favorite: *I'm not racist. I have a black friend.*

I knew that Tristan had taken a step back from Lilith, a deed spurred on by her backhanded comments toward me. However, Lilith was a family friend, and a lobbyist who had singlehandedly generated Tristan's most sizeable sponsorship checks. She couldn't be entirely ignored.

Curiosity got the better of me, and I straightened my head for a better look. Lilith stood tall next to Tristan, her hands wrapped possessively around his bicep. She was determined to fend off the admiring herd surrounding him. Like others, her judgment was clouded by Tristan's external facets.

My brother is absurdly attractive, I grudgingly admitted. He was probably the most attractive man anyone in our circle had seen—chiseled bone structures, strong jaw, locks of dark hair, and amber-gold eyes that stole the show.

One would think he'd be humbled by the good looks gifted to him by God. Instead, Tristan acted like *he* was the gift from God. His vanity knew no bounds.

"You're in college, right?" Tobias asked. His voice came from nowhere. For a minute, I had forgotten altogether that he was here with me.

"Yeah..."

Lilith and Tristan were on the move. Considering his anger from earlier, I had no idea how he planned to make my life miserable and preferred to be on alert.

"Sara?"

"Hmm?" I was busy glancing around to track Lilith and Tristan's movements. My displeasure grew when she dragged him to the dance floor.

"I asked if you were done with your first year of college?"

It was challenging to concentrate on Tobias' words while mentally preparing for battle. "Oh. Yes. Yes, I am."

I tried to focus on Tobias, who appeared annoyed by my inattentiveness. He followed my line of vision. "Isn't that your brother?"

"Umm... yeah."

He said nothing more, grasping that I was no longer in the mood to converse.

It was ironic. I couldn't shut up for the life of me, yet I was tongue-tied when my speaking skills came of use around a hot guy. I was engrossed, searching for a topic to break the ice, and it slipped my mind to track Tristan. The couple next to us moved out of the way, landing me right in the peripheral of Lilith and the devil himself.

Tristan was sizing me up.

Our scorching non-verbal exchanges were nothing new. Bystanders couldn't identify the love-hate relationship we harbored, and our parents never branded our dynamics as anything past sibling rivalry. The world didn't know how we tortured one another. That honor was exclusively reserved for the two of us.

Tris' eyes dripped with something resembling intensity as they roamed my dress. My skin flushed under his heated gaze, but perhaps it was just the aftereffect of dancing. Goosebumps sprung to my skin, counteracting the flush.

I hated how easily Tris unhinged me.

Preposterous.

No one in this world managed to perturb me in the flustering way I felt under his attention. However, the initial antagonism in his eyes flickered when his gaze landed on my dance partner, trailing down to Tobias' arm resting a little too low on my back.

Shit.

The way Tris' eyes blazed, I was shocked the room hadn't caught on fire. He had warned me against cops, and Hell hath no fury like a DC politician scorned. But could this honestly count as a snub to Tris, considering that our parents had orchestrated it, and I was no longer this man's detainee?

The disdain on his face screamed that he could care less about all those valid reasons. Amber eyes lit up, invoking the wrath of my oldest adversary. My imperturbable nature was noteworthy based on the context, knowing trouble was coming my way.

I pulled on Tobias' arm. "Come on, let's go outside. I want to show you something." I didn't wait for a response and dragged a perplexed Tobias away before Tristan took his first long stride toward us.

CHAPTER 5

Tristan

Hello, Mr. Marcolf.

Looking great, Mr. Marcolf.

I've been waiting for you, Mr. Marcolf.

The valet had scarcely grabbed the keys to my Aston Martin when a herd of women arrived to do their bidding. They followed me inside the grand ballroom, uncaring about their shameless gawking.

Why wouldn't they stare?

Four thousand dollar tux.

Ferragamo shoes.

Panty-melting smile and a thick head of inky black hair to go with it.

What's there not to love about me?

But I suspected the real reason women flocked to my side was to bear witness to the amber-gold eyes. The rarity in color preceded my reputation.

Unfortunately, my amber-golds were in the mood to wander,

searching for Sara's silhouette. Sara and I always shared the first dance whenever Mary organized an event. But I couldn't get out of my meeting any sooner, and the event was already in full swing.

Guess there was no first dance tonight. Damnit.

I used to hate being dragged to the dance floor but relented whenever Sara would grab my hand and force me into it. Now, I looked forward to holding Sara for those two minutes and thirty seconds without her purposefully stepping on my feet or doing something equally silly to annoy me.

My drifting eyes finally tracked her down next to the bar area. The crowd parted like the red sea, leaving her in my centerfold.

Sara was fortunate in having extracted the best features from both sets of her parents. Crystal eyes from her dad. Caramel complexion and high cheekbones from her biological mom.

My gaze wafted to her soft waves, framing her heart-shaped face. It was the first time she had relaxed her hair in years, pairing her appearance with a feminine dress that hugged her curves. Inadvertently, my eyes drooped to the slight cleavage she sported. The attire wasn't conservative, nor was it racy.

It was sexy, and I couldn't look away for the life of me.

Fuck, I needed to look away before someone caught me ogling my sister. There were too many eyes here tonight. What would they think if they knew of my lecherous thoughts?

Tristan Marcolf, son of the legendary politician Davis Marcolf, wanted to fuck his little sister's brains out.

If they knew of the things I wanted to do to Sara, I'd be one more worthless DC politician. *This* would become my only legacy.

I wish I could have ascertained that as being my biggest concern.

Men were stealing glances at Sara. Damn infuriating glances. I wanted to rip their eyes out of their sockets because none of them deserved to see her.

Disconcertingly, Sara didn't know to thwart their advances, so I had always been forced to keep an eye on her. And within minutes, my concerns were proven correct. A man came up to her with a drink in hand, but I couldn't see his face from this angle.

Lilith found me before I could nip it in the bud. It wasn't until she dragged me to the dance floor did I recognize the man with Sara. It was that police officer from earlier.

How the hell did the fucker track her down?

A low grumble almost tumbled out of my mouth at the memory of them staring at one another. I had barely managed to drive Sara back without shaking her silly and instead asked her to stay away from cops.

Clearly, she chose not to listen.

Closing my eyes, I counted down from ten. When I opened my eyes again, the sight was no better.

He was drinking her up like she was the only thing that might quench his thirst. And what was she thinking dancing with him so obscenely?

My knuckles whitened with a death grip fist upon noticing his hand resting a little too low on Sara's back. I chanted a mantra in my head that it was only a dance. Nothing more.

The mantra didn't help. But before I could advance toward that man with a death wish, they split. My attempt to do a sweep for them was smothered by a swarm of lobbyists and women adamant about having a word.

Even if I could ditch the lobbyists, it wouldn't be wise to step away. That sister of mine pushed my buttons, and I couldn't afford to make a scene. Not here. I was a congressman for this very state. If I were involved in a brawl, I could say goodbye to my political career.

Instead, I took out my phone and texted one of my staff members to sweep the mansion grounds for my sister. My resolve to let it be didn't last long, and I glanced around once more for Sara and that juvenile boy.

"I think they left," Lilith informed.

For a split second, I had forgotten she was still here. "Excuse me?"

"Your sister," she said in a matter-of-fact tone. "You were looking at her and that man with her."

With furrowed brows, I stared at her with distaste. "Stepsister," I corrected.

"Adopted sister," she corrected my correction.

The response stumped me, and I wondered why she had thought to specify so pointedly. Lilith was a blank slate, but there had been an edge to her voice.

Goddamnit. My irritating sister managed to rattle me every time, unsettling my perfectly laid out plans.

"Right," I conceded. "That's what I meant."

Lilith shrugged. "Don't go all big brother mode tonight. Let the poor girl have some fun."

I shook my head to rid the image of Sara's display of fun. "Do you know of the boy she was with?"

"Umm..." Lilith looked at me unsurely. "I think Tobias something. Your parents had come by earlier to introduce him. Apparently, he was to lead the first dance with Sara."

I froze.

I had dashed here from my meeting to find a dance floor already in full swing. It never crossed my mind that Sara might still opt to perform the first dance without me. Evidently, she didn't care because she had Tobias.

"I don't want to discuss my sister," I lamented. "How's work?" I asked, simultaneously texting my staff for an update on Sara.

I almost nodded off as Lilith unfolded the nitty-gritty details of her work as a lobbyist. Nonetheless, she was the most crucial component of my campaign, so I interjected when a response was appropriate. I wasn't much of a conversationalist other than with Sara and had to learn the cues. A curt response at the right moment indicated to the speaker that you were engaged. It lessened the need to share, signifying your interest in the opposing party.

So was the rule of society and the game of politics. Short of kissing a baby, the art of being a politician was a cliché. Every action was deliberate, planned, and anticipated.

At least there was one upside to my sister. People seldom surprised me, but her ridiculous antics never failed to deliver, constantly shaking the monotony.

My neck craned on its own for the fifteenth time, searching for her. I finally caught a flurry of lace running out of the mansion grounds. She had been gone most of the night. A rage like no other manifested, and I had to let it out before imploding. With a measly excuse to Lilith, I blindly followed Sara, but it was too late.

Sara was already driving away in her car.

CHAPTER 6

Sara

Small wins brought indescribable joy to life, I confirmed.

I tried to convince myself that Tristan's wrath in this matter was inconsequential. But my mind replayed the image when Tobias and I fled the scene. There was something else behind Tris' fury that I couldn't pinpoint. Perhaps it was a flicker of... hurt?

No, that couldn't be right.

So, what if I ignored his wishes? Tris might throw a fit over the trivial offense of sharing a dance with a gentleman caller, but I planned to enjoy the short-lived victory.

Tobias and I lazily strolled hand-in-hand through the manicured gardens of the mansion. Geometric boxwood hedges bordered a gravel walkway, giving it a hidden illusion. The full moon seeped through gaps of the greenery landscape just enough to find our way around. Even if I had custom-designed it, I couldn't have carved out a more romantic night.

"UCLA is impressive."

Tobias bumped my shoulder. "No less impressive than Georgetown."

Throughout the night, I had learned that Tobias was four years older than me and joined the police force shortly after graduating from UCLA. And he recently transferred to a DC precinct.

I also learned that his folks were friends with mine. When they found out about his transfer to DC, Tobias' Dad had suggested looking my family up.

Coincidentally, Tobias happened to be the officer who detained me. He put two and two together shortly after learning my last name and, in a suave move, called my parents to mention our run-in, minus the jail time.

My mother never missed the opportunity when a cute boy called on me. She invited him to this party and asked him to be my dance partner. In Mary's eyes, Tobias was high caliber boyfriend material, a prime prospect because he was from a family like ours.

I shrugged. "If I had my way, I would have gone to Stanford. But my family insisted that I attend college locally."

"But you seem like such a rebel. Can't believe you listened to your family just because they asked nicely."

I scoffed. "No one asked nicely. Haven't you met my brother? He can steamroll over anyone."

I assumed Tristan would've relished sending away his most troubled family member, but he vehemently protested my idea of going out of state for college. With the backing of our parents, he twisted my arm into attending a local university.

Streaks of lights from the fissure of the boxwoods cast on Tobias' face, disbelief painted onto his mien. "So... it was your brother then who wanted you to stay?"

My brows furrowed. "I mean, it was everyone in the family, but Tris truly pushed for it... I guess," I admitted slowly, trying to recall the exact conversation.

If I remembered correctly, Tris appeared in my room one night, listing all the glitches with attending college three thousand miles away.

"Hmm."

"What?"

Tobias rubbed the back of his neck with one hand. "No... it's just, so explain this to me. Tristan isn't really your brother, is he?"

"Excuse me?" I halted in place. More like, I came to a screeching halt. It felt like a snub, an insult, but I didn't know why.

"It's just... you guys aren't blood-related...."

"Blood isn't the only thing that makes someone your family."

Tobias appeared taken aback. "Umm, sorry that came out wrong. I didn't mean to offend you."

Shit. Why was I being so defensive?

"I'm being too sensitive." I shook my head. "I guess it's because I-I don't look like the rest of my family... so when people bring it up...." I looked around, searching for the right way to explain.

He smiled. "Let's forget about this topic. I think our previous conversation was much more interesting." Raising my hand, Tobias kissed the back of it. I nearly gasped from the minute contact, wondering if he'd judge too harshly if my knees gave out.

"What conversation was that?" I breathed, distracted by my fantasies surrounding Tobias. Nothing serious, only a slight future with two dogs, a white picket fence, and five kids.

Yes, I know! I know. Pump the damn brakes, Sara.

But when you had been lonely for so long, all contact was kinder than meant to be. It was easy to lose yourself on a whim and imagine what your babies with the handsome stranger might look like one day.

No one other than my family members had touched me in years.

This small act of intimacy made me want to weep over how badly I had craved sensual touches, insignificant as they might be. I wanted to experience the thing only a man could make a woman feel—desire.

Tilting my face, I stared at Tobias' mouth.

So tempting.

So inviting.

He pulled me closer on cue, my chest bumping against his. A hint of his cologne wafted into my nostrils, making me dizzy with want. His hot breath on my cheek tickled, and I unintentionally held my own in fear of a stronger reaction.

"You're so beautiful, Sara," he murmured.

The last thing I could focus on was a witty response. "Okay." The atrociously ridiculous word tumbled out of my mouth, though Tobias didn't seem to care.

And just like that, his lips were on mine, his body vibrating with meaning.

Adrenaline pumped through my veins, lost and enamored. Two strong hands circled my waist to crush me against his chest, and I barely had the time to wrap my arms around his neck to keep myself upright.

Tobias kissed me softly, licking my lips as his tongue probed for entry. His tongue tangled with mine while his thumb stroked my cheek. It was a soul-crushingly slow kiss, and I cherished every nano-second.

Tobias broke the kiss at long last, palm resting on my nape.

Ever since we met, I had felt this indescribable pull toward him. He was the first man I had kissed in three years, and I felt light-headed at the realization.

"Sara, I want you to know...." He stared at me pensively. "I-I haven't been able to stop thinking about you all day."

"Tobias," I found myself whispering.

He held my face between his hands, searching my eyes. "I mean...

it's insane how we met despite our parents already knowing one another. It feels like a sign that we were supposed to meet, you know?"

I blinked, remembering how pushy my mother could be. "About that. I-I don't know what to say. I'm sorry if Mom harassed you into coming tonight."

He smiled kindly. "Don't be. I love her. When I told her who my dad was, she got him on the line, and they both insisted that I was to be your date for the evening."

Sounded like something Mary Marcolf would do. Her one desire in life was to marry me off so I could give her a bunch of grandchildren.

"But," he said unsurely, "when I asked her for your number or to pick you up, she suggested surprising you here. Apparently, you were not to be given a choice about this date because you're in the business of turning away perfectly good men for no reason. Want to tell me what that's all about?"

Like a cold bucket of water had doused me, I jolted in his hold. In my excitement, I had forgotten about the damned curse and why I chose to stay away from men.

What the fuck was I thinking?

I was doomed from the beginning. Why would I drag someone else into my mess? Why did I risk Tobias' well-being by letting him kiss me?

A blaring memory flashed in my mind.

On a night very much like this one, Mom had tried to present me into society for the second year in a row. This time, my escort was Alex Bowman, another of her friends' sons.

During the formal, I realized that Alex was popular, athletic, gorgeous... and mildly chauvinistic. He bored the mentality that girls should be seen, not heard. Suffice to say, Alex wasn't on track to be the great love of my life. My perception of him only deteriorated when he got handsy after the dance, leading to my hasty exit.

The next day, we discovered that he had been admitted to critical care. A vigilante robbed Alex in the parking lot, shoved him to the ground, then ran over his hands in their haste to drive away.

After the incident, I found Dad studying me skeptically. It was hard to ignore that both the children of Mary's associates were harmed by interacting with me. There wasn't a verbal accusation, although his glances were quite telling.

Alarm bells went off in my head at the memory, and my rational senses returned for the first time tonight.

"I'm so sorry," I said softly. Placing both hands on his chest, I shoved him back. He slightly stumbled before catching himself. Bewildered, Tobias extended his arm to hold me again, but I stepped out of reach.

"What's wrong?"

"I have to go." I turned to leave, but Tobias grabbed my elbow.

"Did I do something wrong?" he frowned in concern.

"N-No," I stuttered. "I-I just have to go."

"Sara," he said softly, "we were just talking, and everything was fine. I-I must have said something to freak you out. Shit, I probably came on too strong. I-I just like you so much, and I don't want to play games."

I covered his hand with my own and slowly removed it from my arm. "It's not that. I-I am so sorry, Tobias. I really have to go." I paused. "Just promise me one thing—you'll be extra careful tonight."

"What?" Tobias asked in disbelief. "What the hell are you talking about?"

Tobias was new in town and didn't know what had happened to all the other boys. I couldn't look him in the eyes. Guilt dripped through every bit of my conscience that I might have put him at risk.

This had been the most romantic night of my life, and perhaps it'd be the only one I'd ever get. I didn't want to taint it by revealing my baggage. I only hoped our time together was so insignificant that nothing terrible would transpire of it.

"I can't explain it." Because you'd never believe me.

How many times had I tried to convince someone of the evil that lurked in my life? Everyone brushed it off as a figment of my imagination or, better yet, accused me of attempted murder.

"Just... don't eat anything you didn't prepare, actually don't eat anything for the rest of the night. And don't talk to strangers. Be very careful crossing the street."

"Sara," he said in a sympathetic tone as if realizing he was speaking to a crazy person.

"Please! Promise me you'll do this for me."

"But—"

"Tobias, please," I cried out, the desperation evident in my voice.

Tobias seemed taken aback but finally gave me a nod. "Only on one condition. You have to go on a date with me."

I almost smiled.

I had lost myself under the starry night and the sway of the warm breeze. I had forgotten that no one was allowed to get close to me. If I truly cared for someone, I had to keep away to protect them from the calamity that followed.

"Goodbye, Tobias." Thank you for the best night of my life.

I tilted my head to the side for one last glance at the beautiful man before bolting toward the parking lot and throwing the door open to my car.

CHAPTER 7

Tristan

"Tristan!" A voice murmured into my ear in the dark of the night.

My eyes refused to adjust to the dim light, displaying only glimpses of my surroundings. The room was painted red, air covered in a mixture of smoke and sin. Amidst the flashes of naked limbs, I made out a figure across the room.

"Who's there?" I demanded.

The figure walked toward me, whispering my name, and tempting me with all sorts of false promises.

I didn't want to buy what he was selling. I tried to back away, but heavy limbs weighed me down, grabbing at me greedily.

"Let go of me," I shouted at the faceless limbs to get away from the figure who had come for my soul.

It was too late.

The horrid face of a demon, with the burnt wings of an angel, stood nose to nose. He looked straight through me.

"It's you," I whispered.

"I see the way you look at her," he uttered softly with a sinister smile carved on his face. "The way you lust after your little sister. You wanted to kill that man for touching her, didn't you?"

My eyes widened, face riddled with guilt.

"It would feel so good to give in, wouldn't it?" He sneered sardonically. "To satisfy your insatiable hunger with her little body."

I shoved him away. "Stop it," I mumbled weakly.

"She wants that man because he is good. A virtuous human. And she wants nothing to do with you because you are just a slave to the pleasures of the flesh. She can see past your beautiful mask and will never want the ugly man underneath."

"Shut up!" I bellowed.

"You're destined to walk this earth alone. You'll never have her! No matter what you do, they'll take her from you."

"Never!" I woke with a start, my body drenched in sweat as I hyperventilated.

Fuck.

I was in my childhood bedroom... alone.

Steve, my right-hand man, confirmed that Sara had driven straight home after the fundraiser. Even so, I felt restless and drove to our parents' to spend the night here.

It was past midnight by the time I arrived. The lights to Sara's room were already turned off. Unable to give her the brunt of my anger for her act of defiance from earlier, I also turned in for the night.

This day had already been a shitty one. First, I discovered that some girls at Sara's school had been bullying her. Sara was generally consistent in her traits—forthright, talkative, proud. My chest had constricted at the thought that there had been lapses in her personality due to those bitches.

My day worsened upon finding some lowly cop escorting her out of the shelter, only for the same fucker to show up at the event tonight. I later found out that he was a family friend, and Mom herself had arranged the damn date.

Sara looked at him like... oh hell. There was a spark of interest in her eyes. And he... he looked at her like she was the divine beauty gracing his undeserving world.

Punching down on the bed, I rose to a sitting position. In the dark, I pulled on a pair of grey sweatpants over my boxers and walked to the sliding doors to step outside on the balcony.

This house was perpetually undergoing renovations, courtesy of our parents' boredom with retired life. My Dad had invested in a collection of hotel casinos in Las Vegas, which now supplied me with a cash stream. I used the money to support Mary and Ragu's lifestyle so they could quit their jobs and invest their time in my campaign instead. Now, they went from city to city to campaign for endorsements and donation checks. In their spare time, they redecorated.

This particular veranda on the second floor had been extended to wrap around the entirety of the second floor. Of all the architectural modifications, this one was my favorite.

I stepped onto the marble floor, hoping the air would do me good.

"What are you doing here?" Sara's voice emerged from the shadows.

All of our bedrooms had two entrances. One door led to the inside of the house, while the other opened up to this massive balcony. Without meaning to do so, I had walked too far and stood next to Sara's bedroom.

I took an involuntary sharp breath as she stepped into my line of sight. My vision blurred, heat reaching me right in the groin.

It had become impossible to dismiss that Sara's body had matured to the point of agony over the last few years. My attempts to subdue the salacious images were in vain, so I stopped trying altogether.

It was easy to outline her figure under the thin white nightshirt.

When Sara stretched to yawn, lifting her shirt high enough to display a set of toned thighs, nothing more was left to the imagination.

Holy fuck.

My cock jerked slightly, and I quickly averted my gaze.

She is your sister. She is your sister. She is your sister.

I swallowed, my previous anger all but forgotten. "It got late after the fundraiser, and DC was a closer drive than my house. I also need a break from the campaign, so I'll stick around until tomorrow."

I owned a property in Virginia as I was a congressman there. Meanwhile, the rest of my family lived less than an hour away in DC. My work consisted of enough time spent in the capital. It wasn't abnormal for me to stay the night at my folks', only difficult to get away from campaigning, even on weekends.

Sara's face was shrouded with disbelief. "Won't your massive empire crumble without their king?"

"The peasants will live to see another day."

With a mocking gape, she pretended to be shocked. "How-the-fuck-ever would they survive without their beloved leader? Do they even have enough bread to eat?"

That managed to extract a smile out of me. "If they don't," I whispered, leaning in, "then let them eat cake."

Throwing her head back, Sara laughed wholeheartedly. The sound punctured through my rib cage to nestle right into my heart. It was sweet and melodic, unlike everything else in this world.

Nothing with Sara should shock me anymore. Only a few hours ago, I wanted to wring her pretty little neck out. And now, here we were—laughing.

Before she came into my life, I had stopped smiling altogether and only spoke out of necessity. I had no substantial relationship with my mother or anyone else for that matter. Over the years, she had chipped away at my reservations. Now, someone resembling a human being stood before her.

"Why are you still up? I thought you went to sleep."

I noted the layout in front of the sliding doors of Sara's room. There was an easel with a canvas propped up on it. Art supplies were scattered in the vicinity, suggesting she was experiencing similar restlessness.

"Couldn't sleep," she confirmed. "I thought painting might help."

Turning her back to me, Sara walked to the easel. She loved to paint whenever she was sad or restless.

At the moment, she was painting the view from our balcony. A man and a woman stood on the very balcony, gazing upon the starry night. The figures depicted multiple ethnicities as chunks of their faces were painted in various colors—white, black, brown, olive, and so forth.

A figure that represents all races, I concluded absentmindedly.

Did she feel excluded from this family? Was this her nonverbal way of disclosing how much she wished we all looked the same?

"Interesting piece," I whispered. "What do you call it?"

"A painting."

"Do you always have to be such a brat?"

She turned to me with a crooked smile. "Only at three in the morning."

"Which brings me to the original question. Why are you up so late?"

"Just thinking of ways to torture you," Sara mumbled absentmindedly.

That little shit.

A few weeks ago, our parents had hosted a large dinner party. The guest list included Lilith, a woman Mom had pushed for me to marry. Lilith had the right build for a politician's wife. Sadly, she did nothing for me. I only kept her around because she was a prominent lobbyist representing the interests of the largest corporations. I needed her support to win not only the upcoming election but to run for the presidency one day.

But it wasn't worth tolerating the backhanded comment I had once overheard her make about Sara. At the time, I gave Lilith her one and only pass. If I saw a repeat in the behavior, I'd ruin her life; campaign be damned.

Sara knew that I only kept up the façade out of obligation, whereas in reality, Lilith annoyed the shit out of me. So, on the night of the dinner party, Sara dutifully waited until the meal commenced to play her hand.

After dinner, the waiters brought out coffee for all the guests. Sara used a permanent marker to write 'marry me' on the bottom of Lilith's cup, then filled it with coffee. Lilith read the words aloud and squealed, convinced that the proposal had come from me.

It was the first time I was speechless, not purposefully quiet.

Sara lived to dish out her own form of vengeance, one that I lived for. It was never violent, only just. She killed two birds with one stone by teaching Lilith a lesson for her micro aggressively charged racist comments while exacting the usual revenge against me.

In retaliation, I donated Sara's clothes to goodwill and replaced her closet with exact replicas, only one size smaller. Sara had a flair for all clothes that were light in color (white or anything in pastel). She was a goddamn princess in that way and refused to wear any other colors. So, this prank was the one I was the proudest of. One she'd probably make me pay for dearly. My lips twitched into half a smile at the thought.

"What have you come up with so far?" I asked conversationally.

"If I tell you, it'll take away the element of surprise, and I'd hate to disappoint you."

"Ah, of course."

Fuck, I loved sparring with her.

When we first met, I was wary of her presence in my life. After all, we were polar opposites.

She was talkative, while I was reserved.

She was sensitive, whereas I was impassive.

She was warm, and I was aloof.

There was only one characteristic we shared—Vengeance.

Our rivalry on the day we met had turned into a lifetime of pranks and schemes to torture one another. Over the years, I began to crave going head to head with her.

Once, I took a whole onion, dipped it into caramel, and told Sara it was a candied apple. The first bite was enough for her to gag and throw up.

She super glued the lids to my shampoo and conditioner, knowing full well of my attachment to my hair and the expensive products I invested in. I kept purchasing new bottles, unable to figure out why they'd work on day one, then mysteriously jam up.

For her retribution, I took the bag of Oreo cookies she had a weakness for and spent hours pulling each cookie apart, replacing the filling with white toothpaste. Sara wasn't happy.

But it wasn't all about our petty rivalry.

When I didn't torture her, Sara could be sweet. In turn, she was the only talkative person I tolerated. Even my childhood friends couldn't pull more than a few syllables out of me. Despite the nearly eleven-year age gap we shared, she was my one meaningful connection to this earth.

When I used to visit home from college, she'd be the first person to greet me at the door. In eighth grade, Sara told everyone that her brother would be the president one day, and anyone to contradict it was met with her wrath.

And every year, on the anniversary of Dad's death, Sara hugged me.

Ever since I hit puberty, everything had been handed to me. People fell at my feet though I'd do very little to charm them. Men wanted to be me. Women kneeled down without knowing a thing about me. No one displayed a morsel of authenticity. The mindless devotion had turned hollow with a voice taunting me that I'd never experience more than these superficial connections. There were no more surprises left... except for Sara.

She became my adopted sister upon Mary and Ragu's matrimony. For all intents and purposes, I was a brother to her, and perhaps that's why she didn't mindlessly bow to me just because of my looks.

For years, our friendly competition had kept me engaged in my otherwise dull life. Not once had she told on me. Instead, she was my worthiest adversary. The only person in this damned world that I respected. And I had come to crave her sweetness as much as I craved her wickedness, although she was always hell-bent on annoying the shit out of me.

Sara turned on her heels and swabbed me with her paintbrush.

"What was that for?" I frowned, irritated.

"I'm furious with you."

"What else is new?"

Grabbing one of the white rags next to her canvas, I wiped the paint off my chest. For a second, I wondered if the moonlight was playing tricks on me or did her gaze linger on my shirtless torso for a second too long?

She looked away much too quick for my liking. "Why are you forcing me to move home?"

Because you lived in a coed dorm, and all the boys wanted to fuck you, and I had been going crazy. "You know why," I replied coolly.

Sara's stone-colored eyes searched mine. "Because you think I hurt those girls?" she asked, bottom lip quivering.

I gaped at her. She couldn't believe that; Could she?

Guilt over the part I had played tore my heart open because her desolate state was apparent. “No, Angel,” I said. “Never,” I reiterated firmly because it was imperative for her to know. “But I think it’ll be best for you to live at home instead of the dorms, so we can protect you if people start talking again.”

Sara’s reluctant eyes returned to the canvas.

I sighed. “Look at it this way. At least there was a silver lining tonight.”

“What’s that?”

“You looked less ugly than usual.”

Sara tried to swab the paintbrush at me again, but I moved back just in time to avoid the attack. “At least my hair wasn’t such a mess that it was all everyone talked about. Your convertible hair gave away which car you drove to the event.”

A slow-motion horror hit me like a train wreck.

Convertible hair? Why didn’t Steve tell me? Did the photographers take pictures of my hair in that condition? Would it be in tomorrow’s papers? Why hadn’t I thought of checking on my hair before entering the grand ballroom?

Always check on the hair, Tristan!

Spinning in place, I caught my reflection in the glass of the double doors to Sara’s room. Everything looked in place where my hair was concerned.

Her melodic laugh confirmed that she was playing with my vanity. I ground my teeth in irritation. How did she always manage to get the better of me? I didn’t even drive my fucking convertible to the event. I had donated that car to one of Sara’s charities.

I gained on her until nominal distance remained between my bare chest and her itty-bitty nightshirt. The smile vanished off her face, and she visibly swallowed. Dilated pupils tried to keep their gaze trained on me. A low growl built inside my chest when her eyes inadvertently drooped to my abs.

It's a nonverbal game we played, one we never admitted to out loud. She teased me for my vanity, and I shut her up with the same ethereal looks even my sister couldn't deny.

Sara's gaze lingered on my torso, and this time there was no uncertainty in the matter. In spite of herself, she was checking me out.

Holy shit, Sara was checking me out. But she swiftly snapped out of it with a head shake.

With smug satisfaction, I yanked at her shirt. "Come on, little monster," I murmured with nothing more to prove. "It's time for bed. You need rest to properly plot my downfall."

"You'll never see it coming." She yawned.

"Uh-huh."

She wasn't surprised when I followed her into the dimly lit bedroom.

"Do you want an Ambien?" Sara and I both struggled with sleep and had prescriptions for sleep medication. She took them on the nights someone got... hurt.

Sara nodded. "On the nightstand."

I grabbed the pack and popped open a pill. She dutifully held out a hand as I passed it over, along with the glass of water sitting on her nightstand.

"Why are *you* up so late? Bad dream?"

I nodded, hauling Sara to bed and pulling the comforter over her.

"What are you doing?" she asked when I climbed in and leaned my back against the headboard.

"Doubt I'll sleep tonight."

"So?"

"So, since I'll be up anyway, I'll keep an eye on you to ensure you don't have any more side effects."

Sara once sleepwalked to our front gate under the influence of these pills. She also had the tendency to talk in her induced state. If she needed help to sleep, I could at least make certain she didn't have dangerous side effects.

"You are such a freak. Get out."

"Shh, go to sleep."

I stroked her hair, which quietened her. She stared blankly but said nothing more. Eventually, her breathing evened out.

Sleep never came for me, just as I knew it wouldn't. Instead, I stared at Sara's motionless form.

God, I wanted to touch her... and not like a brother.

I shouldn't be having these thoughts. Then again, why was she created to be so damn irresistible? She was sex served on a platter. Her voice, her smile, her body; everything about her was so tempting. Especially her mouth. The nude-pink lips were slightly parted in her sleep... and God forgive me because I wanted my dick between them.

I chanted in my head that these thoughts had manifested after seeing her with another man. The motherfucker was salivating after *my* Sara. It was infuriating. I saw the lewd desire in his eyes, and hate had ignited inside me, tearing me up. For once in my life, I wanted a woman's attention on me, but Sara looked past me to stare at *him*.

Part of me wanted to wake her to demand answers. How dare she allow him to touch her, to flirt with her, too?

My annoyance ended when she stirred in sleep. I froze, then watched in astonished disbelief as Sara slipped her hands between her legs.

What.

The.

Fuck.

Never in a million years had I anticipated that Sara unconsciously touched herself. Was this an aftereffect of the sleeping pills?

Watching her during such a private moment felt like I'd somehow fuck her up even if she didn't know. I needed to leave but instead groaned as she aimlessly moved her hands under the comforter. She had this desperate need to get off but could do nothing about it in her state and was practically begging for my assistance.

Please, God, help me. Is this a test? If so, why are you forcing me to fail?

My prayers went unanswered when Sara groaned in frustration. My cock twitched with her next moan, tearing down the last of my reserves. The voice in my ears got louder with each passing second until I could take it no more.

She is yours.

Take her.

She wants you.

Every woman wants you.

She's lucky to be touched by you.

My heart lurched at the idea of someone discovering us at this very moment, with Sara grinding herself against her pussy and me contemplating touching her like a sick fucker. The reputation I had built, it'd be all for nothing. I'd be just another corrupt politician with immoral intentions.

But then the dark voice to haunt me for years whispered, *No one has to know.*

I started praying for divine intervention again because my first thought was about the accuracy of those words. *No one has to know.* Sara was zonked out from the pill, and our parents were fast asleep. How would anyone find out?

Fuck it.

I peeled the covers back and halted, transfixed. She only wore a pair of white boy shorts under her nightshirt. I watched as her hand moved inside her panties. It took every last bit of my remaining self-control not to yank them down for a glance of her soft flesh. I had fantasized about it every night for years.

Before stopping myself, my hand was palming the hard length

through my sweatpants, stroking myself as I watched Sara work herself into a frenzy.

I wanted so much more, but this... what I was doing... was already so wrong. It was against her will, for she only saw me as her brother. But if a time came when I could convince her otherwise, I might have a lucid Sara with desire in her eyes.

The eroticism of such an image spurred on an impulse, and Goddamn if I didn't follow it. I dragged her white panties down with care until exposing her small and beautiful cunt.

It was prettier than I had pictured all those nights while fisting my dick. The years of fantasizing about fucking her. The years of denying myself. Even my God knew that I could do it no longer.

The pad of my thumb lightly grazed her pussy. Before I could come to my senses, I gently shoved her hand away. In their stead, I pressed my digits on her cunt and opened up her folds.

Fuck.

My jaw clenched to suppress the rumble that threatened to break free. Her flesh was so damn tender and hot to my touch. Christ.

I had never pushed the envelope this far with Sara. At most, I watched her from far or didn't let men near her. I had never touched her before.

But it was impossible not to when her nipples were rock hard, standing stout against her nightshirt. With my hand fisted around my cock, I used the other to stroke her hot cunt. I had never felt a pussy so soft or so responsive. Her cunt trembled under my touch, practically ready to fall apart when I pressed down on her throbbing clit.

"Mm," Sara moaned in her sleep.

My eyes widened at the sensual sounds she made. Sara slept like dead under the influence of sleep medication, but no one had fondled her during those other times. Careful not to wake her, I continued to massage her folds.

Shit. This was so fucking hot.

When she pressed her thighs together—keeping my hand tightly locked in her pussy—I growled a *fuck* and jumped on top of her. With my hand massaging her cunt, and the other fisting my dick, I used my knees as leverage to prop myself up, so I could watch both sinful sights. Unable to help myself, I stuffed a finger inside her, practically forcing my way in.

Thank fuck.

No one had been inside my Sara. I could feel her tight walls quaking around my thick finger. When I crooked it slightly to graze her untouched walls, Sara shuddered. She thrashed with her back arched and climaxed right in her sleep. Like clockwork, hot cum spurted out of me and onto her stomach and shirt, covering her.

Marking her.

And that was that.

I had broken the barrier and done something reprehensible. There was no coming back from it, and even though she didn't know any better in her unconscious state, Sara was mine.

Pulling my sopping wet fingers out of her cunt, I brought them to my nose and then dipped them into my mouth. I tasted her before drifting them over Sara's parted lips. She sucked on my fingers subconsciously when they plunged inside the warmth of her moist mouth.

"That's it, baby," I murmured against her ears.

I should have felt guilt over what just happened, but all I felt was utter bliss. And if I stayed any longer, I'd only want to go further. Much further.

Instead, I pulled my sweatpants up and cleaned Sara up with a warm washcloth. With one more longing look at the girl I used to call my sister, I retreated to the safety of my room.

CHAPTER 8

Tristan

Michael sat across from me in his new office, a pristine location in downtown Georgetown. He didn't look up, scribbling away in his notebook.

I woke up early today and prodded him into seeing me for an impromptu session. My mind felt fucked, and I needed him to unscramble it ASAP.

"Are you having doubts about your chances in the election?"

"Huh?" I asked absentmindedly.

"Your campaign," he pressed. "Everything you've worked so hard for."

I blinked. "Right."

I had worked hard for my career and was so close to getting everything I ever wanted. If anyone got wind of what I did last night, my political life would be over before taking off. It was necessary to steer clear of scandals at this stretch to achieve my goals.

Except, the importance of it refused to register with me.

Why had politics been so important to me in the first place?

"How was the fundraiser last night?"

"Fine," I mumbled. The night had gone far from fine.

"Doesn't sound like it. What happened?"

I groaned, running a hand down my face. "Nothing. I just... didn't get as many pledges as I had hoped. And then I saw Sara with this man. This police officer... he was hitting on her." With a twist of my thumb and forefinger, I rotated the tiny globe perched on the side table to drown out the urge to drive my fist through the wall.

"Care to elaborate?"

I paused, unsure whether I should.

Michael noticed my taciturnity. "From what you've told me about her, Sara is a capable young lady. What's so wrong with someone taking an interest in her?"

"I don't want her to become collateral damage."

"How so?"

"Sara is naïve. I'm worried he might be trying to get himself associated with the right family. He is nothing but a two-bit social climber."

Michael quirked his eyebrow, his interest piqued. "We both know your sister isn't naïve. Is this about something else?"

"What's that supposed to mean?"

"Only that you're expressing more than brotherly concerns."

Fuck yeah, I was. I couldn't get the vision of last night out of my head. Part of me was floating on ecstasy after my night with Sara, and the other half was distracted by the residual guilt.

"Tristan, it's clear that you seem to be seeking something more profound than just a one-night stand and are having difficulty finding someone who can provide that."

Oh, I found someone, alright; she just happened to be my sister.

Michael's words disturbed me. The first time I saw Sara as a woman, instead of a little girl, was also the last day I noticed or touched another woman. How the fuck did Michael figure that out? My indiscretions weren't public knowledge.

He answered my unspoken question. "There have been too many changes in... let's call it your dating habits... to overlook the trend. But just because you have given up on..." he waved a hand to describe my previous long strands of one-night stands, menage et trois, orgies, and once more settled on the word, "dating... doesn't mean Sara has to do the same."

Why the hell not? I thought petulantly.

"It's not that," I said dismissively to tackle the root of the issue. "I-I made some impulsive choices last night that might affect Sara negatively," I offered vaguely, remembering how she had moaned around my finger. "But if the outcome is something good, can the ends not justify the means?" Why did it feel so damn good if last night was wrong?

He smiled. "Hmm. Your current dilemma reminds me of another story about Asmodeus. Would you like to hear it?" Michael paused meaningfully, searching my face.

I gave nothing away even as my heart started beating erratically.

Yeah, I fucking want to hear it, and he knows it, too.

Over the years, Michael's stories about Asmodeus sated my curiosity for some untold reason. I had researched this demon. None of the sources I had found matched Michael's version. Perhaps he simply made these stories up in hopes of showing me the light. He was convinced I'd turn into the embodiment of this demon if I weren't careful.

Still, how did Michael learn such intimate details that resonated with my life so acutely?

Michael refused to disclose further. He said that the little mystery guaranteed my weekly return for sessions that now cost me four hundred dollars an hour, claiming inflation caused the rate increase.

Fucking asshole.

Despite my irritation, I didn't protest as he told me yet another story about the demon named Asmodeus.

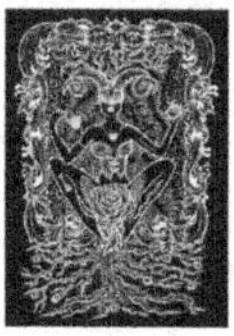

Asmodeus rarely showed himself in form and didn't wreak havoc amongst the mortals through carnage but rather through the power of suggestion. But now, he had fallen in love with a mortal. He was drawn to Sarah like a moth to a flame. The demon strained to hear her voice, yearned to see her at every chance.

But oh, that God, He was as just as He was cruel.

To punish Asmodeus for his follies, God made it so the only women he could touch were the ones to satiate his nefarious desires, never the ones to fill his hollow heart. He was to walk eternity knowing all the pleasures of the body and none about mending his rotten soul.

It infuriated Asmodeus, but there was nothing to be done. Sarah could neither see nor hear the demon. He'd always be a mere feeling to her, watching over her.

All the same, Asmodeus lurked in the shadows to watch his beloved be courted by measly men. When another approached her while she strolled through the gardens, never had Asmodeus' golden eyes flared so lethally from anger. This fly was going to take away his Sarah.

He, the Demon of Lust, could bring any woman to their knees. Yet, the only one he loved was immune to his presence.

His broken heart boomed, beating violently at the thought. It ignited the wrath Asmodeus had never known to possess. And driven by his anger, Asmodeus came apart.

Over the next few years, every man to come near Sarah died mercilessly at his hands until seven mysterious deaths surrounded the same woman. Sarah's reputation was in tatters. Her parents desperately sought to hide evidence that linked their beloved daughter to such atrocious crimes. Still, Sarah wasn't concerned with her reputation, only with the innocent victims who had met their untimely deaths.

Accusing eyes followed Sarah everywhere she went. She tried to drown out the judgment as she walked through her beloved gardens. But two young women sneered at her retreating body.

"Succubus!"

"Harlot!"

"Murderer!"

Sarah's chest constricted with pain as she looked up at Heaven, wailing at God. "Why, God? Why does everyone to come near me die such gruesome deaths? Tell me, Merciful God. What is wrong with me?" she sobbed relentlessly.

God didn't answer. He didn't have to because she already knew the truth.

Sarah was cursed.

Asmodeus' amber eyes glowed with sorrow as he watched her. It was the first time in his forsaken eternity to experience such emotion. Desperation rolled off his shoulders from the powerlessness he felt, unable to comfort her. The arrogant demon, who didn't kneel around the mightiest of all, knelt in front of the woman he loved.

"My dear heart, please don't cry anymore." Asmodeus gently stroked Sarah's cheeks to wipe away the tears, only for his fingers to slip through her skin like hollow nothingness. The moisture remained on her skin, and he cursed at the reminder that he could never touch her.

Sarah jolted at the feel of a lingering coldness on her skin, though she saw no one. She had known something had always lurked in her wake, watching her misery. Swiftly, she closed her eyes, chiding herself for acting like a child who believed in ghosts.

Asmodeus looked longingly at her. He craved to comfort her and vowed to give her the next best thing instead.

Vengeance.

"Don't worry, my love. Their wickedness will never reach your gentle ears again. For angels sacrifice what they love for the sake of humanity. But fallen angels will sacrifice humanity for the sake of their love."

It wasn't until late afternoon when Sarah returned to the gardens, only to find two dead bodies within the tall grass, blood painting the surrounding ground. Their faces and bodies had been clawed with the nails of a mighty beast, one not belonging to this world.

Sarah recognized the bodies. It was the two women who had insulted her and accused her of murder.

Sarah screamed and then screamed again.

Her fragile heart could take no more.

I swallowed several times.

Did he know?

There was a pit in my stomach that Michael knew of my extracurricular activities. There was no other logical reason to tell me this story.

Careful not to disclose any incriminating information, I kept my expression neutral. Instead, I waited for Michael to reveal the lesson he wanted me to take away.

That was our ritual. He'd tell me one of these stories and a lesson to go along with it.

"The end can hardly justify the means if it hurts the thing you care about the most in the process," he said at last. "What might seem like the best decision might simply be your emotions or passions running wild. Maybe it's best to take a step back when you are on the brink of these impulsive spur-of-the-moment decisions. What do you think?"

God, I wanted to give in to my impulses. I *wanted* to touch Sara again. The boy she had mooned over also deserved some rash consequences. My hands shook with the need to make him pay.

But what might that do to Sara?

In the past, she had tried to convince us that she considered herself to be bad luck. Self-reproach coated my conscience. I hated that my actions had made her feel isolated. I had to start controlling these impulses for her sake.

If sparing that boy kept my Sara optimistic about life, then I'd comply. Instead of hurting him, I'd convince her to stay away. And if taking a step back kept my impulses in check, the ones to inadvertently hurt her repeatedly, then I needed to return home and find a new way to control these urges.

I could take up meditation.

Yes.

I'd indulge in meditation to learn better self-control. Maybe I could give myself a week to try a different method.

I'd do anything for Sara because, after last night, I was surer than ever that I'd never work her out of my system. There was no one else for me but her.

Without her, I'd be doomed to walk this earth alone.

CHAPTER 9

Sara

I woke with a start, casting a hand over my eyes to shield them from the unforgiving sun rays.

"Need to stop taking those damn pills," I muttered.

Everything was hazy. Ambien had that effect on me, so I rarely took them. But it was warranted after the "incident" yesterday with those two girls and Tobias.

The girls were currently admitted to Sinai hospital due to their injuries. I wanted to visit them, bring them flowers. However, I had an inkling that their families might object and accuse me of coming with intentions to finish off the job I started.

It was disheartening to learn that my curse had struck again. I thought everyone would be safe if I avoided romantic interests. That policy of mine had worked for years. Now, the future was uncertain once more.

I was also worried sick about Tobias and prayed that nothing terrible happened to him last night. Perhaps Mom would agree to call and ensure he made it safely back to his home?

I sat up with a huff, only to freeze at the sight between my thighs.

Goddamnit.

I had taken my underwear off in sleep. My pussy was red and swollen like I had vigorously rubbed it throughout the night.

I closed my eyes, mortified.

Though I had never been with a man, this sight was far from unfamiliar. I had resorted to touching myself in my sleep in my insatiable craving for physical intimacy. Many a night, I had woken up with my hands between my thighs, furiously working myself to completion.

I groaned, convinced that I was the most sexual human being on earth. After turning fifteen, all I had thought about was sex and not in the typical teenage hormonal way. An overtly sexual ad on television had me running to my room to get myself off. And I had watched so much porn over the years that the images had been ingrained into my mind. Not just the run-of-the-mill porn either; it was dirty, humiliating porn that someone like me had no business watching.

That's the reason God reprimanded me with this suitable punishment. When these urges first popped up, and I started noticing boys, that's also when they started dropping like flies around me.

My lewd thoughts angered God, and anyone to touch me suffered the price. No one in this world believed me, so I stopped bothering to explain and instead stayed away from men.

Befitting, wasn't it?

God had a great sense of humor because my punishment was custom-made. Not only would I never know the touch of a man, but I'd never have children or a family of my own either.

I was destined to walk this earth alone.

With another huff, I shook my head—enough of this pity party. I had a roof over my head while the families in the shelter were about to lose theirs. Instead of wallowing, I needed to head to the shelter. That's why I became involved with charity work in the first place.

When people started getting hurt around me, I went to my pastor and disclosed my loitering suspicion about a curse. He didn't believe me, of course. However, he advised giving back to the community if I was genuinely convinced of inflicting unintentional harm onto others.

Now that my first year of college was over, I could focus my undivided attention on the shelter. The demonstration from yesterday was great for media attention, but many families were soon to be upended. We had no idea where to move them and only had thirty days to evacuate. I had to utilize every one of those days productively.

Shoving my comforter to the side, I swung my legs to the floor, searching for my fluffy pink slippers. I had only just pulled on a pair of shorts and a crop top—both one size too small thanks to my idiotic brother—when the devil himself showed his face.

Tristan pulled open the sliding doors of the veranda entrance to my room and dwarfed it with his gigantic frame. There was such masculine energy about him that he never fit right in my room, where everything was pink, white, fluffy, and sparkly, with one too many pillows on the bed.

My overtly girlie room was the only thing to remain from my previous sunshine and unicorn life. That's before I had turned into a recluse and shut myself away. On some level, I kept the theme of my childhood room because it irritated Tristan. The way his nose crinkled in disgust upon stepping inside fueled my fire.

However, he appeared far from annoyed this morning. In fact, Tristan looked rejuvenated, like he had the best night of his life. The jovial look gave him a boyish charm despite recently turning thirty.

His dark locks were sopping wet from a fresh shower. He appeared so at home in jeans and a heather gray t-shirt that my head felt dizzy. It's like we were kids again and living under the same roof.

The thought saddened me because we'd never live together again. Siblings grew up and went their separate ways. Such was life.

"Any plans for the day?" he asked, looking me up and down. The words were innocent enough, yet his voice sounded... husky?

"Umm... yeah, the shelter," I replied, distracted.

"Every pervert in a ten-mile radius will try to maul you if you go out dressed like that." His eyes flared, glowing like gold in the light.

I blinked at his over-the-top reaction. "I wasn't planning on it. And you're the one who gave away my clothes," I mumbled. "Now, everything is too tight."

That broke the tension. His lips quirked wickedly, pleased with himself at the prank he had concocted. With his index finger, Tris tipped my face up. He was so damn tall that I had to crane my neck to meet his eyes.

"How about I come home again next weekend, and we can go shopping for new clothes? I'm pretty sure it won't bode well for my campaign if I get into fights with a bunch of pervs for eye-fucking you."

I opened my mouth to protest, but he cut me off with another peace offering.

"Oh, and before I forget. I thought of a way to keep your shelter open."

"What?" Surprised by his offer, the hoodie I was toying with slipped from my hands and onto the floor.

With a heavy sigh, Tris bent his knee to pick it up. He seemed to rise at an exceedingly slow pace, and perhaps it was my imagination, but his eyes lingered on my bare legs, heat grazing the skin as he went.

I accepted the hoodie with hands that might have been slightly trembling.

"Steve will research the developers who purchased the shelter," he continued mildly. "I'm sure he can find something to help our appeal with the DC zoning committee. If anything, I'm positive they'll grant the shelter more time if we show due cause."

We? Us? Our?

The shelter didn't fall under Tris' jurisdiction, nor would it benefit his campaign. So, why get involved when he already had so much on his plate?

I shouldn't be surprised. This was our dynamic, after all. Twenty-four hours ago, I was furious with him for giving away my clothes. Now, I loved him for making time in his busy schedule to help with my cause.

This lifeline was why I believed my brother would make a great president someday. Yes, this man was beautiful like every woman claimed, but he also had a beautiful soul that they constantly overlooked. Within the week, Tris and I would likely return to our animosity. In the meanwhile, I reveled in the friendship.

I tackled him at full speed and threw my arms around his neck. "Thank you. Thank you. Thank you."

He chuckled softly at my unsolicited reaction. "Does that mean that I'm off the hook and you're no longer plotting my downfall?"

"Let's not get ahead of ourselves," I rasped out with a sheepish smile.

My response made him laugh, shoulders shaking lightly under my arms.

Leaning back, I stared at his amber orbs. "I can't believe you'd help. I know how busy you are with the campaign. Really, Tris. Thank you."

His gaze locked on my lips for a little too long. It felt like my whole body was lit on fire under his attention, with tiny ants nipping at me. For a moment, I wondered even if my knees would give out. Lately, the way Tristan regarded me—studying every inch of my face as if trying to memorize what I looked like—unnerved me. I took a deep inhale to clear my head and felt nearly overwhelmed by his smell, which was clean and familiar. I guess it was masculine, too, if I had to nitpick.

The daze ended at the feel of an unexpected hardness poking my stomach. My mind was playing tricks on me; I was sure of it. There was no way Tristan was... hard.

No. Of course not.

Tris would never so callously continue to hug his sister if he had a hard-on. My mind was merely dirty, and I wanted everyone else to be just as sinful.

The intimate space between us was unsettling me, that's all. Pulling my hands off his shoulders, I tried to step out of his hold. Tris narrowed his eyes at the hasty retreat but dropped the arm banded around my waist.

My eyes tried to aim for his face but kept failing in their attempts and sought out the broad chest instead, the muscles of his biceps flexing.

I cleared my throat. "I should take a shower before heading to the shelter."

Tris froze at the mention of the shelter, then slowly turned his back to me as he browsed my bookshelf. "Do you know if those cops are still patrolling the shelter?" he asked nonchalantly.

Crap. We never discussed my dance with Tobias. "I-I don't know."

"Hmm."

"I didn't get into more trouble with cops if that's what you're asking."

"Cops are always trouble," he countered.

I held his gaze when he turned around, saying nothing more.

He sighed. "Listen, Angel. I have to return to Virginia," he said remorsefully. He gave me a long look before adding in a low voice, "I'll be back next weekend for our... shopping date."

Oh.

"If you run into that cop in the meantime... I want you to stay away from him. Cops are always sniffing around, trying to get politicians into trouble. You only have to say the wrong thing once, and it can ruin everything for us. You understand, don't you?"

For all intents and purposes, our entire family had staked their lives for Tris' campaign. If he genuinely believed my association might hurt his chances, I wouldn't partake. But it was absurd. Tris wasn't doing anything illegal, and in any case, I wouldn't discuss his campaign with an outsider.

All the same, I remembered the flicker of hurt when I didn't listen to his request about Tobias the first time. So, I knew to be delicate with my words.

"It was only a dance, Tris," I placated.

"Humor me, Angel. Stay away from that cop."

I might not understand why this mattered, but since I had no intention of seeing Tobias again, what difference did it make?

"Fine," I complied.

One of Tris' rare smiles dazzled his face. It's a shame he did it so seldomly because it could stop any woman's heart.

"Thank you, Angel. I'll be back before you know it." Before I could respond, he brushed his lips to my forehead.

I thought he'd pull away immediately, but his lips lingered. I stood there complacent, aware that my heart rate had picked up at an alarming rate. He was so much taller than me that I was eye-level with his broad chest. My distracted gaze trailed from his hard chest to the muscular forearms with defined veins. Other than porn, I had never so languidly inspected a male body, and yet he surpassed all those videos to mimic that of a male model. It wasn't just the sheer size of his six-feet-three frame that screamed all-male, but also the rugged build and rigid lines.

When I tilted my head, my gaze carelessly landed on his lips next.

My mouth dried at the way they parted, his breath quickening against mine. A surge of unwavering shivers curled around my spine, despite the air conditioning in my room being turned off. I shivered again, and two irrationally hard nipples stood to attention.

Disgusted with myself, I crossed my arms over my chest to hide the evidence.

Ridiculous! My hormones were absolutely absurd and entirely out of control. Who acted this way around their family? Before I could further scold myself, Tristan turned on his heels and walked out without another word.

For several moments, I stood there, motionless. "Bye, Tris," I finally said to the empty room.

Shaking my head, I forced myself into the bathroom for a shower. What the fuck was wrong with me today?

After a long shower to wash away my sinful thoughts, I pulled on a robe when it was Mom's turn to run into my room.

"You have a visitor!" she gushed.

Mom's enthusiasm was infectious but misdirected at the wrong offspring. "Do you mean Tristan has a visitor? They'd be disappointed because he already left," I said, feeling a tad bit disappointed about it myself.

"No, *you* have a visitor. It's that handsome cop, Tobias." She put both of her hands next to her lips as if announcing our impending engagement.

I jolted. "W-What? Why is he here?"

"Well, it's certainly not to see me."

I narrowed my eyes.

No doubt Mom was behind this, just like last night. Undeterred by my misfortunes, an ever-so-optimistic Mary Marcolf wanted nothing more than to set me up with a good-looking boy.

Unfortunately for her, I cared about Tobias and couldn't let that happen.

"Tell him I'm not here."

"Sara—"

"Please, Mom."

"Sara, there is a beautiful boy downstairs, the one everyone saw you dancing with last night. All he wants to do is talk to you. The house isn't going to fall on him if you agree."

"We don't know that for sure," I argued.

Mom huffed and started riffling through my closet. She settled on a backless white summer dress. "Here. Change into this."

"Oh, God. You are basically pimping me out."

"Yes. And I don't care. At the rate Tristan is going, I'll never see grandkids. You're my last hope."

"Guilt trip doesn't work on me."

"Worth a shot." She shrugged.

"Tristan doesn't want me hanging out with that cop," I argued again.

"He doesn't want you hanging out with anyone," she countered. "Downstairs. Five minutes."

"Mom—"

"If I don't see you in five minutes, I'll send that boy upstairs," she mused, shutting the door behind.

With an eye roll, I fingered the hem of the dress. Tristan wouldn't be happy about this. But perhaps I could meet with Tobias for only a moment to explain my peculiar Cinderella reenactment last night. I owed him that much before sending him packing.

Reluctantly, I changed to meet with the incredibly tall, dark, and handsome man waiting at the bottom of the stairs. I sauntered down the cascading staircases in my knee-length dress, and it dawned on me that Mom had all but set up a grand entrance for Tobias' benefit.

"Sara!" He tugged me into his warm embrace with his signature heartthrob smile in place.

Unicorns. Sunshine. English Bulldog puppies. My heart burst open with all things that resembled happiness.

Only for a moment, though. "Umm, hi," I said rigidly, wiggling free of his embrace.

He frowned. "Okay. I didn't even kiss you that time, and you're spooked. Hugs are supposed to be friendly territory."

"We are not friends," I pointed out.

"Are we not?" he pondered. "How about I take you out for breakfast so we can change that?"

Oh, he was good.

It wasn't lost on me that I had proposed unfamiliarity, and he had countered it with a date and a panty-melting smile to go with it.

"I can't—"

"Of course, she can." Mom ran into the foyer to cut me off. Had she been listening to our conversation from the other room?

Christ, this woman wasn't kidding about wanting grandchildren. She had been disappointed by Tristan's efforts in that arena, so now her attention was solely focused on me. It didn't matter that I was only shy of twenty years of age.

Since I turned fifteen, mom had had a perfectly laid out plan in place for me. Sadly, it used to be my dream, too, because I tended to romanticize things like my mother. Except, I realized dreams were called just that, for a reason. It was imaginary. Fictional. Lots had changed since then, and I had given up. But Mom never did.

She had planned for me to meet the perfect boy my freshman year. We'd date throughout college, and he'd propose at my graduation. But I'd be twenty-three during the actual nuptials because it'd take one year to plan the dream wedding. And, of course, Mom wanted us to be married for a year before we started trying for kids at the age of twenty-four.

Voila, presenting Mary Marcolf with her first grandchild by the time I was twenty-five. According to her, I was late to the game, and Mom's biological clock for grandkids wasn't just ticking; it was about to burst.

I scolded her with my eyes. "I can't, Mom. I have that thing at the shelter—"

"Oh. I forgot to tell you. The shelter called. They don't want you to come in today," Mom said innocently.

I tried to scorch her nonverbally.

Meanwhile, she turned her attention to the male counterpart in the room. "Tobias, it turns out that I have plans to meet with friends this morning, but our housekeeper has already made breakfast for Sara and me. Would you be so kind as to join Sara for breakfast in our dining room? It'd be a shame to let food go to waste."

Tobias didn't miss a beat. "I hate wasting food."

Mom practically shoved the two of us into the dining room, leaving her own house with the silly excuse. The only thing missing was a sign that flashed, *slay my daughter*.

Tobias wasn't bothered. His handsome face appeared amused as he stepped into the dining room and pulled a chair out for me. Ugh! Even seeing him sip on a simple cup of coffee left me with butterflies and a deep flush.

Inwardly groaning, I mollified myself that it was only one breakfast. Tris wouldn't bear witness to it, and I could spend it making meek excuses for my behavior yesterday.

So, I kept a polite distance throughout the meal, apologized for last night, and said my goodbyes after breakfast concluded. I was adamant that was the end. Hopefully, nothing awful would happen if I kept my heart at bay.

But keeping my heart at bay proved to be a significant challenge, especially when I arrived at the shelter and found a dozen roses waiting for me.

The only person who sent me flowers was Tristan after one of our particularly nasty fights. But these weren't from Tris because he knew my favorite flowers were peonies.

This bouquet of red roses was from the gorgeous cop hell-bent on stealing my heart.

CHAPTER 10

Sara

After that first time Tobias dropped by, Mom invited him over for breakfast, dinner, and every meal I ate at home instead of the shelter. I tried to avoid Tobias, not only for his own good but also out of respect for Tris' wishes.

No matter how much I pushed Tobias away, he was everywhere. And one night, as I was saying my goodbyes, Tobias took me into his arms for a kiss that stole my breath and left my head spinning. He did the same the following day and the day after.

By the fourth day, an odd realization dawned on me.

I had inadvertently allowed Tobias to court me for days, and he had survived to live the tale. It was nothing short of a miracle.

Was it possible I had met someone immune to this curse of mine?

The likelihood had been settling in slowly and surely.

A slight pang of guilt still niggled at the back of my mind because Tristan wouldn't be pleased with my choice of company, especially since Tris had delivered as promised. The shelter had been granted more time to figure out the next step.

The guilt was quickly thwarted by the new hope blossoming in my heart that I didn't have to spend the rest of my days alone.

In the end, I let Tobias drag me away for a lazy afternoon stroll around the streets of Georgetown. The familiar streets of the Capital looked foreign under the spirits of his company.

Tobias slid his hands around the small of my back. "Sara, the last few days have been amazing. But I get the feeling that you... you're still holding back."

I knew it wouldn't be long before Tobias pressed me about the status quo of this relationship. We had been dancing around it for days, and I had been dreading the conversation.

Tobias wanted to progress our relationship—both emotionally and physically. He had asked me on dates outside of the perimeters of my home, and he had asked me back to his apartment.

I had declined both invitations.

I felt safe in his hold and had come to trust him after only a short time together. Tobias was a good man—sweet, moral, a gentleman—and I was the lucky one to have his attention. Not to mention, it turned out that Mom might have been right all along. After days together, nothing terrible had befallen Tobias. Perhaps there'd never been a curse, only a series of unfortunate events surrounding me.

So, why did my heart hold back, refusing to dive in fully?

Perhaps these reservations had to do with Tris. My heart couldn't surrender until he let go of his misgivings about Tobias. Tris and I made plans for this upcoming weekend. I'd disclose the new development, after which my lingering reservations would crumble. I was sure of it.

"I really like you, Sara. In fact..." He shook his head with a smile. "I can't believe I am saying this, but I'm falling for you."

My breath hitched. How could that be? "Tobias, we have known each other for less than a week."

"It's insane, I know." He closed his eyes in defeat. "But I've never felt this way about anyone before."

"Tobias," I tried again. "I-I don't know what to say other than... I-I need my brother's approval before we go any further."

He leaned back in surprise. "Your brother? How could that matter when we have your parents' blessing?"

Shit. He was right. Why did it matter?

"It-It's just... A lot of people in this city know him. It'll be bad if he finds out about us some other way. I want to tell him in person."

Knowing my high and mighty brother, he might already be privy to my ongoing association with Tobias. He had this annoying tendency of learning information when he should have no access to it.

Nevertheless, I hated lying, even by omission. I also understood that sensitive topics should be discussed in person. I planned to tell Tris the truth once he came down for a visit, and I got him in a good enough mood to listen with an open heart.

Tobias didn't appear convinced. "Right," he mumbled. "Your good-looking *brother* that all the girls seem to like."

I glanced discreetly at his eyes which were now filled with suspicion. "I guess," I said cautiously.

"Look, Sara. I would like to take you on a date," he announced abruptly. "And I'm hoping that your parents' blessing is good enough for that cause. Forget your brother. Just say yes to one date with me."

I wanted to say yes. Not only to the date but, *yes,* to experiencing the physical component, too. One I had looked forward to my entire life.

Instead, I tried to gentle the blow. "Can you give me a couple of days to think about it? Please?" A couple of days until Tristan returned.

Tobias didn't bother hiding his disappointment at my answer. "I get it," he whispered. "You're not into me."

"No. That's not it at all." I had an inkling that the hurt in his voice had less to do with me turning down a date and more to do with the mention of Tris. But why?

He sighed, shaking his head. "Until you decide what you want, maybe it's best if I stop coming around."

It's clear that I had made a colossal mistake. The wheels were turning in his head, and he was reconsidering what was between us. I could see it in his eyes.

"Tobias—"

"I have to go," he swiftly cut me off. His eyes were filled with the pain that came from rejection.

Before I could utter another word, he gave me a paltry excuse about an early shift and something about staying in touch. Then he was off.

My stomach dropped.

I was on the brink of losing the best thing that had happened to me in years, and I had no idea why I was letting it happen. My heart tugged heavily with desperation as I watched Tobias walk away and possibly out of my life.

It had been a long day of walking around the city aimlessly. My head was throbbing by the time I returned home; my heart saddened over Tobias. I had hoped for a good night's rest to take my mind off it, but my doomed luck had other plans.

"Tris?"

I opened the door to my room and found my brother on the bed with his elbows resting on his knees. Startled, I froze in place.

"What are you doing here?"

It was late. The room was illuminated with dimmers, but his amber-golds still glowed in the dark with an unholy manifestation. His glare followed me as I dropped my purse on the desk.

My heart was pounding like I had run a marathon. Tristan was here before the weekend, which was near impossible for a congressman. Given his tight agenda, time-off had to be prescheduled. If he was here, it was due to a dire circumstance, possibly even revenge for breaking the promise to stay away from a certain cop.

I had already suspected that Tris knew about Tobias. Reading his current mood, there were no more doubts in my mind that he had been informed of Tobias and was here to dole out my punishment. There was a bad omen in the air, promising retribution for my actions. Whatever he had planned would be his most fierce attack to date.

The thought was arduous, and I simply didn't have the energy to participate in our rivalry.

"Can we not do this tonight?" I asked, not bothering with the pretenses that he wasn't privy about Tobias, nor would I deny what's between us.

Postponing to strike for an opportune moment wasn't the rule of the game. I had a looming suspicion that Tris' plot would force my hand into calling it quits with Tobias altogether, especially if he believed our association might negatively impact his campaign.

This wasn't about rivalry; it was about his ambitions. Nothing took precedence over it, not even my happiness.

"Please, I'm exhausted," I tried again.

He didn't respond. Some time passed without a single syllable, then Tristan slowly rose to his feet.

I did a silent prayer in my head. *Please, God. Please just let him put a lid on it for tonight.*

Instead of exiting the room, he said in the clearest of voices, "Where have you been?"

I blinked at the unexpected question.

"Don't make me repeat myself," he said in a voice of steel.

Something about his tone made my blood run cold. There wasn't an ounce of emotion, the taciturn words reverberating with unkindness. Sweat prickled my scalp, and I wondered if my legs were wobbling under me.

Tristan remained impassive, waiting for a response. And I wondered if he'd go away if I gave him a simple explanation.

"I went for a walk around the waterfront."

"You are lying," he said calmly. Conversely, his fists were clenched, with his jaw ticking visibly. Even his right eye twitched once or twice.

Frowning, I struggled with the accusation. Why would I lie about something so trivial?

Crossing my arms over my chest, I glared at him. "I'm not lying, but it's fine if you don't believe me. Now, can you please leave my room?"

Tristan raised an eyebrow, mocking me with a bemused smile. "Leave? This is my house." Technically the statement was true, but he had never thrown it in my face before. "I have the right to be anywhere in this house, go anywhere I see fit. You, on the other hand, have no rights at all. Don't forget that you live here because I let you."

I stiffened.

Of all the things I could accuse Tristan of, petty was never one of them.

But I could barely focus on the newfound flaw. From the contempt laced in his voice, Tristan was tethering at the edge of something sinister.

With a deep breath, I reminded myself that Tristan wouldn't physically hurt me. There'd always been an invisible line that neither of us had crossed. There was no real danger, especially with our parents under the same roof.

The bravado only lasted until he moved closer, the enormous body towering over me. Without meaning to, I stepped backward and bumped my hip against the edge of my desk so hard that blood gushed to my head.

Tristan stalked me. A few more steps and he'd be at arm's reach. I still didn't know his intentions, but a siren went off to warn me this wouldn't be like all the other times.

Each time we tricked one another, we upped the ante. At some point, we had graduated into the major leagues. Whatever he planned would make those past competitive stakes look like child's play; that much was evident.

I needed to leave immediately if he intended to launch such a vicious attack. "Fine, I'll leave then," I declared with indifference. "Stay here by yourself."

"By myself?" he repeated in a low voice. "That's fitting, isn't it? It's how I was always meant to be—alone," he spoke as if to himself.

I wondered if my mind was playing tricks on me. For a lone moment, it appeared as if Tristan was desolate... sadness clouding over the same man who was too popular for his own good.

As quickly as I had seen the expression, it was gone. He was back to being aloof and cold. With two considerable strides, he took the last steps to reach me.

I took a sharp inhale to suppress the urge to scream. He stood uncomfortably close, closer than two siblings should ever stand, the nominal distance causing his breath to mingle with mine.

Hooking my hand back, I gripped the edge of my desk for support. I tried to breathe but couldn't silence the panic.

"Why are you being this way?" I hissed.

My heart was in my throat. I needed to leave this room at any cost, but Tristan's large frame stood between me and my freedom. Exiting wasn't an option anymore, I determined. But I couldn't help giving my bedroom door a forlorn look.

He noticed. "Don't even think about it. You are not going anywhere till we are done." The calmness on his face surprised me, given the foreboding threats seeping out of his hateful eyes.

"What do you want from me?" I chewed out, ignoring the hint of a spicy smell making me dizzy.

"Only the truth. Where were you today?"

Frustrated, I gritted out, "I told you, Tris. I went to the waterfront. I even bought ice cream if you want to log into my account and look at my credit card statement?"

Tristan frowned. "Who were you with?"

I felt like crying. It was too late in the night for this torture. I gave him the truth multiple times, but he refused to believe me. "I was alone, I swear," my unsteady voice quivered with part exhaustion and part frustration.

Perhaps it was the desperation in my tone that finally invoked sympathy. "You are not lying?" he relented.

"I don't lie, and why the hell would I start with something so stupid?"

Tristan appeared undaunted by my frustration, distracted by something else entirely. His eyes moved over my face before dropping lower to track my neck, my chest, and finally, my exposed legs. When they had tracked my entire body, he only repeated the process more leisurely. A deliberate power move to make me uncomfortable in my own skin.

It wasn't easy to remain composed, but it was imperative to do so. Tristan obliterated anyone who showed weakness. If his opponents didn't give back as good as he doled it out, Tristan lost respect for them. Such was his twisted perspective.

"Why are you staring at me like a perv?"

His brows furrowed with another inexplicable expression. Once more, it was gone before I could dwell on it.

"Little sis, you can't possibly think... or are you truly so delusional? Have you seen the women I have been with? You look like an ugly duckling in comparison."

My lips curved smugly. Tristan appeared perplexed over the lack of effect his statement had. I should be crying over being called ugly, but Tristan's vanity was his downfall. Not mine.

"At least my supposed ugliness is only on the outside. What do you plan to do when your physical beauty wanes, and the outside matches the inside? You'll lose everything you've built based on looks—the women will leave, and your precious career will end." Leaning closer, I added, "You'll have no one once the world realizes that you're nothing but a pretty face."

Tristan didn't hesitate, grabbing my wrists and pinning me against the wall behind us. This time I didn't flinch, nor did I have the urge to scream. The attack wasn't deliberate. It was an unplanned reaction because he feared it to be true.

He was on me, pressed against me to imprison me in place. The furnace-like body emitted heat, like a warm hug on a cold night. He constrained me with minimal effort, his impressive size reminding me that he could snap me like a twig if he pleased.

A storm raged in my chest, but it wasn't from fear or excitement. I should have been terrified—I was during our initial exchange—but now there was also triumph.

My self-satisfied grin brought on Tris' look of determination. "At least I'll have things *to* lose," he spoke in an unsteady voice. "But you'll never know what it's like to be admired or loved. Tell me, how long before that cop gets hurt because he was around you for too long?"

The reminder of that lingering possibility wiped the smirk off my face. I had no more interest in playing this game with Tristan.

"He doesn't know you," he muttered quietly. "The real you."

"Let go," I ordered coldly, turning my face away from Tristan. My nose landed at the base of his neck— it smelled like a mixture of musk and vanilla. It was fitting that even his smell was spicy and sweet.

Tristan did the opposite, pressing me harder against the wall with his body weight until I almost wanted to yelp from the pressure. Every part of my body was indecently covered by his; chest, face, and hips. His face was inches away from mine. He watched me intensely as if he had every right to do so.

I couldn't breathe and closed my eyes to stop the suffocating feeling of his body pressed tightly against mine. Our hearts were beating against one another and somehow synchronized into one loud heart-beat. I could hear it distinctly in the silent room and wondered if he could, too.

"Let go!" I repeated, this time more urgently. An odd, tightening sensation was turning my legs into jelly. I was only upright because he had me pinned. Even that was torturous. It was crucial to put an end to whatever was happening.

"Please," I pleaded, surprising him.

He didn't let go. Instead, he dropped his face in my hair to audibly inhale.

Our irregular breathing filled the room, but neither of us spoke. With my every breath, I inhaled more of the musky-vanilla smell, feeling lightheaded from it. His shallow breaths fanned my cheek, my stomach dipping indescribably.

Vague anguish broke out all over my body, begging to be released. The back of his fingers grazed the side of my face so tenderly that I almost burst into flames. There was a desperate screeching inside my brain that whatever this new form of torture was, it needed to end.

CHAPTER II

Tristan

Thoughts of Sara from that night had consumed me for days. I hadn't been able to stop thinking about her while driving back to Virginia. I couldn't stop thinking about Sara's soft moans throughout the next day either or upon returning to my office.

I especially couldn't stop thinking about her when Steve called me with an update.

I occasionally had him watch over Sara whenever I was indisposed. I needed to take a step back from Sara to control my impulses. Steve was to watch her in my stead, a feat he complained about because her life had turned too boring to allocate such resources.

But suddenly, there was an update to report.

Sara broke her promise. She was seen walking hand in hand with that boy Tobias—the same man I had promised to spare for her sake.

Red.

Jealous, possessive red had flashed in front of my eyes for the entirety of my drive back to Washington DC upon hearing the news.

And in that fit of jealous rage, I had made another impulsive decision, and fuck, I couldn't take it back.

The evidence of my arousal and desire lay at Sara's feet. She squeezed her eyes tightly to block out our indiscretions in the dark. Irritation pestered me at her tentative nature. Making a fist into her hair, I yanked at it.

"Open your fucking eyes."

She obliged, chest rising and falling. My peripheral vision betrayed me to glance at her exposed legs in a dress that was both tight and short.

My mouth went dry at the sight of her cleavage outlined by her heavy breaths. She was beautiful with her full lips, bouncy hair, and honey skin that I could gorge on for days.

Without meaning to, I leaned in. My nose dug into the side of her neck and inhaled like it was the very nourishment I needed to stay alive. The smell of Jasmine, the one reminding me of home, engulfed me.

"Tris, I don't want to play this game anymore," Sara croaked, placing both palms on my chest to push me away. "Please, stop."

I would have given up my seat in Senate and the chance to win the presidency rather than stop. Grabbing her hands, I moved them out of the way to once more crush her with my body because, by God, she felt so right. She felt like home. Like comfort. Like warmth.

I came alive, blood thumping in my chest as if it were beating for the first time. And it craved all the unsavory things she wished to deny me.

Her inability to articulate this desire wasn't enough to stop me from acting on the impulse. Removing one hand from the wrist I had imprisoned, I slowly traced the collarbone with my thumb. Her skin, God, it was warm and soft. So soft. I had forgotten to breathe, focused solely on the delicate skin. I kissed her collarbone, skimming my lips over it.

"Tris!" Sara pushed my shoulders with both hands. "What the fuck are you doing? Have you lost your goddamn mind?"

With a deep inhale, I lifted my head to kiss her.

Sara turned her face, body resonating with perplexity. "Tris, what are you—"

Her words of protest were cut short as my lips found hers. Circling my hands around her back, I dragged her closer, leaving not even the space for air between our two bodies, kissing her fervently, desperately.

I wedged my leg between her thighs, wondering what the hell I was doing.

I hadn't a clue, only that I had gone mad upon hearing about that cop and somehow needed to solidify what's between us by any means necessary.

Sara made one more attempt to break free, which I ignored. My hands roamed her back, waist, and hips; I couldn't stop touching her. A rough tug on her hair made her gasp, and I took full advantage, exploring her mouth hungrily and without bounds. Her taste was invigorating, firing up every one of my nerves until the sensations buzzed through my body.

She protested when my insatiable mouth moved to her neck, behind her ears, only to return to her parted lips, licking to savor the taste of cherry from her lip balm.

"Get off me, you freak!"

Sara shoved against my chest with all her force, but it didn't make a difference. Her hateful eyes gleamed with shock and revulsion.

"Are you really that hell-bent on revenge that you'd kiss your own sister just to make a point? You have stooped to a new low," she hissed, careful to keep her voice low because who wanted to scream from the roof of their house that their brother was kissing them?

Sara continued to hurl all types of profanities at me. It was difficult to concentrate when she was so warm and inviting. Consuming.

My mouth covered hers again, this time more urgently. I trapped her hands between our chests, her body molding perfectly into my hold. My groin ground against her in rhythmic motion, separated by her panties under that dress and my slacks. They were so thin that I could outline the flesh underneath her panties. My bulge rubbed against her to create the perfect tempo to complement the mouthwatering kisses.

And God, that Jasmine scent—what was she doing to me?

I groaned, shaking in a last-ditch effort to maintain control before giving up any attempts to rectify the situation. That incessant voice kept whispering, *take, take, take.*

Fuck it.

Life was too hard, but everything was right in Sara's arms, though her arms weren't around my neck nor my waist. They had gone limp at her sides, not the sign of a woman in the throes of passion.

It was challenging to focus on that tidbit while my body was on fire with a need so primal that it'd be unnatural to let the call go unanswered. I didn't have a choice in the matter; I didn't. I had to continue even when Sara restarted her efforts to wiggle out of my grip.

"I don't know why you are doing this, but enough," she rasped between broken kisses, body squirming violently to escape. "Whatever your play is, you win. Now get off me."

I was in a trance. The wild beats of my heart nearly broke my rib cage open. The desire was sadistically demanding. My body trembled with an urgency to suppress them, but it was as if I had lost all control. I tilted my head to suck on her neck, my thumb resting on her racing pulse. Her skin tasted salty-sweet, setting my insides ablaze.

At that moment, I lost all control and entirely succumbed to the demon residing inside me.

I sucked on her neck desperately, the skin there wet from my tongue. She was driving me mad with her taste and her smell. If there were a way to transport both, I wouldn't hesitate to do so.

"You are sick." The revulsion in her high-pitched voice rose with every passing minute.

Sara wasn't concerned with the other residents of this home anymore. She was disturbed, traumatized, and unable to comprehend. A desperate plea was forming to escape her situation.

"Tristan, stop. You don't mean to do this... something's wrong with you... please, Tris."

I was drowning in her scent, grabbing at her frantically even while she resisted. I squeezed her soft breasts, thumb moving restlessly over her nipple. It gradually peaked, her heart beating uncontrollably under my palm.

Unable to help myself, I reached inside her dress.

"Stop!" Sara screamed this time, her voice laced with panic. It was definitely loud enough to carry. "Tris, please, please just stop."

I would if I could.

But I was desperate to find out what color panties she wore today. I needed to know if her nipples had peaked from my attention or because the room was cold. I needed to satiate the demon inside me.

"Please, Tristan. Please, stop. You are my brother. How could you do something like this?" Sara said in a manner of defeat. She wasn't physically fighting me anymore; she was entirely hysterical. "Stop! Stop! Stop! You are crazy. What is wrong with you?"

I repeatedly blinked, panting to steady my heart. The axis to my world had tilted while it triggered Sara's panic, which was the last thing I wanted.

I pulled my hand out from underneath her dress and took three steps back, but my efforts to subdue her were in vain. "Breathe, Angel. Just breathe, or you'll start hyperventilating."

"You are crazy! You are crazy!" she screamed over and over.

The lights in the hallway turned on suddenly. Within two seconds, Raguel and Mary came pouring into the room.

"What the hell is going on here?" Mary screamed with Raguel in tow.

A traumatized Sara refused to calm down. Blinded by terror, she didn't notice our parents had entered the room. "Stop. You're insane. How could you? You're my brother."

Both parents looked back and forth, eyes widening in bewilderment. Raguel had the pistol locked and loaded, the one he concealed inside the safe in their bedroom. It was pointed right at me.

God, this was tedious.

"What the fuck is going on here?" he asked.

"What the hell are you doing, Ragu?" Mom wailed, tears streaming down her cheeks as Raguel threatened her firstborn. "That's Tris. Have you lost your mind? Put the gun down."

But he didn't. Ragu silently waited for his daughter's signal, which I admired despite his tendency to be tough on Sara.

Meanwhile, all I wanted was to return to kissing Sara. Only a mild curiosity kept me engaged in the otherwise tiresome seconds to pass as I wondered if this would be the moment Sara broke our tradition of protecting one another.

Instead, she regained her wits upon seeing the gun. Her shock subsided only for a new one to take its place.

"Dad," she uttered, horrified, "Are you insane? Put the gun down."

"What's going on in here?" he asked instead of putting the gun away.

"Nothing," Sara said quickly, stepping forward and forcing her father to lower the gun. "I-I... Tris was... playing a prank on me... and it freaked me out," she finished lamely.

Even now, she couldn't lie and thought I had played a prank. Come tonight, she'd realize it wasn't a prank but a confession of my feelings.

No brother kissed their sister as a way of a prank.

God, that kiss. I wasn't sure how I had managed to stop myself in the first place, but I smothered the raging temptation for another taste of her lips. Fueling the fire right now wouldn't bode well. Ragu was already displeased by Sara's half-hearted explanations. Sara had screamed things that had explicitly hinted at my less than honorable intentions.

Mom tried to diffuse the situation. "You kids scared us half to death," she scolded sternly. "We thought someone had broken in. These pranks have got to stop. You're both adults now; act like it."

We managed to nod, though Sara was still shaken, and Ragu watched me closely. Suspicion was brewing in his mind. Despite Mom's lecture, which went on and on, he uttered not one word. This might be my *house*, but I felt that I had suddenly worn out my welcome in his *home*. At least for the near future until this storm had passed.

Reading the room, I left my parents and Sara with some puny pretext for popping up unexpectedly and an even worse excuse for being unable to stay. Frustration consumed me because my key to Heaven was being revoked, but it was best to let the dust settle.

With that affirmation in mind, I strolled to my Aston Martin parked outside and redialed the last number on my phone.

"Steve, I need you to take care of a few things."

I listed off instructions, starting with booking a nearby hotel for the night and dropping off an overnight bag. The gatekeepers to what I desired the most could hardly keep me away for long. Ragu and Mary were due to start their travels for my campaign, so I only had to wait them out.

Hope remained that by this time tomorrow, Sara would be at my side. I had made her aware of my feelings; I only wished it had gone down differently. But after the initial shock dwindled, she'd come to the same conclusion I had years ago.

We belonged together.

"The fundraiser tonight is a black-tie affair." Steve stared at the notebook. He had the build of Captain America's body double and looked odd reciting an agenda and working on time management. "I've scheduled to have your tux dropped off by seven."

"Cancel it."

"Sir," he protested. "Tonight's event is very—"

"Cancel it," I snapped. My leg tapped restlessly against the floor of the presidential suite. The comfortable couch in the living room failed to ease my fidgety limbs. With eyes masking the agitation, I pressed on the only topic that mattered, "Do you have the updates I asked you for?"

Steve's blue eyes gleamed at the question but gave nothing away. As an ex-Navy SEAL, his credentials could stretch past the responsibilities of my chief staff member and into dubiously legal activities if I so desired.

His best asset? Discretion. Steve didn't ask many questions or even bat an eye when I had ordered him to follow a police officer or record his communications with Sara.

I gave Sara the night to digest, then anxiously awaited her apology. She saw Tobias behind my back after specifically instructing her against it. Surely, she was never interested in him, merely confused by her emotions for me. She'd apologize for the folly now that I had expressed my feelings.

But Sara never reached out.

Frustrated, I texted her with my hotel details, asking to meet so we could talk. I kept the text vague in case a wary Raguel went through her phone.

More radio silence.

Impatient with the progress, I enlisted Steve's help. There was no way Sara would communicate with that boy after what transpired between us but... just to be safe.

Heaving a sigh, Steve put down the agenda notebook and grabbed a manila folder instead. He passed it along without a word.

And that's how I learned of Sara's betrayal.

That's how I knew she had planned for the night.

And that's how I lost my mind.

Sara sent a text to Tobias with instructions and the code to the front door of our house.

My house.

In another text, she expressed her excitement for tonight.

I was wrong. Sara's misgivings were about me, not Tobias, for she had promised to give herself to him.

My throat closed from suffocation. My eyes blurred with the red I saw. Jealousy, as I had never experienced, clawed my insides. I was fucking choking on it. Coughing, Heimlich, nothing, absolutely nothing could cure me. I was so twisted up from the fit of envy that I blindly stood and headed for the mini-fridge.

Steve watched me from afar. Something resembling pity might have followed me. Fuck. Did he know?

"What do you want me to do?" was all he asked in his professional demeanor that never demanded more than I wanted to share.

I said nothing for several seconds as I threw open the fridge door, searching for mini alcohol bottles.

Two warring voices had guided me all these years. A demonic one pushing me toward giving in to my impulses and Michael's pacifying voice to rethink those choices. I fought to crank up the volume on Michael because he sounded so very much like the good angel. But he rarely won because the way of the fallen angels was more gratifying.

So, I felt no remorse when saying, “Nip it in the bud. Accident. Brutal enough to incapacitate the boy for a few days. Let’s call it a warning shot.”

He asked no more questions because my insinuation was loud and clear. Other than that, the less I knew, the better.

Once he left, I familiarized myself with the remaining tiny liquor bottles in the fridge. Sara’s betrayal stung like nothing before, and I was buried in self-pity, misery, and defeat.

The self-destructive tendencies Sara had chipped away had now started to rebuild themselves without her presence. And fuck, I couldn’t breathe without her. Couldn’t think of taking one more step.

Don’t think about her. Don’t. Think about anything but Sara’s betrayal.

But how could I not when she was all I had thought about for years? I never wanted anything so badly in my life; I had never looked at a woman and gone mad with desire the way I did with her. She had become my singular obsession to the point I breathed, ate, and slept around thoughts of Sara.

Meanwhile, she planned to move on with Tobias and leave me behind.

Over my dead fucking body.

Stumbling out of the hotel room, I decided to give voice to the demon instead of the angel. Because at least demons were forthright about their intentions. Because anything was better than feeling this way. Because I had to smother the whisper that this was to be my life for trading away love.

And for the first time in my adult life, I suffered what hundreds of women had claimed to experience at my hands.

Heartbreak.

CHAPTER 12

Sara

"I don't know," Tobias said unsurely over the phone.

"Please, Tobias. Give me a chance to fix things."

"I don't think you understand," he said quietly. "It's not only that I'm falling for you, but I'm *in* love. I love you, Sara."

My stomach rocked. It was too fast, but he said the word with such absolution that I believed him. I didn't know how to respond, so instead, I waited for him to continue.

"And if you're not even attracted to me, then why am I torturing myself by being around you—"

"No, Tobias. That's not the case at all."

I was jittery over what happened last night and needed a Wet Nap to wipe my dirty mind clean. Tristan had officially lost it, and I hadn't processed it. In a fit of rage and anger, he tackled my lips. Even he didn't know what he planned to achieve from it. After our parents barged in, Tris appeared mortified over his actions and made for an abrupt escape.

Luckily, our parents left today for another one of Tris' campaigns, saving me the embarrassment of any further discussions. Hopefully, by the time they returned, it'd all be a distant memory.

Only, I had no idea how Tris and I could recover from the setback.

My salacious mind was out-of-control because there was a moment last night when I didn't fight back. It had scared me so terribly that I couldn't stop screaming. Only the gun pointed at Tris had snapped me out of it.

When you started acting indecently around your own damn family, that's when you were in serious need of finding God. Since God had left me, I needed to take matters into my own hands.

"Tobias, I am attracted to you. Come over tonight after your shift. My parents are gone, and we'll have the house to ourselves. I want to take the next step with you," I blurted.

The whole ordeal with Tristan solidified one thing for me. I needed to redirect my sexually charged energy toward a healthier counterpart. All the signs were pointing at Tobias.

A curse that had haunted me for years had been lifted, and the most sexual virgin on earth was being given the green light to have sex.

A hot guy was in love with me. Tobias was a beacon of hope, and I worried about losing him if I didn't show that I was into him, too.

And my parents were due to visit a few districts in deep Virginia for Tris' campaign, so we had an empty house.

The universe was screaming for me to lose my virginity, and I had zero reasons to hold back.

Tobias paused on the other side. "Sara, that's not what I meant. I want to take you out on a date, but you have been so hesitant—"

"I have just been nervous about starting something new. That's done with now. I'm tired of being scared, and I am tired of waiting."

"I don't mind waiting—"

"But I do," I interrupted. "I don't want to wait any longer. We'll go on a date... after. I-I want this with you."

He was quiet for so long that I wondered if he'd say no. "Losing your virginity is a big deal, Sara. You sure about this?"

"Positive." Because there was no way I should let a man like him go, right?

I flicked off the non-existent lint for the hundredth time.

It was a nervous tick.

I had put the memory of last night entirely out of my mind. And Tobias, the perfect man, was due here at any minute. I needed to stay focused on him.

Tobias will be a sweet and gentle lover, I reiterated in my mind to calm my nerves.

But what if it turned out I was terrible at sex? It'd be ironic if I were an awkward lover after spending years fantasizing about it.

Wringing my hands together, I fell backward on my bed and stared up at the white ceiling. I had imagined this moment on countless occasions—my first time—and replayed the fantasy one last time before I was officially *deflowered.*

Tobias would probably start with sweet words of affirmations to put my mind at ease as he leaned in for the perfect kiss. Then he'd move onto soft caresses before undressing me gently. The act would make me shy, and I'd turn away from him. At long last, he'd take me so tenderly that it'd be neither painful nor harsh. Just everything I had dreamt of and more because Tobias was perfect and unflawed and everything good.

After making love to me, he'd stroke my hair lovingly while I laid on his chest, and we'd speak of our hopes and dreams and a beautiful future.

I'd had the tendency of romanticizing things in the past. But I was sure that my daydreaming ways were appropriate for this instant. Our time together would be nothing short of perfection.

I smiled, a grin stretching over my face until it hurt. Keeping my eyes closed, I replayed the images and only jolted from my fictional whimsy at the sound of harsh footsteps in the hallway. I had left the front door open and let Tobias know to head straight to my bedroom.

The shuffling didn't sound like Tobias' usual footwork. These were urgent, as if the world were on the cusp of despair and he was coming to the rescue.

He is just as eager, I realized.

A shyness like I had never known befell me at the thought, and I turned my face away from the door, looking out the window. The orange glow of dusk dazzled me with a serene peace at the same time I heard the twist of the doorknob.

It's really happening.

The door creaked open, and footsteps entered my room. I squeezed my eyes shut, anticipation overwhelming every cell of my body.

He was silent, watching me in my white baby doll lace nightie. Yes, it was extra to wear white like I was some virginal bride. But the color complimented me, and I wanted to look my best.

Did he like it? Did he desire me?

I hadn't a clue because I couldn't force myself to face him, nor could I open my eyes. My inexperience was showing, and I didn't know how to behave.

"Angel!" said a deep voice.

For a moment, my mind went blank. Was my mind playing tricks on me?

And then came the senseless terror.

I whipped my face toward the voice to find an unwelcome guest. My vision blurred at the sight of Tristan's thinned lips. Amber-gold eyes flared with the lethal fury they harbored inside. The muscles on his face were tight, with clenched hands at his sides.

I sat up speedily with my hand on my abdomen. "Tris?" I muttered under my breath, face ridden with shock. "What the hell are you doing in here?"

It couldn't be. He wouldn't have the guts to return here after what happened last night.

Tristan didn't care to explain. There was only a flicker in his face, eyes clouding with an atrocious premonition.

A small voice whispered in my ear, *Run.*

For some reason, I didn't hesitate to listen.

Jumping off the bed, I made a start for the sliding doors and into the balcony. The fresh air had barely registered when Tristan tackled me. We fell forward, my face hitting the rough ground on impact.

"Ow!" I cried out, pain shooting through my busted lip as the metallic taste of blood exploded inside my mouth. "Tris, what the fuck are you doing?"

Instead of answering, he took advantage of my momentary lapse and mercilessly dragged me across the grand veranda. He slid the door open to his bedroom and tossed me inside with ease. I face-planted onto the hardwood floor of Tristan's room. When I tried to scramble to my feet, his weight was instinctively on my back to pin me down.

"Get off me!" I jabbed an elbow to his stomach. Only, it made no impact, the hard wall shooting a bout of pain to my elbow instead.

The hemline of my short baby doll nightie rose to my ass while my legs chafed mercilessly against the ground. We wrestled viciously as I attempted to break free, but striking effectively—while faced away from him—was no easy task.

Tristan held my face down to the cool floor. With a knee lodged between my thighs, he managed to part them to make space for himself. As he pinned my wrists to the floor, an alarm went off that my fate had been sealed.

CHAPTER 13

Tristan

She fought with spirit, like always. Even when I spread her legs wide and pinned her to the ground, she twisted her body, ready to spit in my face. The plethora of curse words she hurled was colorful, to say the least.

God, she was a tigress; my beautiful, fearless, wild tigress.

What the fuck am I doing to this tigress of mine? I didn't want to see Sara this way—defeated or beaten. Had I lost my mind?

The contriteness disturbed me deeply, just not enough to stop the madness. I had spent the last two hours drinking in my hotel room until the time came when Tobias was to meet her. Except, he wouldn't go near her again. Not tonight, not ever.

I showed up in his stead, still unsure what I'd do to Sara. The question was answered the moment I saw her sprawled on the bed.

Heat had exploded inside me at first sight of her white lingerie. The lace barely covered her ass, displaying her sexy as fuck thighs. Small, firm tits were presented through the scoop neckline that dipped a little too low. The see-through material took my breath away, and I had stared at her tight body like a man possessed. Then I remembered that she wore the lingerie for *him.*

Sara made a run for it, having recognized the ire in my eyes. Not only had she betrayed me, but she had taken careful measures in preparation for the step.

The thought turned me manic. I hated her for the perverse way she made me want her—like a man unleashed, driven mad in my need for her—while she was ready to offer herself up to another.

Sara managed to lift her torso, but I pressed her down with a hand between her shoulder blades. Her right cheek dug against the hard floor, eyes filled with panic. Even in this state, she was beautiful with messy hair with her expensive tattered lingerie.

"Tristan! Have you completely lost your shit?" she screamed. "Get the fuck off me!"

I didn't respond. My eyes were glued to her hemline, which had risen to her butt to display a matching white lacy thong.

Fuck.

Me.

My rapid breathing increased, and my heart was ready to explode from anticipation as I drank in the miles of caramel skin. I wanted to memorize every inch of her body before dipping my head between her toned thighs for a taste.

Sara momentarily stopped thrashing. "Oh my God, are you..." Her voice faltered when she felt my hard bulge digging into her ass. She was unsure before, but my body gave me away. She stiffened upon discovery and instantly went from a tigress to prey.

A trapped prey.

In a shocking turn of events, Sara started crying. "Please, Tris," she pleaded in a broken voice. "I don't know what's wrong with you, but you're scaring me. Please, stop this." Those were the only words she successfully got out before turning her face to the side and sobbing uncontrollably.

It was a side of Sara I had never seen—one that begged for mercy—nor had I seen her cry before. For a moment, I wondered if I could fight this demon lurking inside me. Perhaps I was strong enough to take on this dark force.

My hands trembled with the need for control. *Please, God, make me stop. Mine was gone but spare this girl her soul.*

My prayer went unanswered as the smell of jasmine entered my lungs, and I dug my nose into her tresses. The smell was so overpowering that I slanted my face and greedily inhaled more of the sweet aroma until my mind went dizzy with an unquenchable thirst. Dismissing the minute effort to stop, I tightened my grip to restrain her wrists instead.

"I can't stop, Angel. I need you," I whispered with sincerity, snuffing out the raw emotions. I was floating in a mist of lust and sorrow. I couldn't stop these demonic desires for her, even if my life depended on it. "I have no one else other than you."

"What are you talking about?" she cried out, sobbing so hysterically that my heart lurched. Her tears rolled to the hardwood floor, pooling beneath.

I lowered my face between her shoulder blades. Placing a small kiss on the bare skin, I trailed my lips to her neck, sticking my tongue out to taste her salty skin.

"Please stop," desperation rolled off her tongue.

I let go of her wrists. Sara stiffened in shock that I actually listened to her pleas. However, when I slipped my hand between her legs, she jolted out of her trance and restarted her struggles.

"NO!" she screamed, flaying. "Please, Tris. Snap out of this. I'm sorry for not telling you about him sooner. I won't do it again. Please, please, please let me go."

She thrashed without restraint, completely wild. She used every one of her limbs to strike me, finally bobbing her head backward to hit my face. I barely felt the attacks, my heart racing as my fingers dipped between the fabric of her thong.

"Please. Tris, please don't do this! You are my brother. Stop!"

I ripped her underwear down with force, exposing her to the cold floor.

"NO!" Sara shrieked so loud that the sound echoed and bounced off all four corners of the room. Even with her face turned away from me, I knew horror was etched in her expression. A second wind kicked in, sparked by my touch. Raising her feet, Sara kicked back donkey style, making contact with my shin.

The momentary shock was enough to release her wrists, and she used the small window to place both palms on the ground to crawl away. I grabbed her ankle to drag her back with potent force but stopped dead in my tracks at the sound of a loud thud.

Sara had hit her forehead on the wooden floor, falling flat on the ground.

Fuck.

She laid perfectly still, body stretched out underneath me as I loomed over her. Once more, I prayed for divine intervention to save her from these evil clutches, but when she groaned and moved her head side to side—indicating her consciousness—the hardly honorable intentions vanished. Before Sara could regain her full bearing, I flipped her on her back and climbed on top. Crushing her with my full weight, I reached between her thighs to feel the warm heat once more.

Jeans, buttons, flyers, every barrier of mine flew open to free my cock. I grabbed my dick with violent energy and sought out her entrance.

The act turned her lucid. Sara returned to fight mode and grabbed fistfuls of my hair. Driven entirely by rage, she dragged her nails across my arms hard enough to draw blood.

Shaking with my own urge, I bit her shoulder. Hard. Sara let out another bloody murder scream, nearly cracking her raspy voice.

I ground her hips, digging my fingers into her flesh to keep her still, and brutally parted her legs, lining my groin against hers. The moment I made contact, any residual doubt over my actions disappeared. My focus was lasered on the heat coming off her sex, the soft flesh, and the tight opening.

"Tristan, stop!" she shouted desperately, attempting to clamp her thighs together. "Why are you doing this?" she wailed desperately. Sara continued her efforts, using every bargaining chip to break loose. She repeatedly called out for help while I trailed my lips across her hot skin.

I muttered some mumbo jumbo of my own, voice thick with desire. "Because you are mine. Because I can't walk this earth without you..." I plunged inside Sara mid-thought with one punishing stroke, feeling every bit of resistance from her intact opening.

Before I could process the ecstasy, Sara's limbs were flailing again. Pain burst at the sites she made contact with, but I blocked out all distractions, oblivious to the physical assaults. While her body inherently fought the intrusion, I determinedly forced myself past the barrier.

I expected her to scream, but she surprised me again.

Radio silence.

CHAPTER 14

Sara

The pain was so overpowering that my mind went temporarily numb. It took several seconds to register the sting, and then I screamed at the top of my lungs. My cries filled the room, brought on by the ache from the thick girth ripping me in half.

I wondered if I had passed out from the agony of the piercing shards of blades cutting me open. And for one interveinal moment, I felt no other movements except for his body shaking against mine with tremors. Almost as if he were waiting for me to acclimate, and the effort he exercised was monumental on his part.

Hot breath tickled my cheeks while droplets of sweat from his forehead dripped down. Panting heavily, Tristan trailed his lips over the column of my neck, frantically nibbling on the skin. He tilted his face and kissed me, shoving his tongue inside to explore my mouth greedily.

I weakly threw my limbs about, but the fight in me had grown weak. The insurmountable pain had drained the last of my energy. Even my voice was too hoarse to cry for help, but the inability to use my vocal cords didn't decrease the piercing throb ripping my insides, torn apart beyond repair. Excruciating tears seeped out of the corner of my eyes, rolling down my cheeks, and when his cheeks brushed against mine, he stilled upon the feel of damp moisture.

I took the lifeline, grappling to form words that might evoke his sympathy. "Tris," I croaked. "Please, stop. It hurts so much."

He rested his forehead against mine while stroking my baby hairs with a thumb. For an instant, I let myself believe he was about to snap out of this insanity, and my nightmare was to come to an end.

Instead, he spoke in a gruff voice, "Stop fighting me. Then it won't hurt so damn much."

The harsh words settled inside my chest like ice. My stomach churned from the lack of empathy he projected, devoid of humanity. No longer did I bother fighting back. Partly, I was depleted from the earlier exertions, but mostly because I believed him.

"That's a good girl," he breathed the gentle encouragement, content that I had stopped screaming and thrashing.

I didn't respond, wanting this to be over with at any cost. Having agreed to pay the price, I merely drew in bated breaths in preparation for what was to come and braced for the worst.

But there was nothing punishing about what happened next. Whereas the initial penetration had been angry, every move after was made with purpose. Tristan stroked my hair tenderly, amber eyes burning with desire. The gesture reverberated with the deep meaning of stealing my soul. His actions turned so abruptly affectionate and familiar that fresh tears sprung to my eyes.

"It's okay, Angel. Don't cry," he murmured against the tears leaking from my eyes, kissing them away with faux reassurance.

With no more protests to voice, I took the abuse as he drew his hips back and plunged forward, this time at a mercifully slow pace. He waited before repeating until finding a rhythm that was neither painful nor enjoyable.

I could tell he was watching me even with my eyes closed shut. I didn't want to bear witness to his pleasure. The physical anguish couldn't compare to the emotional turmoil, and a visual would only prove more disturbing. Tristan didn't seem to mind and took his fill until he was shuddering from head to toe.

"Fuck, you feel so good," he whispered gravely as he ground into me over and over before grabbing the nape of my neck for a kiss.

I turned away, but he dragged my face back, lips finding the center of mine for an unrestraint kiss. He squeezed my breast, an earthy groan reverberating.

"God, Angel. These are perfect. I've wanted a taste of this for so fucking long."

He yanked down the built-in bra of the lingerie piece even as I tried to pull the fabric up to cover myself. Goosebumps from the cold exposure sprung to my hot, flushed skin, creating a contrasting sensation. Kissing down the valley of my breasts, he swiped his tongue along the outline of my cleavage. His mouth landed on my nipple, and he sucked so hard that I screamed again. But when he moved to the other one for repeat treatment, I was hit with a hot and cool combination. The odd sensation muddled my mind, and for the first time since the start of his horrific experience, the pain between my thighs dulled away.

"So close, baby," he rasped. "But I need you with me when I come inside you."

Lascivious intents dripped from his voice before another obscene act came into play. Dropping his hands between us, Tristan firmly rubbed my sex, which was no doubt mingled with fluids and blood. He hugged me to his body as his fingers circled my swollen clit, keeping with the rhythm of his gentle thrusts.

"You're gorgeous," he whispered as the fingers between my thighs sped up, resolute to finish what they started.

Surrendering, I let him have at it, transporting myself to somewhere else entirely in my mind. It was difficult to escape his lewd hands on my body. No skin was left unturned in his explorations. He was so intentional with the touches that it seeped deeper and deeper until he reached my mind and violated my thoughts.

Dazed, I could only focus on his deep moans, the hot breath fanning my cheeks, and the peppered kisses along my breasts. My lubrication coated his fingers while I felt dizzy enough to pass out.

"Fuck, baby, does that feel good?" he said frantically, pleasure spiking in his voice.

Feeling light-headed, I closed my eyes. The haze was so thick that I didn't realize Tristan had returned to my parted lips, brutally taking my mouth. There were too many stimuli and far too many caresses to keep track of, and I forgot to jerk away.

"That's it, Angel."

He was no longer moving inside me, only the insistent fingers rubbing between my lips with determination. The warmth emanating from them inflamed the heat spreading in my core.

An intense pressure grew with the urgency to break free. My mind turned into a blank slate, sweat beads covering my furrowed brows. In my lethargy, I could no longer stop what was threatening to implode inside me and transport me to the abyss.

Tristan kept kissing me all the while, tongue licking my bottom lip with a silent encouragement to let it happen. It was impossible not to under his relentless fingers, and the being that threatened to break loose finally did so with an explosive scream that came from my startled shock and Tristan's awestruck words. "That's it, baby. That's it. Come for me. Come for me so hard."

He started thrusting inside me, unleashed. I didn't feel any more pain, only a throbbing that stretched each time he hit my swollen cunt.

"Fuck, yes!" he groaned, his heavy weight deflating over me with the warmth of his seed spreading inside my belly.

CHAPTER 15

Tristan

Not a single word passed between us.

What in the hell could I say anyways to make it better? *Sorry I raped you,* wouldn't exactly cut it.

I shifted slightly so my weight wouldn't crush her. For several minutes, I fumbled with my clothes while Sara said nothing.

"Angel?" I coaxed when she still hadn't moved.

Sara was stretched out on the floor and noiseless other than the rapid sound of harsh breaths. Her indifference was so unprecedented that I panicked.

First, I made sure she was conscious. Next, I checked her pulse, which was thrumming at an alarming rate. I searched for other signs of trauma when I caught sight of... blood. There was blood between her thighs.

Fuck.

My windpipes tightened to the point of choking me.

I did that. I used the only woman I cherished to satisfy my demented needs, leaving her broken in the process.

Hastily, I picked her up in bridal style and laid her on my bed. I darted to the bathroom for a washcloth and returned promptly to clean her. The act of wiping away blood and semen with a damp cloth turned into the equivalent of a sponge bath. I ran it over her body like a devoted servant, peeling off the tattered lingerie to replace it with one of my oversized T-shirts that went down to her thighs. Finally, I pulled the covers to her chest.

I had assumed she'd snap out of it by now, but Sara lay there with her eyes closed as if dead. *Or perhaps she wished for death.*

I swallowed the lump in my throat.

No.

That would never happen. I wouldn't let it. Sara was the strongest person I knew. The only person strong enough to survive the monster to live inside me.

Unsure how to proceed, I waited for an indication of what else she needed. The deafening silence only stretched between us. With my knees drawn, I sat next to her on the bed, incapable of providing a single consolation after what I had done.

Hours went by like this, with my back pressed against the headboard while Sara refused to open her eyes.

"Do you want something to eat, Angel?"

Such a ridiculously stupid question. No, she didn't want to fucking eat. She wanted me to leave, not wanting me to be the first thing she saw after opening her eyes. But there was no one else here. Even if I were the man she hated, I couldn't leave her alone in this state without knowing how she might react.

Her breathing evened out at long last, and she fell asleep. Upon realizing she was stuck with me, Sara distanced herself from me by escaping into her subconscious.

I brushed the hair back from her forehead, staring intently at a face that seemed shattered. It was never supposed to happen this way between us. Now that it had, I couldn't take away the pain of what I did, nor could I erase the memory of her tight cunt squeezing my cock.

No longer could I live without the feel of her around me. Only one truth remained in our lives—Sara was mine, whether she liked it or not.

I stirred in the dark, moonlit room. At some point, I had shifted to lie next to Sara, cradling her in my arms. The gentle rise and fall of her chest indicated she was still fast asleep. I had no concept of how much time had elapsed, but the sound of a scream interrupted my slumber.

An entity emerged from the dark shadows with hints of a clipped wing dragging behind him. Immediately, I knew it was that demon who had taunted me for years. There was no escaping him because there was no escaping your own self.

For the rest of the night, he replayed Sara's screams from earlier and made me listen to them even as I put a pillow over my ears to drown out the sounds. I told myself that the atrocious screams were a figment of my imagination. A nightmare. All the same, I saw his wicked smile because we both knew the truth.

The fallen angel had bested the good angel. I had failed Michael by letting Asmodeus win.

CHAPTER 16

Sara

I never wanted to wake again. I could suspend the truth with my eyes tightly shut, but the soreness between my thighs wouldn't let me live the lie. Once I opened my eyes, I had to face the reality of what had happened.

At some point, a warm embrace cocooned me. Marred with shock and trauma, I let myself believe that Tobias was comforting me.

Why had he arrived so late? What had kept him for so long?

The thought of him finding out about what happened made my heart lurch, especially after he had professed his love for me. But I had to come clean because, surely, he'd notice if I was no longer a virgin. What if his perception changed after finding out the truth? What if he no longer viewed me as a woman he desired and pitied me instead?

I didn't want anyone treating me like a porcelain doll. The preconceived rejection shut down my brain, and I continued to keep my eyes shut to deny what had happened.

Later, the realization dawned on me that it wasn't Tobias at all but Tristan holding me through the night.

Stunned with the fear of rousing the monster from earlier, I didn't make a single sound. I prayed to God for his touch to vanish, waiting for him to fall asleep so I could make my escape. But he never did.

Instead, sleep took me under, and images of a carnal beast flashed in the minds of my slumber, promising this was only the beginning of my nightmares.

When I woke next, the pulsating pain and the cruelly bright sunlight against my closed lids rushed back memories from last night. Bewildered, I leaped out of bed and frantically searched my surroundings.

No sound, nor was there anyone else in sight. Tristan's room was bare with minimal furnishing—a modern, white bed with two matching nightstands. Everything had been tidied up as if the appalling act from a mere twelve hours ago never took place.

Did he do this?

With soft feet, I walked toward the sliding doors to the veranda, but it was locked from the outside.

Odd.

Desperate to leave, I checked the bedroom door next and rattled the doorknob. Also locked.

What the fuck?

"Hello," I called out.

No response.

My head throbbed in pain and confusion, but at least it didn't sound like Tristan was around. Disoriented, I fumbled into the bathroom to relieve myself, then gurgled with mouthwash and splashed water on my face.

Having gotten a hold of my faculties, I returned to the room, optimistic that I could think of a way out with a clearer head. However, I spun in panic at the unmistakable shuffling of Tristan's footsteps coming from the hallway. When the bedroom doorknob rattled, I pressed my back against the wall and suddenly wished for nothing more than to stay locked in here by my lonesome self.

CHAPTER 17

Tristan

Balancing the tray with one hand, I unlocked the door and turned the knob. It was preposterous to bring her breakfast like we were lovers. But Sara had slept past dinner time last night. The French Toast was for nourishment and sustenance purposes rather than a grand romantic gesture.

She would no doubt try to run for the hills, so I had locked both the doors to my room while preparing breakfast. Once we discussed the extent of our new relationship, my mind would be at ease.

She will agree, I repeated the mantra to myself.

To entice her into my proposal, I had straightened myself out. My face was marred from Sara's assault, a hangover, a day-old stubble, and eyes sunken deep from a restless night. It was the first time the ladies were more likely to use the word ghoulish—rather than ethereal—to describe my physical appearance. It was also the first time I couldn't stand the sight of my own reflection. I had almost punched the mirror to shatter the evidence of my undeserving face, to feel the shards cut deep in my skin. I wanted to erase my reflection because it wasn't the evidence of God after all—like they claimed—it was the reflection of a monster who hurt the only woman to matter.

It was Sara who had made me feel human, who had brought me back from the brink of nothingness. So why had I done such an awful thing to her?

Unfortunately, my contemplations paled in comparison to Sara's trauma. With a deep breath, I pushed the door open to find her pressed against the wall in an innate response to my presence.

"Morning, Angel," I said hoarsely.

Sara said nothing, her head hung loosely to stare at a spot on the ground.

She looked like a gift from God in my oversized shirt that only reached past her thighs. My heart started beating so erratically at the suffocatingly appealing sight of her that I wondered if the damn thing might break loose.

But when she pushed away handfuls of curly mounds covering her face, it revealed the swelled bruising on her forehead. Rays of the morning sun cast light on the dark marks glinting on her beige skin. And I certainly didn't miss the trembling or the remnants of fear evaporating from her.

I dropped my gaze and replayed the horrors from last night in my mind to fight away this temptation. She wouldn't survive another bout of my attack—physically or emotionally—so soon after the fact.

Instead, I set the tray on the nightstand and reached into my dresser for a pair of sweatpants. When I solemnly held them out for her, she looked suspiciously at my outstretched hand. Taking the hint, I placed the pants on the corner of the bed and stepped backward until I was far enough that she didn't fear an attack. Like an animal worried about their last morsel of food being taken away, she grabbed for the pants and pulled them on. Sara flinched at the movement, an aftereffect of the physical injuries she had sustained.

The ones I had caused.

My chest ached in self-deprecation, unsure if I'd ever succeed in erasing her forlorn looks. Blinded by a haze of sorrow, I watched her swim in pants much too large for her petite frame. Meanwhile, Sara eyed the bedroom door.

Well, this was going great.

I sighed. "Even with a head start, I'll catch you within seconds. Not to mention, you have neither your car keys nor cell phone on hand. So, can we skip the part where you try to run and discuss last night instead?"

I knew she heard me by the barren expression. "You can't keep me locked up in here for long. Mom and Dad will return home soon." My heart skipped at the raspy way she spoke, having lost her voice after last night's screaming match.

"I don't intend on keeping you locked up."

"So, you plan on letting me walk out of here; just like that?" She stared out the window, giving me the nonverbal permission to divulge. Clearly, she was only focused on escaping this room and me. So much so, she hadn't demanded an explanation about last night or even so much as cursed me out.

Sadistically, her numb mood worked in my favor since she might be just shaken up enough to listen to my proposal. "That's right," I replied softly.

"Then why did you lock the doors?"

"I wanted us to speak before you ran off."

"You mean, before I ran to the authorities," was her rebuttal. The composed nature of her tone stunned me.

"I'm not worried about you going to the cops."

"And what do you plan to do to stop me?"

The insinuation astounded me. She made it sound like I was going to take a hit out on her in order to silence her. "Nothing. I just assumed you don't want our parents finding out." I raised my brows, challenging her to refute.

She didn't respond; her face turned away. It wasn't lost on me that she hadn't glanced my way once during the entirety of this conversation. My breathing became labored at the emotional damage I had inflicted on her—on top of the physical—and I swallowed the lump in my throat.

"This wasn't how it was supposed to happen," I said gently.

"Oh? Did you want to take me on a seven-course dinner date before raping me?" she snapped.

"I regret the way... I hate that I hurt you," I worded carefully. "I was... I was angry last night. The thought of you with that boy..." I closed my eyes.

Fuck.

An irrepressible ire was beating inside my chest, one I couldn't satiate or quieten. It didn't stem from hatred, only anger over her damned choice to be with that boy and the temptation she aroused in me.

"I told you how I felt about Tobias, but that didn't stop you—" I gritted out, unable to finish the thought without losing my mind. "I snapped, okay? As long as you end things with that boy, I'll keep myself in check." No matter the case, she would leave him. That much was final.

Sara huffed at my declaration, shaking her head in disbelief. "Thank you for your input in my love life. I'll take that into advisement."

God, she wasn't going to make this easy. Tobias was beneath her, but she refused to see reason. Much too soon, the carnal rage from last night returned at her deplorable stance, one I had barely suppressed for this conversation.

"Whether you like it or not, you're mine," I growled. "And that's all there is to it. Surely, you know me well enough to realize that I don't share."

Sara stiffened, eyebrows lowered suspiciously over my usage of continuous tense. When realization dawned on her, she pressed herself further against the wall.

"S-Share... y-you mean... what the fuck?" She ran two frantic hands down her hair. "You plan to do that a-again...." Dread and desperation surrounded her, and she couldn't finish the sentence.

I took a step toward her. The way her eyes flared with fear, I almost gave up on the idea midway. However, she had to get used to my proximity. I closed the distance between us. "It'll be okay, Angel—"

Her hand moved in a flash. It was only when my face tilted to the side did I realize the force behind her slap. "If you touch me again or even come near me, I swear to God I'll chop your fucking dick off."

All other emotions were tampered down by the abrupt humor in her words, and I had to bite down on a sardonic smile.

I knew it.

I hadn't broken my little angel. The fire inside her burnt bright. It only solidified my previous conviction that we could find a new normal, one to fit our evolving dynamic.

Anger glinted in her eyes, defiance pulsing in her body language. "And if I were you, I'd tread carefully. Otherwise, I'll blab to everyone about what you did to me."

"Will you now?" I asked coldly. "You have worked in that shelter long enough to know that raising hell will only leave you with a target on your back. Not to mention, you'll also be dragging our parents through the mud, not just me."

She stared at me ruefully. "Don't bring them into this. It'll kill Mom if she finds out."

"No. *You* will kill Mom if you go public with what happened."

Sadness coated her beautiful face. "I'd never break her heart like that," she relented softly, eyes lowered. "But you already knew that."

Giving her a momentary reprieve, I explained my stance softly. "Sara, listen to me. I don't want to hurt you. I only want to be *with* you, not force myself on you." *But I will if you don't agree,* I heinously admitted to myself.

"Thanks. That's comforting to know."

Irritation surged. *This* was what I had been reduced to over something I received offers for in plentiful. I only had to go outside for women to kneel before me, begging to pleasure me with their mouth, ass, pussy, anything.

Yet, she looked at me as if the thought of being touched by anyone other than her precious Toby was sickening.

"You don't have a choice in this matter, Sara."

"What's that supposed to mean?"

"It means that I have leverage over you," I responded without an ounce of emotion in my voice. "The shelter," I added.

Sara narrowed her eyes, perplexed. "Why are you bringing up the shelter?" she asked carefully.

"Because... If you don't break things off with that boy, I'll make sure that your precious shelter is torn down a lot sooner. If I have the resources to keep the place open for longer, then I also have the resources to shut it down. I don't give a damn if they all become homeless—"

"No," Sara screamed, distressed. "Please, Tris, don't."

"Then do as I say and leave Tobias."

The slight widening of her pretty gray eyes held more fear than last night. There were no tears in them, only a dilemma. She had accounted for more time to evacuate and was well aware that I didn't hand out idle threats.

Jackpot.

"At any rate, how will you explain losing your virginity to dear Toby? Your only option is to either tell him that you cheated on him or the truth. At which point, I'm going to run your damn shelter to the ground so fast that you won't have time to find another alternative for housing."

The way Sara opened and closed her fist confirmed my suspicion that these thoughts had already occurred to her, and the choices were far from appealing.

Remorseless, I perused ahead. "Do everything I ask of you, and I'll find a way to keep your shelter open."

Her palm lay flat on her stomach as if she had been punched in the gut. I hated seeing Sara in this state—cornered with the sting of defeat—as I had no interest in crushing her spirit. I only wanted her to share her soul with me.

Still, the depressing truth to the matter was that the world was ugly. Her bottom lip quivered. She looked around with incredulity, hardly believing this conversation possible after what went down between us last night.

"W-what... Where the hell is all of this coming from? When did you start harboring this sick need to hurt women... to hurt *me*? After last night, how could you stand there so calmly and suggest doing that to me again? Why did you do it in the first place?"

The four W's and one H—the pillar of any good interrogation.

These were all great questions, ones that I should answer.

On the other hand, Sara's emotions were escalating. It dawned on me that she was crumbling. She was angry about last night and scared over my future intentions. I shouldn't have piled on so much at once. It was overloading her, so I decided to tackle a couple of questions at a time.

"I want to clarify some things. First of all, I hurt *you*, yes, but last night was a singular experience—a fluke. I drank a lot, was pissed about that boy, and snapped. It's not an excuse, but you have known me your entire life. This isn't my M.O. If you don't believe me, answer me this. Women throw themselves at me. What need would I have to force one?"

She was worried that I might do this to other women, but despite our most recent interaction, Sara couldn't contradict the logic in my statement. Neither of us had ever come across a woman who wouldn't willingly open their legs for me... except for Sara. In fact, we had diverted several women who were caught stalking me.

Now that I had put her mind at ease over the issue, I tackled the other questions—when and the why.

"Secondly, I stopped seeing you as my sister a long time ago, which is why I know you can get there too." Though a sick part of me enjoyed how twisted good it felt to fuck my sister. "This thing between us," I wiggled my index finger, "this heat... It's been there for the last few years. We both feel it, so don't tell me that the thought hasn't occurred to you."

"You're my brother," she retorted incredulously. Technically, Sara didn't outright refute my declaration; only pointed out our relation and how society viewed us.

I took a step forward. "I'm not your brother. Not by blood."

"Just in every other way," she countered.

"I understand it's a difficult adjustment—"

"Difficult adjustment? I have known you since I was five. I don't even remember a time when you were *not* my brother."

Herein lay the problem.

We were nearly eleven years apart. I was almost sixteen when I met Sara, and she was introduced to me as a stranger.

Whereas Sara had only turned five when she met me. Her earliest memories were of the four of us as a family. She had never known me in a role other than the one of her brother.

I closed my eyes, unsure what I wanted out of Sara, given that wasn't even the only problem. We could never marry, nor could we be together publicly without ridicule and shame. Letting her be with another was not an option either. So, here we were, stagnant.

Our silent glaring was interrupted by the sound of the garage door opening.

"What the hell?" Dashing to the window, I noticed our parents' car pulling into the driveway.

Fuck. They weren't supposed to arrive for a few more hours.

Sara appeared at the window and equally paled at the sight. There was also relief in her features because we were no longer alone.

"Your bruises," I said without glancing at her.

"Yours too," she whispered back.

I lightly touched the scratches on my face and cursed under my breath.

"They'll want to know how... Fuck, Dad's going to pull out his gun again. What should we say?"

A tiny spark of hope dared to linger in the back of my mind at the way she wanted to plot with me to conceal what had happened.

"Go back to your room and pretend to be asleep. I didn't drive here, so I doubt they'll come to my room if they don't see my car in the driveway. I'll leave after the coast is clear."

She nodded, then rushed toward the veranda door as I procured a key from my pocket to unlock it. She stopped midway when I spoke again.

"Everything I said from earlier still stands. I'll give you a few days to... adjust. I want an answer by the time I return. Either lose everything by choosing him or be with me, and I'll give you everything you ever wanted." I might be the man to paint her sunny disposition into the color gray, but if she let me, I could also make it bright again.

Sara stared straight ahead. "Go to Hell, Tris."

I smiled self-deprecatingly. "Only if I can take you with me."

CHAPTER 18

Tristan

"Something the matter, Tristan?" Michael inquired, eyes trekking my strides as I impatiently paced the length of my office.

Yeah, something's the matter. I was a depraved fuck who indulged in his little sister's body without permission. Worse yet, I only granted her a few days—under the pretenses of giving her the time to process—while planning how to take her again as soon as she was healed enough.

As I said, depraved fuck.

I had tried hard not to be a stereotypical DC politician. Dad was known for his work ethic, and for years, I was successful in following suit. Stayed away from scandals, never engaged in a workplace romance, and was one of few politicians who hadn't been threatened with a sexual harassment lawsuit (a miracle for the likes of us). In spite of my previous voracious sexual appetite, I was no longer hankered down by the same lowly, uncontrollable desires... other than for Sara.

A lifetime of goals. A role I had been groomed for since birth. The possibility of becoming a senator and the hopes of running for Presidency if I played my cards right. I flushed it all down the drain for thirty minutes with Sara.

The worse part?

I didn't care.

I'd give up everything and do it all over again for thirty more minutes with her. My mind had been plagued with only dark thoughts, and after days of endless torture, I had my assistant schedule a session with Michael in my office.

At my extended silence, Michael scribbled something in his notebook. God, how I hated when he wrote shit down. It was ammunition against a politician's career, and I almost demanded that he show me the notes.

"You know, everything you say here is confidential," he reminded, having caught the drift of my suspicious eyes.

I scoffed. "Unless it's illegal, then you have to report it."

Michael wrinkled his brows with a contemplative look. "You are right. Legally, I do have to report it if you plan to harm yourself or others." He paused, uncrossing his legs. "However, if you were to tell me of a hypothetical situation... I don't see any reason for reporting something that never happened."

I smiled sardonically. That's how Michael catered to his affluent and morally ambiguous clientele. After all, what's so bad about a fantasy? I could hardly go through this mental hell alone. The entity inside of me was getting progressively stronger. It had become a part of my existence, the way my organs were a part of my body. While I didn't believe in the embodiment of evil, I had still carried out the Devil's biddings. So, I needed help, and Michael always seemed to have the answers.

Stomping on my paranoia, I joined him on the sectional leather couch with a heavy sigh. Blinding morning light from the windows probably highlighted the guilt etched on my face.

"Okay." I nodded, relinquishing control. "I had a dream that I did something terrible," I said the words all in one breath.

Dropping his notebook on the coffee table, Michael made it clear that he'd no longer take notes or keep a paper trail of this session. "Go on."

I cleared my throat, uncomfortable. Churning the next words in my head, I realized it was damn near impossible to disclose fantasies of raping my adopted sister without implicating my career.

Never mind. I couldn't disclose it even under the guise of a dream.

Michael sighed. "Was this dream about your sister?"

I frowned, irritated at being figured out so easily. "Why would you automatically assume this is about my...." I paused, suddenly not wanting to use the word sister in therapy. "Why would you assume this is about Sara?"

Michael didn't miss the omission in my rewording and studied me carefully. "Because your moods are generally linked to her."

I wanted to wring his neck out. "Not this time. I'm just stressed about the upcoming election and need to stay sharp for the campaign." Not entirely untrue. My looks gave me a competitive edge, but appearances alone didn't entice voters into casting their ballot.

"We'll get to the campaign." Michael eyed me sideways. "But first, let's circle back to this dream of yours. Judging by your appearance, I'd say this dream has been bothering you for a few nights."

Four sleepless nights, to be precise. I had managed to keep my word and give her space, returning to my own home for the intermittent. However, my efforts to check in with her had been futile due to Sara's refusal to answer my calls or text. Steve had men with eyes on her round the clock and even dropped by once under the guise of checking on my parents. Apparently, she had kept to herself for three straight days and finally left the house today to resume her role at the shelter.

"So, tell me. What happened with Sara in this dream of yours?"

Michael was a dog with a bone, but it was best to discuss it rather than give in to one more of my rash episodes. Perhaps, he could help me get these impulses under control.

I sighed. "I dreamt that I hurt Sara." I glanced at him, refusing to elaborate on how I hurt her. "And I don't want to hurt Sara," I said remorsefully.

His expression remained neutral. "Have you considered making it up to her?" Then he added with a smile, "In your dream, that is."

"How?"

"From what you tell me, Sara is a creature of sacrifice. She's devoted her life to helping others. If you want to fix things with her, show her that you can also sacrifice what you desire for those in dire circumstances. After all, love itself is the ultimate sacrifice. Even the words *falling in love* carry the connotation that one must *fall*, potentially hurting and sacrificing themselves in the process, to love another."

My heart palpitation spiked, eyes flickering at the word *love*.

"While you consider my words, I want to tell you another story about Asmodeus' Sarah. Is that alright?"

I said nothing, which he took for acquiescence, and dove in.

Sarah's fragile heart was tired of the pain she caused. She recalled every insult hurled her way, the accusations, the condemning eyes, and those who called for her death in order to spare the lives of others. They were right.

To shield those around her from suffering more misfortunes, she had to end her own life. Leaving behind her loved ones was a thought more agonizing than death itself, but what choice did Sarah have? This was the only way out, so no longer would others suffer the wrath of the curse she brought.

Filled with desolation, Sarah stared contritely at the view from the roof, where she was likely to meet her end.

No longer did she fear her mortality. Only the horrid looks of her doting parents upon finding her motionless body kept her from jumping. Fervent tears streaked down her face. Taking one's life was a mortal sin, one her parents would have to bear the shame of carrying forever.

The thought kept her rooted at the ledge of the roof.

Instead, she asked for God's help in taking away her life. "Please, God, take my life in exchange for others. Grant me the gift of death."

But death never came.

"Sarah offered to sacrifice herself in order to save those around her."

Never had I been so annoyed by one of Michael's stories. Exactly what in the fuck was he suggesting? That *my* Sara would try to bargain away her life?

Not a chance.

Michael caught the drift in my narrowed eyes and swiftly explained. "Asmodeus' toxic love caused Sarah to seek out her own death. Whereas Sarah's sacrificial love was to protect those around her."

Tap. Tap. Tap. He tapped his pen against his thigh, and for the first time in years, showed signs of nervousness. For some reason, it was imperative to him that I saw the light now more than ever. As if we were on the verge of a massive breakthrough.

"If you find yourself at a similar crossroads with *your* Sara," he said quietly, "maybe it'll be helpful to remember that toxic love will only push her over the edge. Sacrifice is the only way to true love, even if that means letting her go in the process."

"What the hell is that supposed to mean?"

"We have known each other for more than a decade, Tristan. Surely, we can have a frank conversation. I can no longer overlook that your celibacy in recent years is tied to your love for Sara. These passionate feelings you harbor for her are spiraling out of control—"

I stood instantly, mouth dry. How the fuck did Michael always manage to figure this shit out?

He spoke before I could throw him out of my office. "If I had any interest in blabbing to the press, I would have done so long ago. So, can we drop the pretenses in hopes of an honest conversation?" When I still hadn't sat down, he continued, "Tristan, I'm not worried about your feelings for Sara, only troubled by how you might act upon it. As far as I'm concerned, there is nothing wrong with how you feel. She is an adult, and you aren't related by blood."

"Marrying someone from your own family is still illegal," I snapped before I could stop myself.

Sara and I weren't *stepsiblings*; we were *adopted siblings*. In this country, it was illegal to marry your adopted sister. I had already researched for a loophole in the law.

Add that to the growing pile of reasons I had initially fought my feelings. Sara wanted a family of her own, and I could never give her one she could proudly show off. I swallowed the pill that had left me bitter for years.

"I think perhaps it's best if you leave. I have a lot of work to do."

Michael urged me to sit by waving a hand in the direction of the sofa. "Please. Let's talk about this some more. I just want to help my patient."

But I didn't sit, overwhelmed with this conversation and his suggestion of letting her go.

Fuck that. I'd never let her go. If she wanted sacrifice, I'd show her sacrifice—anything in exchange for not letting her go.

"Michael, it's time for you to leave," I spoke each word with such precision that he didn't argue.

With great reluctance, Michael rose to his feet. He glanced at me upon reaching the door to my office. I assumed he'd be angry over how I was cutting this session short after he had made the long drive. Except, it wasn't anger sparkling in his eyes—only pity.

Eight children sat in a linear arrangement around the tiny, torn-down classroom inside the shelter. They each had a blank canvas in front, holding paintbrushes in their hands like powerful weapons.

At the front of the class, a very patient Sara was perched on a high bar stool with a canvas of her own. She was dressed in an ivory, thigh-length dress-shirt with a belt looped around the waist. Where it should have been conservative, the attire sent hot blood right to my cock.

With immense self-control, I snuffed out the burning desire to take the five necessary strides to yank her into my hold. Instead, I watched her give the kids instructions in a soft voice, walking them through the process of recreating the piece she was drawing.

She'd make a great mom one day; I couldn't help but muse.

After the miserable week away from her, the weekend had finally arrived. I'd given Sara the time to process. It was time to face the music. With that resolution, I drove here with a plan cooking in the oven.

To my relief, she seemed better than I had expected. She was lost in the process of art therapy, while I was lost in watching her from the shadows. However, I wasn't granted the luxury of studying her uninterrupted for more than a few serene seconds.

"Mr. Marcolf!" came a shrill gasp.

I clenched my teeth over having been discovered.

With her reverie interrupted, Sara's attention snapped toward me.

CHAPTER 19

Sara

"Mr. Marcolf!" Jen, the manager for this shelter, all but curtsied.

"Tris?" It took me several seconds to register his presence, though his God-like façade stood out so distinctly that it hardly escaped the attention of bystanders.

"Oh my God, it is you," Jen gushed. "I recognized you from the posters. It's so good to finally meet you in person. Sara's told us so much." Did she just pocket her hand to conceal her wedding ring?

Smart women turned into brainless idiots around Tristan. I knew from experience that this situation might escalate for Jen if I didn't intervene.

I turned to face the room. "Everyone, finish drawing your vases while I step outside."

I had been entertaining the kids at the shelter with various weekend and afterschool activities to distract them from an obscure future. It was imperative since many of them didn't want to return to their previously abusive homes.

I nodded at the pre-teen sitting in the back. "Ray, you're in charge."

Ray stood on cue. At twelve, he was the oldest and was also incredibly mature for his age.

Stephanie, an outspoken nine-year-old in the bunch, grumbled bitterly that she'd make a better leader. Nora, her shy younger sister, disagreed. Meanwhile, Sam, the youngest at seven, tried to sample the paint from the tip of his brush.

Ray was at his side without missing a beat, turning the brush around to face the canvas instead. "Ms. Sara said to paint, not eat."

And that's why he was my right-hand man when it came to helping out with the other kids. Unfortunately, Ray was too good for this place. All of them were.

With a deep sigh, I stood from the barstool, feeling terribly weary. Finding suitable accommodation to relocate these families was near impossible. Many zoning committees didn't want a shelter in their community as it brought down housing prices. I had exhausted every resource for potential sponsors, only to come up short or to hear gentle rejections. It had left me utterly drained.

Shelving away the feelings of defeat, I moved to the doorsill. Jen twirled the wispy tendrils of her brown hair, shuffling her feet nervously from left to right as she addressed Tristan. "If you aren't doing anything, I was just about to—"

"Jen!" I interrupted her shameless gawking as her eyes trailed from Tris' biceps flexing against the sleeves of his Polo shirt and down to the waist of his jeans. "Mike called the office to see if you needed anything from the store?"

Without looking away from Tristan, she asked absentmindedly, "Who?"

I sighed. "Mike! Your husband of four years."

Jen shook her head as if remembering her wedding vows. "Right. Yes... Mike. Right. Of course. Okay, then. I-I'll go call him back."

Tris said nothing. The faint cocky smile was indicative, nevertheless. He knew of the power he held over women.

"It-it was nice meeting you." With one last glance at Tristan, Jen hastily walked down the hallway before rounding the corner. She was confused by her own reactions and slightly embarrassed.

I turned my attention to Tristan, unable to meet his gaze. He studied me with such intense scrutiny that I felt flushed from the inspection, and my gaze was cast down in search of discrepancies in my outfit. Rookie mistake. It's how he found weaknesses in his adversaries.

Tristan guided me away from prying eyes and to a secluded corner. Our steps were slow, meaningful, and sounded loud in the deserted hallways. There was now an awkwardness between us that was simply cringeworthy.

"What are you doing here?" I inquired tersely.

"Time's up, Angel."

I had no idea what bout of insanity started this, but Tristan had granted me the week to adjust. One week to get over the trauma. One week to break things off with Tobias. And one week to willingly open my legs for the Devil.

Otherwise, he'd run this shelter to the ground.

I had considered defying his wishes and going to the police instead. Then I had snorted at the mere thought.

Not only was I used to seeing powerful men get away with crimes far viler than the one Tristan had committed, but more often, the victims suffered for coming forward.

I was at the protests when Dr. Christine Blasey Ford came to DC and accused Judge Kavanaugh of sexual assault during his Supreme Court campaign. I was also there when she was publicly shunned and ridiculed for coming forward and by other women, no less. They believed she made up lies to destroy a good man's career.

Ultimately, she had to move out of her home, quit her job, and was plagued with death threats to this day. Meanwhile, Judge Kavanaugh was an associate justice of the United States Supreme Court.

Welcome to the reality of this ugly world.

I couldn't tell a single soul of what had happened. Even after an expensive and humiliating public trial, not one person would believe the assault. Instead, Mom might finally believe that I was the mental one if I accused Tristan of foul play a second time.

I had already cried wolf, I realized bitterly.

Regrettably, I also couldn't inflict any actual damage on Tristan without shattering Mom in the process. It would kill her if anything terrible happened to her only son. I had already brought enough misfortunes to Mom's life. I might want to hurt Tristan, but I could never hurt Mary Marcolf.

If I wanted justice, my real-life choices were limited, if not non-existent.

I could kill myself than live with a pain I could never get retribution for.

I had shuddered when the thought had crossed my mind. At times, my need for justice trumped logic. Such thoughts had no place circling the perimeters of my mind. I was the one to counsel girls away from morbid ideas.

No. I was determined to survive this. The nightmare of what happened would eventually cease to exist and become a distant memory. By God, I'd get past it and achieve the only thing that mattered anymore.

Vengeance.

In the days following that awful night, I spent the first few huddled in my bed. My mind was jam-packed with nightmares. By the third day, the shock subsided, and a new emotion took root instead. Anger.

As the week ended, I left my mourning behind and became consumed by my need for revenge. I returned to work with only one vendetta in mind—to make Tristan Marcolf pay for his crimes.

However, there was a slight complication.

Tristan wasn't in the business of handing out idle threats. If he suggested running this shelter to the ground, he meant it.

Ray and his mother arrived at our organization because the local government shelters were overcrowded with waiting lists. At the time, Ray had a broken arm while his mother was covered in bruises. The thought of forcing them back to the same abusive household or into a broken system made me shudder worse than anything Tristan could do to me.

Although my parents were initially the primary sponsors for this private shelter, they later became too busy for it. I was the only Marcolf actively involved in the proceedings of this place and begged Mom and Tristan to continue hosting fundraisers to keep it open.

Even so, cash flow was an issue. The charity functions barely collected enough funds to pay the discounted rent for this building, the staff of five (including Jen), upkeep, etc.

None of those fundraisers could possibly raise enough money to purchase this lot. Even if I sold everything I owned, it only equated to a monetary value of fewer than thirty thousand dollars. Whereas the property this building was located on cost upwards of two million.

My parents retired to work on Tristan's campaign. They had no income of their own, other than the stipend he paid them. Their home belonged to Tristan, along with their cars. All three of us put any other expenses on credit cards, paid off by the same man.

The only person I knew with deep enough pockets and connections to keep this shelter open for longer was, in fact, Tristan. So, I had to keep him on an even keel unless I could figure something out for this place.

Unfortunately, Tristan wasn't a patient man. "You owe me an answer."

"I-I need more time."

"I'm not giving you more time so you can find a way to be with *him*," he barked.

"This has nothing to do with... It's over with Tobias."

I got too comfortable with Tobias' short-lived fortunes and dismissed this jinx that followed me around. Like always, my curse had struck lightning. On the same day Tobias admitted to being in love with me, he got into a car accident. Presumably, a drunk driver had tried to veer him off the road.

Tobias escaped the crash thanks to a bystander, who called for an ambulance. Luckily, there were no serious injuries. The hospital discharged him after an overnight stay, and he got a hold of me the following day to explain what had happened.

By that point, I was an emotional wreck. Tobias' account of his night only solidified the need to break things off in order to save him from further danger. Not to mention, I felt too tainted for his pure and unadulterated form of love after what happened with Tristan.

The mere idea of hurting Tobias squeezed my heart, and my deflection only left him more confused than ever.

Tobias: *"I don't understand. I thought you wanted to progress our relationship. Did something happen that I don't know about?"*

Tobias: *"Please, Princess. Don't shut me out."*

Tobias: *"Does your brother have anything to do with this?"*

It had become abundantly clear that a breakup without pain was impossible, and last night, I ripped off the Band-Aid.

Sara: *"I'm sorry. We aren't right for each other. Please accept that it's over."*

The heartbreak wasn't good enough for my brother. Tristan gripped my hips with two firm hands and glared. "If I find him with you again

—" My heart iced over when he stepped forward, forcing my back against the wall behind me. "Don't forget our deal, Sara."

"Deal?"

"Break things off with *Toby* and be with me. Or defy my wishes and pay with the things you care about."

My eyes searched his with trepidation.

"If you don't agree, I'll ensure every zoning committee you apply to will be met with obstacle after obstacle."

I winced.

"And that's only the start. I'll go after *Toby* and blacklist him from every precinct, too."

"My God." I covered my mouth with a hand.

His actions only fortified my determination to peruse ahead with the terrible yet just form of vengeance I had conjured. Where real-life options for justice had failed me, there remained a mystical power at play.

Every man to desire me is met with disaster. What better way to exact revenge than by giving Tristan precisely what he had asked for?

The retribution was poetic—downfall brought on by the very thing he desired.

None of the men to 'court' me were met with irreversible damages, such as death, but there had been considerable pain. If I genuinely believed that I was cursed, all I had to do was let Tristan touch me. Not so much that it might shatter my mother. Only enough to trigger whatever misfortune befell those other men.

Generally, I sought justice, not violence, but dealing with this trauma had left me bitter. And Tristan wasn't helping with his charming personality.

"What's gotten into you, Tris?"

"You!" he spat. "You must have understood by now there isn't a whole lot that's off-limits for me when it comes to you."

I gulped.

While I had decided to let him have me, I didn't know if I could handle proximity to Tristan quite yet. The wound was too fresh, and the idea of that man penetrating me again made me shrivel. Tristan concealed a promiscuous side from his family and quite possibly had a sexual appetite that I wasn't equipped to handle. Perhaps if I had a bit more time, I could adjust.

"I told you that it's over with Tobias. This has nothing to do with him. I-I just... All of this is so insane. You're my brother."

"I *was* your brother," he countered. "And now, I want to be the man in your life. Just try to compartmentalize."

"Compartmentalize? I-I am still trying to process what happened between us. How am I supposed to just forget?"

My answer wasn't a yes, or a no, but Tristan had shown a side of himself that's entirely unpredictable. So, I fully expected his wrath.

Except, his eyes softened with understanding. He ran a hand over the back of his neck... a nervous tick that he never displayed in public. He sighed in defeat. "I know all of this can't be easy for you... but being away from you isn't working for me, Angel. We need to find a middle ground."

The unexpectedly tender voice caught me off guard. Tristan was either vain or vengeful. This softer side of him flared up on rare occasions. The women who chased after him had never seen the vulnerable side. To be honest, no one had other than me.

"Such as?" I asked.

"We can start with something simple. You are almost done for the day. Let's go to dinner and talk."

"No," I immediately declined.

Disappointment coated his eyes, but he didn't waver. "I hate to pull this card, but you don't have a choice. Don't forget, I'm the one making concessions, and you're the one in need of something. If you don't wish for me to go after Toby and want me to extend the dates to keep this shelter open, then I expect you to meet me halfway."

I gritted my teeth in anger. God, I couldn't wait to make him pay.

When I was in high school, this boy, Sasha Ivanov, tried to woo me. Sasha was the artsy, dreamy type who loved to write poetry under the birch tree. We used to make out behind the bleachers and the empty corridors of the school. We had barely ventured into second base when Sasha was expelled for hiding contraband in his locker and promptly shipped off to military school.

Perhaps if I could bear it enough to let Tristan touch me, the same fate would befall him. Nothing violent that might make Mom sad, but hopefully it'd result in him being condemned and sent off to a land far, far away.

"No dinners, no romance." Dinners and niceties had no part in our twisted relationship. If I wanted to avenge the crimes committed against me, I couldn't falter by viewing my perpetrator in a humane light. "If you refuse to give me more time, then all I can agree to is something purely physical."

No longer did I fear Tristan repeating the same horrors. A man who planned to use violence wouldn't have bothered with blackmail. I suspected he was telling the truth about wanting a willing participant to his lustful desires.

Don't get me wrong. I wasn't naïve and knew Tristan to distort the lines of morality if it fit him. And just because he didn't want to inflict violence didn't mean he wouldn't be coercive in his pursuits.

Tris' eyes widened at my suggestion, finding it unbelievable that I'd concede so easily. He questioned my ulterior motives, but the greed glinting in his eyes also told me that he didn't care. He stepped forward, raising his fingers to my cheek. I closed my eyes in anticipation of someone sucking the very soul out of my body.

I reminded myself that it was for the greater good. One stone, two birds—the revenge I sought while keeping him at bay until something panned out for the shelter.

However, when he slanted his face for a kiss, I exclaimed. "Stop!"

An ensuing panic was rising. It subsided when Tris dropped his hand and took a step back, a flash of hurt in his eyes.

I blew out a breath. "I-I can't... I don't know if I can do this... I'm not ready for what you want." I twisted my hands together, hoping he'd accept my answer. Images of pain from that horrible day flashed through my mind. I couldn't imagine his body on top of mine. It made me shrivel up from the inside.

As if he knew what I was thinking, he soothed, "That's understandable, Angel. What if we start with something else instead? Something easy."

"Something easy?"

He nodded. "What if all we do is touch? Until you get used to me, we can just... play around. I won't go inside you, but I want to be able to at least touch you. Can you manage if I limit myself to only that?"

My eyes rounded. Here?

He caught my drift and shook his head. "I didn't mean here or right now. I meant when you get home."

I frowned. "But our parents are there—"

"They are gone," he informed. "Steve mapped out a campaign trail for them. They'll be gone for a couple of weeks. Maybe we can spend that time getting used to each other?" he asked with hope in his voice.

"I-I don't know if it's a good idea for you to stay over while they are gone."

"Then I won't. I'll only stay on the nights you want me there." He stepped forward. "I'll keep my promise, and I won't go inside you... not until you want me. But I want to try other things... things that might not scare you."

Tristan patiently waited for my response until I finally gave him a curt nod. I promised to meet him at home, swallowing the dread.

Remember, Sara. It's the only way for payback.

Vengeance consumed my mind as I dismissed the painting class, collected my things, and drove home to give my soul to the Devil.

CHAPTER 20

Tristan

I had never been so damn nervous. Not while waiting for the results of the last election or even announcing my intent to run for Senate as one of the youngest in history.

Our parents were traveling to campaign on my behalf, leaving the house deserted for our use. And though Sara had agreed to oblige (much to my shock), her nerves were shot at the idea I might use this window to my advantage instead of keeping to my word.

In short, tonight was pivotal.

I asked her to meet me in one of the guest rooms, after she showered, in the hopes that a neutral territory might alleviate her reservations. Despite Sara's lackluster introduction to it, sex was one department where I excelled.

Sara might not be impressed by the things other women were in my past, but my abilities in the bedroom were something even she couldn't deny. Perhaps those capabilities were a gift like my physical appearance or merely owed to my experience. Either way, Sara came amidst my largest act of cruelty against her and even in her sleep.

If Sara agreed to our deal, I could teleport her body to an entirely different dimension while her mind remained for me to bend.

My muscles locked when I heard her soft steps gracing the room.

She came.

The moonlight streaming through the floor-to-ceiling glass panel doors of the veranda was the only source of illumination. I was on high alert when the fragrant smell of jasmine moved closer, my back stiffening from anticipation. I stood by the two-tier bar trolley of the room, home to an overabundance of expensive liquor. I pretended to do something to the extent of making a selection. In reality, my hooded eyes were fixated on her like a predator in shallow water. There wasn't a single sarcastic bone in my body, a hint of a prank, nor a sneer at the tip of my tongue. I was too stunned by this sight—a willing and vulnerable Sara.

I was being handed a gift, one I didn't deserve. And God, did I want to unwrap this gift because Christmas had come early, and thank you, thank you, thank you to the Heavens for it.

Sara's unruly curls cascaded down her shoulders, framing her face softly. She was wearing nothing but a silky blush-colored bathrobe that reached her knees. An ankle bracelet that had tortured me for years framed her delicate feet, and the exposed skin glowed like shimmery gold. All I could think of was how it'd look when she bared it all for me.

While I had seen women in expensive lingerie and all kinds of sexy costumes, Sara in a bathrobe was somehow more provocative. She tiptoed wordlessly. Her eyes wandered around the room on everything except for me. Wrapping her arms tightly around her middle, Sara appeared defensive. If only she'd allow herself, if only she'd open her heart, she'd know things could be different between us.

With a deep breath, I took a swig of the drink I had poured into my glass. To my surprise, she moved closer to the trolly. I had planned on starting with a reassurance or pep talk to put her at ease, but Sara beat me to it.

"Before we..." she didn't know how to end the sentence and rephrased it. "I want to discuss a few things with you before we go any further."

My back tightened. Fuck. Was she going to change her mind? Come on, Angel. You have come so far, don't turn your back on us now.

"First, you're going to disclose everything Steve has uncovered about the developers so far. Then you'll find me sponsors to fund the upkeep of the shelter, and you'll get all of this done by the end of the week."

My jaw ticked. "As long as our agreement still stands—"

"And you won't threaten the shelter again," she cut me off. "It's a cheap shot; we both know it. I don't want you holding that over my head so long as I fulfill my... obligations."

I glanced at her, perplexed.

She rolled her eyes. "As long as I keep..." she waved her hands in the air in search of a better word, "warming your bed... but only by doing things that I condone. You'll keep your promise not to... go inside me until I agree to it. For tonight, I don't want to go any further than touching. Oral or penetration of any type is off the table."

The immense control it took for me to mask my expressions was noteworthy. After what seemed like days, I was finally able to let out a breath of relief. I took in the oxygen wholeheartedly, welcoming the feeling. Not only was Sara willing, but she had laid down her terms. She had thought it through.

"Fair enough," I forced the words out.

Sara fiddled with the belt tying her robe in place. My eyes inadvertently landed on it, wondering how easy it'd be to rip that thing off her.

"Would you like a drink?" I asked instead.

She nodded absentmindedly. I had purposefully taken off my shirt in preparation, leaving me in only my blue jeans that hung low. I had caught her eyeing my torso before. It remained to be seen whether it was fascination over the male anatomy, or she was simply impressed by the eight-pack I sported, but I knew it affected her.

The theory was proven correct when I poured her a glass of wine and stepped a little too close to hand it over. Her eyes widened at the proximity, though she tried to keep the apathetic look in place.

Her curiosity betrayed her, and her gaze dropped. She trailed my eight-pack stacked one over another in symmetry. I didn't relish in anything less than perfection when it came to my body and paid a celebrity trainer an insane amount of money to ensure just that —perfection.

Sara's thirsty eyes roaming every bit of exposed skin were worth the no-pain-no-gain philosophy I had adopted at the gym. It was so fucking hot that my dick stirred... No, Tristan, focus.

Tonight was about getting her drunk on me for a change.

What had made me a 'good lay' back in the day was my ability to read women. I'd get in their heads, figure out their kinks and simply deliver. It had a transporting effect on women, after which they'd do anything for me.

If I could get into Sara's head, it wouldn't matter how she felt about me. She'd be too addicted to care because everyone had a weak spot. Mine was Sara. So, what was hers?

"Do you want to touch me?" I suddenly asked. Sara was a shit liar, so she had decided to omit that part of herself altogether at an early age. If I wanted to know what might work on her, all I had to do was ask.

She peered up at me quizzically, having snapped out of the trance. There was a slight flush to her golden beige skin over being caught checking me out.

"Just because you are agreeing to this doesn't mean you can't enjoy it. You are allowed to enjoy this," I pressed.

Sara couldn't refute this attraction (however deplorable and sick she might find the fact). She had denied her feelings thus far, locked them up deep inside her head, but they were slowly unraveling. The knowledge sent a hot rush of blood to my groin, fingers itching to part that robe to see what was underneath. The need to touch her was escalating out of control... For fuck's sake, Tristan. Focus!

What the fuck was wrong with me? I was dubbed the sex icon in the DMV, the youngest elected Congressman in my district, and I couldn't play it cool around this nineteen-year-old for five minutes to execute one lousy seduction plan?

"Have you touched a man's naked body before, Angel?" The words sent a rush of anger through my system, but I swallowed it down because I knew the answer.

Sara shook her head, glancing at my torso several times while trying to avert her eyes, too.

If she had never properly touched a man's body, then she must be itching to experience it. After all, curiosity was a bitch.

Sara had panicked when I tried to kiss her earlier at the shelter, so I had to do this very cautiously by distracting her. Gently, so as not to spook her, I grabbed the wine glass out of her hand and laid it back on the trolly. I placed her right hand over my heart. The slight touch sent a jolt to my cock, but I kept my eye on the prize. I dragged her hand down. I did it repeatedly until I saw a hint of fascination in her eyes. Her pouty mouth formed the perfect O while tracing the curves of my abs, the edges of my waist, and the slopes of my V.

"Do you want to touch more of me, little Angel?"

The only response was her pink tongue darting out to lick her bottom lip. It glistened in the moonlight, and what the fuck were we talking about?

I took half a step closer. Her stunned expression had my body buzzing with excitement, aware of every way her gaze roved and my jeans that were too tight for comfort now. Unzipping myself, I slid the jeans down and kicked them to the side, leaving me in a pair of black boxers—another piece of clothing I had picked out with Sara in mind.

Once, she was standing on the balcony and had glanced inside my room. I was in a pair of black boxers. The way she had inadvertently checked out my ass and abs confirmed that brother or not, she couldn't deny what she thought of my body.

She was staring at my cock now, which had never been this hard.

"That's what you do to me, Angel. Touch me there." How could she deny it when she had never touched a man's cock, and it was right here to satiate her inquisitiveness?

Sara didn't oblige.

Touch me, I mentally willed her. I was about to lose my shit if she didn't touch me right fucking now.

With a sigh, I moved her hand down slowly. Oh fuck, so slowly. She didn't pull away. At long last, her delicate fingers grazed the top of my black boxers, and my legs nearly caved in. All from one damn touch. My restless legs wanted to bounce, every nerve ending shooting off signals of pleasure, and fuck, this was torture. I had seen my body's effect on plenty of women, but not the other way around. It was different. Intoxicating.

My heart pounded against my rib cage, my hard cock seeking freedom. Letting go of her hand, I dragged my boxers down reverently slow and held my breath should even a sound break the trance she was under. I kicked them to the side as soon as they slid down my hips and onto the floor. My dick sprung free, bobbing up and down with an urgent need only she could satiate. Drops of pre-cum gathered at the tip, and Sara stared in awe.

There was something more than curiosity in her eyes now—something I had seen in passing but couldn't always verify.

It was hunger.

I was convinced it was at that moment I'd die of the blood rushing to my head with the look of desire in Sara's eyes as I revealed my engorged cock. And if I died right now, what a way to go.

My theory had been confirmed. Sara touched herself in her sleep because she was dying for an outlet. She was a sexual person without a channel to redirect her energy. Now that the opportunity had presented itself, she was conflicted about passing it up despite all of the reservations she harbored.

That's the only confirmation I required to execute my plans for the night.

"Come on." I was shocked when the words came out coherently. "I want to show you something." I grabbed her hand and walked her over to the bed.

Confused by the turn of events, Sara glanced at the set-up on the nightstand next to the bed. A couple of sex toys. Lube. Blindfold. Handcuffs.

"What is all this?" She visibly gulped as if I had laid forth the tools for a torture chamber.

I couldn't help but want to laugh at her adorable face, yet I decided it best to explain. "Thought these items might help you ease into... more. Have you ever used a vibrator before?" I murmured.

"None that went inside me."

"None of these will go inside you either," I promised, blindly reaching for one of the items on the nightstand. Every piece had been curated for the purposes of tonight, and the first one on the agenda was the blindfolds.

Her breath quickened, body strained with the tension of doubt when I rounded her and brought forth the blindfold to tie around her eyes.

"Wait!"

I paused, the scrap of long, rectangular fabric in front of her face.

"Why do I have to be blindfolded?"

It was important.

Currently, the girl was exercising a monumental effort to meet my gaze. Her fear stemmed from my recent bouts of cruelty but the reservations cultivated from the lifelong role of the brother I had played in her life.

If I blindfolded her, I'd take away both of those factors to enjoy this without constant reminders. Afterward, she'd be acclimated enough and wouldn't need the blindfold.

It was all about jumping over the initial hump.

However, if I explained all of that, it'd defeat the purpose. The point was for her to be so lost in the moment that she wouldn't realize it was me playing her body like a marionette.

"It'll heighten your other senses so you can feel more." It was part of the larger truth. "But if you don't like it at any point, tell me to stop. I'll do so like I just did," I reminded her to build trust.

I was still holding the piece of fabric without having tied it around her. I had stopped midway because she had voiced a request.

"I'll stop if you change your mind."

After another hesitant pause, she nodded.

"This won't hurt," I whispered, placing a reassuring kiss on her shoulders to help her realize she was in control.

Sara was breathing heavily, chest rising and falling with mine, as I tied the blindfold at the back of her head. I led her to stand at the edge of the bed and stood stoutly behind, so she wouldn't stumble, then reached for the next item. This one might be a fight to get her to agree. I took the handcuffs and rubbed them within my palm to warm up the cold steel so that it wouldn't shock her.

Sara heard the rattle.

I spoke before she could inquire, wording my sentence very carefully. "Sara, I'd like your permission to handcuff you."

She froze against me. It wasn't the mention of the handcuffs that surprised her; it was my request for permission. I wasn't known for it, but Michael's voice nagged in my ears. If I bothered to humble myself enough to ask for permission, I wouldn't deny her request if she wanted out.

"I-I don't know about this," she spoke at long last.

"The importance of this might be difficult to understand," I breathed in her ear. "But just like the blindfold, I'll take it off if you change your mind."

The handcuffs were a fail-safe. In case the blindfold came off, or it broke Sara's trance, I could make her come before her mind could process it.

"Feel this contraption." I dropped the handcuffs in her palms to let her feel. They were fairly large for her tiny wrists, and if she so pleased, she could wiggle out of them with minimal effort. "Your hands are small, so you can get out of these if you pull at them. I have been forthright with you all night. I wouldn't buy this kind if I planned to do something you didn't want."

Sara remained hesitantly quiet for many moments. I could feel the vibration from her body. She was placing a considerable amount of trust in me. Trust I had broken in the past. It was a small victory when Sara gave me the curtest of nods.

"Remember, let me know if you want me to take any of this off at any point. I'm right here."

That soothed her nerves while I handcuffed her hands behind her back. I urged her to hop onto the edge of the mattress on her knees. I stepped between her parted thighs, rounding one arm around her waist. She was securely in place with her back firmly against my chest. She let out a shuddering breath when my hard length dug into her ass.

"Hold onto my arm if you feel like you're about to fall."

She nodded without voicing any protests. Good girl.

"Spread your legs wider, Angel."

After another momentary pause, Sara obeyed. The back of her knees flexed as she pressed her left knee into the mattress to move the right one further apart.

Fuck.

Sara was cuffed and blindfolded and spread in front of me. The amount of self-control I was exerting ... Focus, I chided myself.

I grabbed the next item off the table. Before turning on the vibrator, I decided to let her feel it and get accustomed to the feel. I moved the wand over her palm that was restrained in the back.

"Just a vibrator," I confirmed against the shell of her ear.

She blew out a breath as if bracing for a nasty shock. "It's big," she commented when I turned it on, startling her.

"It won't go inside you," I promised.

I grabbed the bottle of lube off the nightstand and slathered the liquid over the head of the wand to give her an extra push with that slick feel. Very slowly, I undid the belt of her silky robe and parted it.

I couldn't see Sara's naked front, but my hand grazed against her bare breast, making me groan. From the back, I lifted the fabric to slide the head of the buzzing wand under her from behind and between her parted thighs. When it grazed her sex, the immediate jolt in Sara sent a shiver down my own spine.

"Oh," Sara reacted immediately.

Keeping my arm firmly locked around her waist, I rotated the head of the vibrator until finding an angle that rubbed her clit. I held it there while the base of the wand rubbed between her ass cheeks.

Initially, Sara gave nothing away, as if this were purely transactional or she was doing this out of an ulterior reason I hadn't quite figured out. But soon, something shifted.

With her eyes blindfolded, hands cuffed behind her back, Sara had no worries of this world, no judgment to face, and no inhibitions to hold back. She slowly relaxed as I massaged her clit and trailed my lips over her neck to suck on the flesh.

I whispered all sorts of sweet words in her ears, but they did nothing for Sara. If anything, they kept snapping her out of the daze.

I quickly altered course. Where sweet words had failed, perhaps it'd be the wicked ones to take her breath away.

"Fuck, Angel. Your body is amazing. It makes me so hard that I might come just from looking at you."

Sara drew in a ragged breath, surprising me. Was that her kink? Slight objectification, or perhaps she simply liked all things dirty and filthy.

I decided to test the waters.

"Look at what you're doing to me." I dug my length against her ass. My cock was past hard, ready to combust for this queen. "This was what you'd wanted all along, wasn't it? That I lose it, that I forget everything because I can't think straight around you?"

Sara gasped even as her mouth objected. "Of course not. What the hell are you talking about—"

"All this time, you were fluttering your lashes at me, playing pranks, prancing around the house in nothing but a shirt. Were those things not for my benefit, little Angel?"

"I never saw you as anything past my brother... oh God... Oh, God. Oh, God," she moaned when I found a sensitive spot, her protests all but forgotten. She rocked against the vibrator on her own accord, unable to help herself.

I felt her attempt to clench her thighs at my words, but the wand separating her cheeks wouldn't allow for it. It only made her mercilessly writhe against the vibrator, forcing my bare dick to grind against her ass every time she moved.

My fingers wrapped around her pretty neck to keep her still. "Stay fucking still and take it the way I give it to you."

Unhinged, Sara's head rolled back to land in the crook of my neck. She gave in completely, reflexively riding the vibrator to get herself off, working her body so unforgivably that sweat trickled down her back. With her hands restricted, she had limited mobility but kept moving her hips back and forth until a shudder rolled down her back.

"Can't stay still, can you, baby? It's because of how badly you want this. You act like a perfect little angel in front of everyone else, secretly wishing someone would give it to you the way you want it—dirty and filthy. You like being a slut while no one's looking. Is that it?"

Sara screamed.

This was the hottest thing I had done, and all I'd done was hold a vibrator while she took her pleasure. I wasn't even the one getting her off. Consumed, she didn't care that she was pressing her ass against my cock. I felt every bit of her torment to get to that finish line as her curly mounds bobbed. The hand around her slender neck slid to her perky tits, which bounced in my hold. Grinding my dick against her ass was enough to have my balls draw up painfully for the release I sought.

I bit her neck, then grabbed hold of her perfect globe of an ass. "Fuck, your ass is perfect. Bet you want me to fuck you here too, don't you?"

Sara's entire body tightened with pent-up tension before letting go. "Oh my God, oh my God, oh my God." She ferociously thrashed and let go with a scream, all the while grinding her ass against my cock that was throbbing for its own release.

And just like that, cum spurt out of my cock, ropes and ropes landing everywhere, covering her, marking her, dribbling from her back to her thighs. The wave was so indescribable that I let go of the arm I had banded around her, and Sara fell forward onto the mattress.

There wasn't a yelp or a cry as she fell forward. Instead, Sara seemed sated and content with her cheek resting against the soft mattress. She was so far gone; she didn't even care that her legs were now parted wide open while I stood at the edge of the bed with the vibrating wand still in hand, a sticky mess, and shaky knees.

She didn't care about the cum dripping down her back and legs, and, if I was being honest, neither did I. I only cared about seeing her fall apart again.

I climbed onto the bed to first undo the handcuffs and then untie the blindfold, relieved that the little plan had worked. The sight of her was so damningly erotic that I couldn't help asking between bated breaths, "Again?"

Sara looked zonked out from the best orgasm of her life—similarly to me—her thighs trembling. There was no way she could withstand another orgasm so soon after.

But Sara simply stared at me with unfathomable eyes as if expecting me to spontaneously combust. I could make no sense of her expressions and simply waited until she said, "Fuck yes."

I separated her thighs further. Sara faced away from me, with her cheek on the mattress. The silky robe was now covered in more of my cum than it covered inches of her skin. Separating her perfectly smooth ass cheeks, I grazed her asshole with the head of the wand.

"Oh, fuck," Sara screamed at the new sensation.

I held it there, sliding it back and forth, as her body tremored, quaking uncontrollably. She called out to the Lord over and over, moving her ass back to chase the friction while I pressed the vibrator into her puckered hole. And then it happened again.

Sara climaxed earth-shatteringly from the vibrator that was stimulating her asshole.

I leaned in and slanted my face against hers, breathing unbelievably hard. The axis of my world tilted when Sara moved her head to the side and said, "Again."

CHAPTER 21

Tristan

"You seem more relaxed today," Michael commented as soon as I sat.

Was I so obvious?

A serenity had befallen me after days of mental torture. I felt like an entirely different man after only one night with Sara.

However, she wasn't ready to spend the night in my arms, nor was she comfortable with me sleeping over. I had promised to respect her boundaries and said goodnight like a gentleman, then spent the night at a nearby hotel.

Steve had vehemently protested when I asked him to clear my schedule for today. It was time off I couldn't afford with the elections around the corner, though the only thing that seemed to matter anymore was this insatiable hunger Sara had stirred inside me.

I only mollified Steve by having him bring the office to me. But Michael turned out to be a greater pest than Steve and kept texting me nonstop.

***Michael:** Please call me to schedule another session. You might lose Sara forever if we don't resolve these feelings.*

Lose Sara?

Never. We had only just begun, but the words hit me hard enough to return for a follow-up session.

"I assume things are better with Sara... In your dreams, that is."

I smirked. "I'm working on making it up to Sara... in my dreams."

"That's great to hear, Tristan. Are you ready to acknowledge your feelings for Sara now?"

"Maybe." I wasn't ready to say it out loud quite yet. "But first, why don't you tell me one more of your stories? I always find them... enlightening." Michael always seemed to know of my conundrums and would pluck a silly story out of his ass to show me the light. It kind of worked last night, but Sara continued to be hesitant. She didn't want me sleeping over because she was worried about being unconscious around me.

How do I get her to let go? How do I get her to return my affections without holding back?

Michael frowned, perplexed over losing the usual upper hand he exercised by being the one to suggest it. "What story would you like to hear?"

I glanced out the window and toward the busy streets of Georgetown. "We know how Asmodeus feels about Sarah, but does she ever fall in love?"

"Oh, she does. She does, indeed."

As the years passed, the fear surrounding Sarah became palpable. Some believed her to be mad. Others thought her to be a murderer. Some thought she was both.

Nonetheless, tales of her beauty were widespread and brought the most curious of men to her doorsteps for a distant peek. One such man was Tobias, the son of Tobit.

His father was an old family friend and had sent Tobias to meet with Sarah's parents. At first sight, he became enamored with Sarah's beauty and demure alike.

Others warned Tobias of the catastrophe to follow the girl, but Tobias and Sarah felt a pull toward one another that was as unexplainable as it was undeniable.

Sarah had never dared to hope for love. Now, it had come knocking at her door, and her lonely heart sang loudly for Tobias.

However, when a lovestruck Tobias asked for her hand in marriage, Sarah slinked away. And when he told her that he loved her, dread like she had never known coiled inside her. For any man to love Sarah always died a painful death, and she could never allow Tobias to meet such a fate.

Of course, Asmodeus' Sarah was in love with another Tobias. If Michael was hell-bent on teaching me a lesson with these stories, couldn't he at least change the names?

For four hundred dollars an hour, I expected a bit more originality.

"Tobias and Sarah couldn't fight their attraction, whereas Asmodeus did everything to tip the scale in his favor. Sometimes it's best not to force matters of the heart and let things take their natural progression."

"Didn't matter, did it?" I snapped. "Sarah still turned Tobias down."

He tilted his head thoughtfully. "Only because she cared for him."

I scoffed. "Are you about to say some shit like, if you love something, let it go?" I gripped the edges of the sofa but kept my face thoroughly placid. If he thought I'd let Sara go off into the sunset with Toby, Michael had another thing coming for even suggesting it.

If I couldn't have Sara, no one could.

He looked at me innocently. "Hmm. I was only suggesting not to force matters of the heart. Whereas the first thought to pop into your head was about letting Sara go. What do you suppose that's about?"

My eyes rounded. Inadvertent or not, for the first time, I had voiced the idea of letting Sara go for the sake of her happiness.

Michael won that round.

Where was she?

After leaving Michael's office, I had driven straight to the shelter, his words ringing in my ears. Sara was nowhere to be found. She wasn't in her office or in any of the usual classrooms. Then I remembered the project in the basement she planned to take on.

As I shifted gears, children's laughter drifted from afar in the otherwise empty hallways. My steps were rushed, making their way through the doors leading to the basement. I felt restless.

Why had I gone to Michael in hopes for advice to lure Sara? All he had done was sprinkle doubt.

Tobias and Sarah felt a pull toward one another that was as unexplainable as it was undeniable.

Lava had churned inside my stomach.

No. It was over between them. If she tried to go back to him by leaving me behind, I'd take her down with me. I'd do anything to avoid spending the rest of my days alone.

The overwhelming possibility was raw on my mind, invoking an urgent need to see her face.

But when I reached the abandoned floor and turned the corner of the hallway, my vision blurred from the blood rushing to my head. Two lone figures stood in an intimate huddle, and for several moments, I could do nothing more than watch Sara and Tobias whisper in low voices.

My mind had already gone to a dark place. A voice had whispered in my ears, promising the possibility that Sara would never have me because her heart belonged to another. And while Michael's story might have annoyed the shit out of me, I now wondered for the umpteenth time if he had any insight that I may be unaware of and had known exactly what's between them from the beginning.

My worst fears had come to life, and the only color I saw was red.

CHAPTER 22

Sara

Tobias tracked me down to the same basement we had first met. It seemed like a lifetime ago, and I was a different person then. Life had turned complicated since, but one detail had been made certain for me throughout the various ordeals.

I didn't love Tobias.

"Sara," he greeted me in a low voice, concern etched on his beautiful dark features.

I deserved his full wrath, but I couldn't digest his kindness. I managed to return a curt nod.

"How are you?"

"Fine," I said with a forced smile.

"You don't seem fine. You haven't returned any of my calls or texts..." His voice trailed off, fingers drifting over my forehead. With brows drawn together, his eyes narrowed with anger. "What the fuck. How did you get that bruise?"

I realized a little too late that the bruise from that awful night had persisted. Why did I forego makeup this morning?

"I knew something was wrong," he said with urgency. "This isn't like you, Sara. You wouldn't have dropped off the face of earth unless something bad happened. Are you in trouble? Talk to me, Princess."

My heart shattered at the tender nickname I no longer deserved. And before I could say more, another figure emerged from the shadows.

Of course, Tristan found me at the exact moment Tobias had done the same. His steps appeared frenzied, yet he was perfectly manicured in a light blue button-down shirt with gray slacks. The attire didn't match the flared amber orbs, confirming that he had heard Tobias' endearing reference.

"Tris?"

Angry, accusatory eyes stared back; the promise of retribution written in them. His stern expression made me want to disappear into thin air.

Instead of acknowledging me, he chose to goad the male competition standing in front. "Toby," he said, knowing full well that his name was Tobias. "What a pleasant surprise to find you here."

Luckily, Tobias didn't take the bait, focused solely on my welfare. "Sara, tell me what's going on. I can help."

Tristan stepped in front of me, blocking me from Tobias' view. "We don't need your help," he snapped.

"I believe I was speaking to your *sister*," Tobias retorted.

Male testosterone pulsated in the air, and I interfered to subdue some of the escalating tension. "Tobias, really, don't worry about me," I said over Tristan's shoulder.

Tobias' suspicious expression spoke volumes. "Sara, may I speak to you alone?"

"No," was the only word Tristan spoke, but the clench in it informed me he was hanging on by a thread. Other than that awful night, Tristan had never demonstrated violence. But now, his body language reflected the same atrocious premonition.

I glanced around nervously, panic forming inside me.

Tobias caught the drift. "I just want to make sure you're safe, Sara," he said softly. "Don't worry. I'm not going to interrogate you about..." The way he glanced at the minuscule space between Tristan and me made me wince at his insinuation. "...anything else."

I had an inkling that he could sense something was off in my relationship with my brother. Oh God, what the fuck was my life? I yearned for the days when I was the 'untouchable girl' instead of the girl who'd now be known for fucking her brother.

My distraught thoughts must have been apparent because Tobias tried to round Tristan to reach me.

The punch was so loud that I heard it before finding Tobias sprawled on the ground.

"What the hell, Tris?" I shrieked.

Tristan had punched Tobias so hard that he had gone flying on the floor. A drop of blood dribbled from Tobias' busted lips. He wiped it off with the back of his hand and was back on his feet within seconds.

Meanwhile, Tristan charged at him like a bull toward a red flag.

Tobias blocked Tristan's next punch before it could make contact and socked Tristan on the jaw instead. I ran to separate them, but their repressed anger outweighed rationality. My pleas to stop fell on deaf ears.

"Stay the fuck away from her." Tristan punched Tobias in the gut, forcing him to hunch over.

Tobias returned with an attempted headlock but was met with another one of Tristan's blows. "You're the one who needs to stay the fuck away. Even that first time, I saw the way you looked at her. Do you think I'm blind?"

"Please stop!" I hysterically pulled at Tristan's bicep to stop the assaults.

They both yelled simultaneously, asking for me to back off. With a quick inspection of my surroundings, I quickly realized no one ever came down to the basement.

Punches of fury flew into the air like missiles, and it became abundantly clear that Tristan was winning by a long shot. At this rate, he might kill Tobias. The scariest part was the blank eyes, once more devoid of humanity.

The carnal beast to reside inside only understood one thing—hunger. I didn't know when or how it started, but at that moment, I knew it to be my truth. Tristan would go through murder without regret if another man so much as touched me.

In a moment of clarity, I saw the choices laid forth.

This floor was abandoned and completely separated from the rest of the shelter. By the time I reached the main halls to retrieve my phone, Tris would have beaten Tobias to a pulp, and his cronies would be here to clean up the mess. Quite possibly, he'd bury the scandalous story and get away with it, too, especially if he threatened Tobias with his job or his family back home.

I didn't put anything past Tristan anymore.

My options were limited if I didn't want him murdering an unconscious man since Tobias had now passed out.

Last night, I allowed Tristan to touch me, hoping the repercussions would keep him at bay without irreversible damages. But now, I had to go further because Tristan had left me with no other choices. My heart came to a complete stop as I watched his enraged blackout assaults on an unconscious man. If I truly believed to be cursed, all I had to do was touch him more, and this time, enough to trigger a grander aftermath.

With a tranquility I had never known, I stepped forward. Tristan had Tobias pinned to the ground, landing punch after punch. When he raised his fist in the air once again, I wrapped my hands around it.

Tristan stopped and turned to me, surprised by the calm demeanor.

From the corner of my eye, I tried to assess Tobias' injuries. Nothing appeared broken thus far, but he'd need a few butterfly stitches, and the bruises would need to be iced.

Biting down the sob that threatened to break free, I ensured my sideway gaze didn't linger. If I showed Tobias even a morsel of empathy, Tristan would finish the job he started. I had never seen such wrath in a man's eyes.

"Please, Tris," I said softly. "Enough. Leave him."

"Let. Go," he chewed out, ready to kill an unconscious man.

My stomach rocked with the need to comfort Tobias, but I held my resolve and only looked at Tristan. My intention would otherwise break.

"Tris," I began quietly. "Tobias wasn't supposed to be here." My voice shook with the effort of the sentence.

"I don't know how else to communicate this with you except that I. Don't. Share," he gritted out. "You should have remembered that."

"I swear, he came here unannounced because I had broken things off so abruptly. He only wanted to make sure I was alright." I felt unsure how else to voice Tobias' act of kindness.

"I don't care."

"I'll make sure he doesn't come near me again. Please, Tris. Don't hurt him anymore."

He shook his head. "The time for compromises has passed. I gave you time to get used to me, but all you have done so far is string me along."

"Then let me prove myself to you," I said faintly. "My phone is upstairs. Just let me call him an ambulance, and you have my word that things will be different."

"Different, how?" he asked, failing to keep the huskiness out of his voice, while the meaning of this conversation was becoming clear to him.

I conceded my soul. "You know how."

CHAPTER 23

Tristan

Slowly rising to stand, I moved away from that asshole's unconscious body. Sara wisely followed me instead of rushing to poor Toby's side. I suspected she was attempting to keep me at an even keel by acting indifferent.

It was a smart move.

Plus, Sara was familiar with enough assault and battery cases at the shelter to realize Tobias' injuries were superficial. He had merely passed out and would be fine after sleeping it off. She had intervened before I could cause any severe harm.

Perhaps it was the concern she harbored for 'poor Toby' that made me turn around abruptly and tug her into my arms. There were no protests, nor did Sara pull away. Only a gasp when I yanked at her hair with manic force before my mouth crashed down to hers.

The things I wanted to do right now didn't stem from love, only from a vicious need to possess. Be it forcing her to crawl naked across this hallway while begging to suck my dick or fucking her in front of her unconscious lover.

Instead of doing either, I kissed her violently until there were no such thoughts left to be dissected. I growled when she detached our mouths.

"Tris," she beseeched. "Please let me get my phone and call him an ambulance before we go any further."

Ambulance?

Suddenly, my eyes widened, remembering that dear Toby laid not fifteen feet from us.

Tedious detail.

Steve could get here in twenty minutes to take care of the problem and find a way to keep good old Toby from talking to the press. Either way, I doubted he'd file a report. Cops relished in portraying the alpha male. His big ego couldn't handle how poorly he got his ass handed, let alone go public with the information.

Anger surged once more at how he had come here in search of *my* girl, but it quickly died away when Sara looked up at me with sadness in her gray eyes. They held me captive.

I might have tortured her for years with our rivalry, but I had indulged her all the same. I handed over the keys to my new car when one of her charities needed transportation, and all because Sara asked sweetly. Not once had I been able to deny her if only she batted her eyelashes at me. Our dynamics might have changed, but the power she yielded over me hadn't. I didn't want her to be sad or remorseful. And if I didn't take care of this, she'd be doused in both.

Fuck.

"No ambulances," I informed Sara. "He just needs to sleep it off. Steve will take him home and fix him up..." I nodded my head at Toby. "But I'll only call him if you follow through with what you just offered.

If I have Steve take care of that boy, what exactly am I getting in return?"

"I-I can't have sex with you. I-I am not ready." She looked down at her interlaced fingers. "What if I do something else instead? You can show me how to do other stuff... other ways to pleasure..." she couldn't finish the sentence, drifting off.

My brow quirked. Last night, she was hesitant over letting me touch her. Now, she was offering to learn how to pleasure me and all because of another man.

The thought had me tethering at the edge.

"Teach you stuff? How about instead I put you over my lap and spank your ass for that little stunt. Or maybe I'll tie you up and fuck you until you learn your lesson. Or maybe," I lowered my voice sadistically, "I should fuck you in front of your unconscious lover until the only name you remember is mine."

If she felt any horror at the graphic images I painted, she didn't show it. Sara held her chin high. "I already told you. Sex is off the table."

My jaw ticked. "Then this isn't an offer worth considering."

"You asked me to meet you halfway. That's what I'm trying to do. I'm open to a one-time deal in exchange for you to squash this with Tobias. You won't threaten his job or so much as touch a hair on his body again."

Two days ago, I would have taken her up on the offer. But now, it stung. Her concession was covered with the stench of love, just not for me. The fists at my sides tightened, driven mad because Sara's negotiations were all tied to saving another man.

"I agree to your terms, but only if you let me do what I want *before* Steve's arrival. Right here. Right now." I licked my bottom lip, hands shaking.

"Here? As in, in front of..." Sara glanced around nervously, her gaze landing on Tobias.

"That's right. There're no cameras, and we both know no one's coming down here."

"You agree to my no-sex policy?"

"As long as you satisfy me in other ways."

Sara swallowed but voiced no more protests. She patiently waited while I resentfully took out my phone and texted Steve with instructions.

"We have thirty minutes until he gets here." Thirty minutes to play. I nodded toward the wall next to me. "Put your back against that wall."

We stood fifteen feet from Tobias' unconscious body. It was far enough that he couldn't witness us should he rouse, but close enough to disrespect him with what I had planned.

Sara's eyes drifted toward him, and after a moment's hesitation, she shocked me by conceding. Her footsteps were light as air, cognizant about drawing unwanted attention from dear Toby, who was out cold.

With her back to the wall, she pressed into it. My breathing was coming fast now. Hers, too, pushing her tits against the off-white sleeveless dress she wore today. It looked warm against her brown skin, reaching past her thighs.

My hands trembled as I moved closer. This was so wrong. I shouldn't be doing this with Tobias here. Sara loathed violence, and I had just beat the shit out of that cumbersome cop. The blood was still fresh on my hands.

If anything, I should be making it up to her after the pain I had caused thus far. She was the college kid, and I was the thirty-year-old congressman who should know better than to subject her to these kinds of things.

Only, my desire for this woman was so suffocating it was manifesting into a being of its own, melting my insides into Jell-O. I had this need to influence her with an experience that was unmatched. The same one that made me a god in the eyes of other women. If Sara was willing, I could compel her into the addiction that came with my body.

This was my opportunity to up the ante.

If our future relations continued to be out of body experiences for her, she'd soon forget all about precious Toby. In fact, I'd make her experience it right here in front of him.

From the corner of my eyes, I saw Tobias' horizontal body in the empty hallway. Satisfaction ran cold in my blood. Ideally, I'd like to fuck her over his corpse, but I guess I could settle for this in its place.

My hands shook as I gripped her waist to nuzzle her neck. She gasped, not having anticipated it when I sucked on her flesh and then wedged my thigh to part her legs.

Slowly, I knelt in front of her.

Sara looked down, perplexed, as I reached for the hem of her dress and peeled it until it was hiked around her waist. My concentration almost broke at the sight of her white thong. What I would do to rip it off and fuck her raw... I shook my head.

No. Concentrate.

This was about the long game.

I reached for her panties and moved the crotch to one side in search of her pussy lips, never having tasted her before. Yet, now, the need to suck and lick and feel her tremble against my tongue nearly overwhelmed me. With heavy breaths, I leaned forward and parted her lips with two fingers.

"What—oh my God." Sara jolted in surprise.

God, I had never felt anyone with such tender pussy flesh before. She was so soft that the texture almost melted against my fingers.

A slight tremor vibrated through her body, along with another small shudder, when I ran my fingertips over her slit. I rubbed her clit, extracting a hiss out of Sara.

A growl tumbled out as I dove in for the first taste of her. "Fuck." I groaned when her taste exploded onto my tongue. Sweet jasmine mixed with the perfect amount of sin. Nothing, absolutely nothing, on earth had tasted so fucking good.

"Oh my God." She hadn't meant to moan but was too lost to care.

The sound hit me right in my cock. My tongue lapped faster against her slick heat, running along her lips. She was wet, dripping, drenched, practically shaking. The visual of her arousal was as erotic as the feel of it. Despite herself, Sara parted her legs wider, allowing me more access. And before she could control her reaction, Sara pushed herself further into my face and ground ruthlessly against my tongue while her hands weaved into my hair to hold on for support.

I knew the moment her head had knocked back. The moment her body quivered uncontrollably as I began to eat her out, and the moment she started to clench in preparation for take-off.

I sucked on her clit desperately, then flicked it before swirling my tongue, finally spearing her opening. When I plunged a finger inside, Sara jerked forward, her thighs shaking against the sides of my head.

She mumbled something to the extent of *oh God* before she could hold back no longer and started actively fucking herself against my tongue.

There were no more pretenses left. Sara was enjoying this, and I was living for every moment of it.

And then it happened.

Sara came loudly against the pressures of my tongue and finger, grinding herself against my mouth without holding back. A tremor ran down her body as sweet wetness trickled down her thighs and onto my chin.

Gasping and squirming, she moaned over and over until she was a lithe body barely able to hold herself up against the wall. I rose to circle my arm around her before she could slide down the wall, wiping my chin with the back of my other hand, a cocky smile in place.

"You like that, baby?" I asked against the shell of her ear.

She couldn't form a response, panting heavily. Evidence of her arousal was slick on my slacks when I hugged her close, leaving wet spots behind. My cock was so hard and throbbing that it might burst from that minimal contact.

Nothing compared to hearing this girl fall apart. God, the sounds she made... they made me want to fuck her until neither of us could move, until we forgot the world, or everyone forgot about us along with our last names, and until I made her love me.

This animalistic need for her made my slacks impossibly tight. Nothing else mattered apart from sinking into her and feeling that pussy fit me like a glove. It'd be so easy to unzip my pants and find that slit of hers that was wet and slippery enough to take my thick cock. It was only the promise I had made to her that kept me from acting on the impulse.

Instead, I held her while Sara calmed her excitable heart. As soon as she recovered enough, I'd take her home and do something nice for her... a reward for the acquiescence she showed today. Sara had come further than I had dared to hope.

I dropped my face in her hair as I fixed her underwear and smoothed her dress down. "Come on, Angel. I'll take you home."

Sara stiffened in my hold. Her gaze involuntarily flickered to Toby.

"I told you," I said with my jaw clenched. "Steve will fix him up."

She didn't budge, nor did she argue. However, her body language gave away the nonverbal answer. She didn't want to leave poor Toby in this condition and was exercising immense self-control not to flock to his side.

Even after that mind-boggling experience, one that women called me a God for, Sara was unmoved. For fuck's sake, I made her come in less than five minutes, and I didn't even try to fuck her. For once, I wanted to do the honorable thing and take care of her despite the fact that I had time on my side. I only wanted to give her a taste of how good it could be between us, so she wouldn't feel the need to do this out of desperation next time.

I wanted her to want this, to want *me*.

My past had consisted of so many women and sexual conquests that I could hardly put a number to it. The encounters had left me hollow, and after my mid-twenties, I gave up on the shallow pursuits altogether. In all that time, I'd never let anyone affect my pride to this extent.

But now, at the age of thirty, a teenager was dangling the hope of a fulfilling experience and pulling at every one of my strings. The balance in our power dynamics was unfair.

I was risking my life's goals, my career, everything this family had staked, and all for a girl who couldn't bear to be away from another man. A woman who continued to betray me, despite my numerous warnings against seeing that man.

Fine.

If that's how she wanted to play it, I could be just as selfish. Maybe I wasn't processing things coherently, which made me say it. "If you aren't leaving with me, then get on your knees."

"What?" Her head jerked up, stunned.

We now had twenty minutes to spare, and I planned to use every second of it.

"You heard me," I said silkily. "Kneel!"

Sara swallowed, her bravado faltering at the order to do something so demeaning. Once more, she shocked me by complying.

"Wait," I said before her knees could touch the ground. "Put your knees on my feet." The dirty basement was hardly how I imagined this, but I didn't need her scuffing up her pretty little knees.

She scooted forward, so that when she sank to the floor, the weight of her knees landed on my dress shoes. My gaze fixated on her crown while hers was straight at my crotch. The angle gave me an unfiltered view of her plunge neckline and the black bra under her dress. A slick of sweat formed at the top of her mounds, and God, I almost bit my fist to stop the urge from tearing that dress open right down the middle.

She was so damn pretty.

Excitement coursed through me because the only thing better than Sara kneeling in front of me was the victory of taking her in front of the man I despised the most in this world. I resisted the urge to smirk with sly satisfaction.

My hardening length pushed painfully against my slacks. Instead of adjusting, I undid my belt and zipper to free my cock. If only she knew how wildly the blood in my veins was thrumming in anticipation.

"Suck," I ordered, holding myself out for her.

After a moment's hesitation, Sara leaned forward with her mouth open, taking my tip between her lips.

I rumbled at the first touch.

Oh, God, that felt so fucking good.

The offers might have been in plenty, but I had been quick to deny women in the recent years. I had forgotten the feel of a silky-smooth tongue tracing my crown with saliva. It felt so fucking good that my head dropped backward with an open growl.

Holy shit. Holy shit. The warm mouth welcomed me inside, greeting my cock like it had come home.

"Close your lips," I instructed with heavy panting, watching her under hooded eyes.

I guided my cock further inside, both hands on her nape as that silky tongue coated the underside of my length. Slowly and slowly, I slid myself down the moist cave and was only halfway in when Sara laid her hands flat on my thighs.

Presumably, she hadn't done this before, and someone my size was hardly the best introduction to ease into it. Her inexperience didn't matter to me. Everything with Sara felt unbelievably good because it was *her*. I couldn't even count the number of times this very fantasy had me fisting my dick. It was taking everything in me not to show my hand, not to admit that she might be the one kneeling, but it was me who had submitted to her by losing my cool and breaking the restraints that I never otherwise let loose.

It made me want to spank her ass because her fantasy of the same included *him*. The thought made me want to unleash the demon inside.

"Look at me, Sara," I growled, and she obeyed. Beautiful gray eyes peeped up through dark lashes.

I pushed myself forward with a hand on the crown of her head. I wanted to go harder, to throb at the back of her throat until I was shooting down.

"Fuck, you're driving me crazy."

I shoved inside harder, and Sara choked a little. I pulled back, giving her a slight reprieve, only to return for more. She needed a longer break, but I couldn't mollify the urgent need to thrust deep enough to find the back of her throat. The carnal desire contradicted the tender ways I wiped away the moisture when her eyes watered or praised her for being so good.

Dark tresses bobbed between my legs while I growled at the sky. I had never been so hard before, so swollen that every vein stood to attention with the need for her. My legs vibrated, and I gripped her nape again to hold her in place while I fucked her mouth. I drove into her over and over, back and forth, until my cock throbbed painfully and until I exploded with my cum spilling down her throat.

Sara let go of my cock with a pop, and I had to hold up a hand against the wall next to me so I wouldn't stumble. She rose to her feet, observing me as if she were expecting me to drop dead at any moment.

Although this moment should have felt like a victory, her scrumptious look made it seem there was more at play than what meets the eye. And because she was such a shitty liar, the answer was readily available if I wanted her to divulge it.

"Tell me, Angel," I drawled. "It couldn't have been just concern for little Toby that made you drop to your knees. Why did you really do it?"

"I was hoping something bad would happen to you if I gave in," she said reflexively with no humor in her tone.

My fists clenched at the sides.

That's been her genius plan all along?

Sara's easy acquiescence last night contradicted vastly with her otherwise combative nature. It made sense now. She gave in, hoping it'd be my demise because of this damn curse she believed in. She was convinced everyone who came near her was met with disaster, while overlooking it was simply *me* keeping her safe.

I ground my teeth, barely keeping myself under control. This infuriating woman knew how to push every one of my damn buttons.

A slow, sarcastic smile graced my face. "Too bad for you, I'm invincible."

She shrugged. "Let's find out."

Our glaring contest ended when my phone buzzed. "Steve's here to take care of him," I informed, looking at my text. "Let's go," I said stoically.

Once more, Sara didn't move.

I frowned. "Steve's here to take care of him," I repeated. "What's the problem now?"

When she hadn't moved, I realized that she wasn't leaving until she saw Tobias home safely. I closed my eyes, the ragged breaths not enough to subdue a new wave of anger. I forced the words out of my mouth to give her one last chance, "Sara. I just let it go after you told me why you had agreed to blow me. I'm not in the best headspace. If you choose to stay behind now to take care of that boy instead of leaving with me, I promise you won't like the consequences."

Sara's unwavering stance was the only answer I received.

Grinding my jaw, I stepped back before I lost it entirely. I only had one solace—Toby was in no condition to so much as speak to her, and Steve would limit any unnecessary interaction between them, though all of those things did little to mollify my wrath.

I had tried to fix things the way Michael had suggested. I sacrificed what I wanted in order to make her happy. None of it worked. At the end of the day, she refused to leave that boy's side, and the only reason she wanted to be with me was in the hopes of destroying me.

So, fuck it. I was done.

Fuck sacrificing for love. Fuck giving up my selfish desires in exchange for her wishes. And most of all, fuck Michael.

I was now ready to try it Asmodeus' way.

CHAPTER 24

Tristan

I dutifully waited for the lights to Sara's room to turn off before letting myself into my parents' manor and, subsequently, her bedroom. A sleepy sigh escaped her as I opened her door and approached her unconscious form on the bed. I dared not to breathe, maintaining distance since no more than an hour had passed. She might not have reached deep sleep even with a pill in her system.

For a moment, guilt clenched my heart. If she took a sleeping pill tonight, it was only to dispel the nightmares I had aroused as of late.

Don't do this to her again, I repeated the mantra.

I hadn't wanted it this way between us. I yearned for her to need me like the air she'd suffocate without. I wanted her to crave my touch the way a vampire craved blood, as if she'd die without my cock stuffed inside her.

But Sara continued to do stupid shit like using her body as a revenge ploy or keeping acquaintance with Toby. She insisted on accompanying Steve to get precious Toby situated in his apartment. She refused to leave his side while Steve fixed him up and only agreed to return after receiving assurance that he was perfectly fine.

The whole thing was damn irritating.

Sara was the closest I had felt to Heaven. No longer could I take these kinds of divides between us. And no longer could I go on without experiencing her body nightly. After the stunt she pulled today, I felt little reinforcement to do things the right way.

Hours, it must have been, that I stared at her while questioning my very humanity. What kind of man would do this after the trauma I had already caused her?

A terrible man, a familiar whisper responded in my ear before turning my gaze toward the gift lying on the bed.

Sara had thrown the covers to one side, irritated by the summer heat. She wore nothing except a flannel sleeping shirt that only reached her waist and a pair of boy shorts that were indecently riding up her ass, revealing every inch of thigh she had to bare. Her legs were sprawled open in an unladylike fashion. And just like the time before, her hand was on her pussy.

Fuck.

She was so filthy and naughty in her sleep.

The sight sent a jolt straight to my dick. No man on earth could resist such a woman.

I took off my clothes, except for the boxers, and dropped them on the floor before cautiously sliding into the bed. Tilting my head, I inhaled from her pulse point and bit my bottom lip from letting out a groan. I took another deep inhale, nearly overwhelmed this time from the smell.

It still wasn't enough.

My hands lowered to the fabric of her boy shorts. I moved slowly in case the drugs hadn't adequately taken effect yet.

God help me and my awful thoughts.

Pressing my knees against the mattress, I moved lower down her body. Inhaling her jasmine scent, I followed the swell of her breast to the dip of her waist, stopping at the skin between her thighs.

As if she could feel me there, Sara's breath quickened, and the hand caressing herself fell away.

God, I could almost taste my salvation. All I could imagine since earlier was soaking my tongue inside her pussy again and doing nothing else for the rest of my days.

I removed her panties very gently and nearly came in my pants at the sight. I parted her beautiful beige lips to stare at the pink flesh between them and inhaled her in. She had this distinct female scent, fucking sensuous. And her pussy was so drenched. Shit.

I knelt between her spread legs, further exposing her glistening cunt. "How are you so wet, Angel?" I rasped in a painstakingly hoarse voice.

She was soaked, dying for relief. Here I was, begging to give it to her.

I justified myself.

I did warn her that she'd pay for staying back with Toby. And technically, she had agreed to explore more, so long as explicit penetration wasn't involved.

However, if sex were involved, the chips could only fall into place. Steve disclosed that Sara had visited the doctor's office last week for birth control shots. Those shots took up to ten days to become effective, meaning there was a small window for pregnancy in the interim.

Ragu and Sara were devout Catholics. If Sara were pregnant, the struggles to alter her perception of me as her brother would take a back seat. I already came inside her once, and here was one last opportunity to double the chances.

Despite Mom's many requests that I settle down with a nice girl and give her grandchildren, I had never considered passing down my genetics. My emotions were limited, and I rarely felt connected to this earth. Why the hell would I subject a child to that cold, aloof upbringing?

However, I laughed, smiled, played pranks, felt joy and all kinds of emotions in Sara's presence. If we had a child together, the kid would be brought up in a warm, loving household because of her.

Not to mention, our kid would be darn cute with her curly hair and marble-slate eyes and that gentle heart of hers, too. She'd pad around with my child in her swollen belly and complain nonstop about the injustices women suffered by carrying a child while males got away scot-free. She'd probably play a prank on me as her own form of justice so that I'd be equally miserable.

The imagery satisfied the male ego in me, and an ear-to-ear grin stretched over my face. If she were pregnant, Sara would instantly become mine. And the possibility to impregnate her was being served up on a platter.

I looked away.

No. No. No.

I promised Sara that I'd control myself and wait for her acquiescence. No matter how angry I might be with her, I shouldn't be here.

I needed to leave before she woke instead of sucking on her sweet clit. And I definitely shouldn't incline my face to lick the juices flowing to her thighs. No. I should leave instead of giving her exactly what she sought in her sleep.

But my chest expanded at the thought she might be dreaming of *him,* and that's why she was dripping wet. Driven by jealousy, all I could think of was dipping my face into her cunt to mark it with my tongue.

Surely, one lick wouldn't be the end-all.

Just one lick, and I'd never do this again without her permission. It was right there—the gates to my Heaven. She was ripe for the taking, so mouthwateringly delicious that I was practically drooling over her pussy.

"Just one taste. Please, God. That's all I will do. I won't go inside her."

Her cunt wasn't just sopping wet now; it was trembling like a needy bitch demanding relief. The pink flesh was so damn tender and inviting that it quaked against my parted lips.

"Fuck." I tilted my head before I could talk myself out of it.

Sweet jasmine mixed with the perfect amount of sin, exactly as I remember from earlier. So. Fucking. Good.

I drew a path with my tongue, swiping over her entire cunt. My breath shuddered against her tender pink flesh during the slow lap.

"One more taste," I murmured. "Please. Just one more."

I flattened my tongue on her clit, sucking on the delicious juices flowing freely now. Then, I begged my God to let me do it once more, and one more time after that, again and again, until it became clear that I was lying to myself. Once, twice, thrice was never going to be enough. A thousand times wouldn't be enough because I'd rather go to Hell than be denied this taste.

I dove in, spreading her legs as I fucked her with my tongue, grazing her clit with my teeth. I lapped at her like a man possessed, hungry, and starved, taking in his last meal as I slipped a finger inside her.

Even in her sleep, she was insatiable, brazenly grinding against my face, thrashing from her uncontrollable urges. The moan was stuck in her throat while my eyes drifted to the locked door even though our parents weren't home.

"Fuuuuck!" Sara orgasmed in her sleep with an earth-shattering scream, absolving me of guilt. Her cries hit me right in the groin as her pussy clamped down on my finger, my cock impossibly hard against my boxers now.

Unable to hold off any longer, I pulled my boxers down, fisting my cock while forcing her to come on my face.

I was surrounded by her scent and taste and didn't know how it was possible she hadn't wakened. But if I had already sinned, I needed more. I palmed my erection and stroked it punishingly hard, watching her pussy in a trance while I got off.

Shifting, I stretched out over her and rubbed my cock against her hot, swollen clit. God, she was so warm down there, and I groaned when her clit throbbed against my dick.

I was so fucking close to her entrance that I could slip inside and take her. Only that damning promise stopped me from fucking her, costing me every effort in my bone.

"Not like this," I reminded myself, grazing her cheek with the back of my hand. I kissed and nipped at her, inhaling her jasmine scent with my face buried in her neck. I peppered kisses all over her body. Her tits were easy to outline under my hand, and I delicately peeled her top up enough to expose them.

I groaned again.

While they weren't overly large, I loved the size and shape of her breasts. Fascinated, I watched the perfect olive-colored areolas and nipples stand erect under the attention of my tongue running over them.

Sara writhed underneath me, the hot and cool sensation making her gasp. Her cunt was still wet against my cock, and every time I rubbed it, she cried out in her sleep.

"Oh, fuck!" Cute little moans escaped her parted lips.

Yes, I determined, I would happily go to Hell for eternity if I could hear that sound for the rest of my mortal life.

My balls drew up painfully, cock pulsing hard in my closed fist as her back arched for one more climax. Her breasts brushed against my bare chest, and I dipped my head for another taste of her nipples.

Everything of hers tasted so damn sweet. She tasted like a goddamn princess. Perversely, the thought of how I was dirtying the virtuous princess in her sleep was what had me coming all over her plump, juicy cunt. White drops sprayed against her pussy, her thighs, and her stomach, dripping down to the mattress.

"Shit. Shit. Shit."

There was so much of it that I could hardly believe it. My head dropped in the crook of her neck, breathing loudly, matching her sleepy moans. When the orgasm finally subsided, I groaned, falling to the side and running both hands over my face.

Dipping two fingers inside her cunt, I gathered her juices and brought the fingers to my mouth. My perversion had a mind of its own and would never be satiated because my cock jumped again at her taste, and I turned my face to stare at her sleepy form. She was breathing softly, haphazard after how I had used her body.

I cleaned her off with a washcloth but couldn't force myself to leave.

"Forgive me, Angel," I murmured. Not only for what I had done to her but for what I wanted to *keep* doing. Before long, I had undressed her entirely as the need for her outweighed my sanity.

CHAPTER 25

Sara

With my fingers to my temple, I tried to orient myself. I had only taken half a pill tonight to decrease a potential hangover as I planned on tackling a big project tomorrow. The effects of the small dose must be wearing off because I generally slept through everything while under the influence.

However, a gentle caress between my legs and the ruffling of sheets made me groan. My eyes fluttered at the feel of the fingers between my thighs, gently thrusting in and out while a thumb massaged my folds.

Great. Another bout of my sleep-induced horniness.

Given my introduction to sex, one would think I would have given up on sex entirely. Instead, I had woken up with my hand between my legs every single night.

However, something about tonight's scene niggled me in my subconscious. My fingers weren't so thick, and I wasn't quite as... advanced at playing my body so well.

But I could barely focus on logic when my body had been so

perfectly prepped for the sendoff. My pussy clamped down, thighs quaking with an immense need to release the budding heat. My back arched, head moving side to side.

"Fuck. Fuck. Fuck," I chanted mindlessly, ready to give up my soul in exchange for reaching that peak. "Oh God, oh God. That feels so good."

The perfect unison was joined by a wet tongue flattening against my clit that was desperate for attention.

My eyes flew open as soon as I realized someone was giving me oral.

Earlier, I had a dream of coming in my sleep, but now it was clear as day. It wasn't a dream, and those weren't my fingers. Someone was in my bed, caressing me between my legs while I was unconscious and stark naked.

I swallowed several times in the dark. My body—that was tethering at the edge of an ecstasy forced on me—warred with the terror gripping my insides.

In a swift move, I tried to jump off the bed to dislodge the fingers and tongue. The man in my bed reacted faster. He was on me, tackling me back to the mattress. And when I parted my lips to scream at the sight of an equally naked Tristan, he slapped a hand over my mouth.

No.

No.

No.

After the first time—when he didn't go inside me even while I was cuffed and blindfolded—hope had budded that Tris would oblige to my boundaries. I had stupidly believed that the violence between us was a one-off for him and that I was the one in control. That I could hurt him with my body, not the other way around.

What an idiot I must have been.

That small piece of trust he had regained was replaced by the raw emotions from the week's events. The assault. The false promises. Poor Tobias. And now this betrayal.

Heartbroken, I turned my face away to quietly sob into the pillow.

Tristan allowed me the small reprieve and let his hand fall away from my mouth. "Angel—"

"Even after everything you did, I wanted to believe you wouldn't do this without my say," I whimpered. His hardening cock brushed against my sex. The liquid dragging over my bare skin was indicative of what he had done. "You promised not to force yourself on me. That's all I had asked—"

"I didn't go inside you," he said it like it was the epitome of chivalry. "I touched you because after what happened today... I can't stay away from you anymore."

"Get off me!" I screamed.

I struggled against him as he parted my legs with force. And although my mind had alerted me of danger, my body hadn't quite caught up. I was swimming at the edge of what he had started earlier and couldn't turn it off.

I was too far gone to put up a more vigorous fight and had only had one weak protest left to voice. "This is all so sick. You're my *brother*."

"It turns out that you like fucking your brother," he retorted. "Even in your sleep, your body responded to me. You're soaked, Sara."

"I hate you," I spat in response.

"Then take your revenge by giving yourself to me. You're the one plotting my demise because you think letting me have you will hurt me. You can't rest until exacting justice, and I can't go another night without you. So, do it. Get your revenge and put us both out of this misery."

The sting of betrayal gave root to the ugly suggestion. I had spent my life wanting to experience sex, and it was finally in my reach along with my justice. I had concluded that the only ill-wish I could bestow upon Tristan was giving myself to him. Now that he had hurt an innocent man, I could do this with him every day without feeling an ounce of remorse until every one of my salacious desires had been fulfilled.

The last of my guilt vanished when his hard shaft thickened against my sex. Languid kisses and licks caressed my neck at a mercilessly slow pace. The small touches had my pussy spasming, high from the fire he had ignited.

He had raped me, hurt Tobias, touched me while I was unconscious, broken my heart, and yet I got off on him. Nothing made sense except that I was all fucked in the head and deplorable... and wholly consumed by him.

"You feel it, too. So good, you're being so good, Angel," he praised.

I let him have me, eyes fluttering when his fingers slipped between us and moved against my swollen clit. He sucked on my stiff nipples until the conflicts in my mind waned altogether.

"That's it, baby," he murmured in awe. "Let me in."

"God." A low moan ripped out of my throat, surprising us both.

Victory danced in his eyes. "You want this, don't you, Sara? You want me to shove this cock inside you while my fingers play with your little pussy."

I could only focus on the heat bubbling inside my veins and the sweat prickling my temple. "Yes."

No sooner had I said it than Tristan slammed his cock inside me. Unlike last time, the dripping wetness between my thighs eased the entry, but he was still too big and stretched me until I couldn't breathe.

He remained still, stroking my hair tenderly. And when I moaned again, he whispered, "This is how it should have been during our first time."

My eyes opened wide, unsure how to feel about his confession. Luckily, it didn't matter as he started running his hands over my body, instilling some unknown entity with his touch.

I had overheard women boasting of their conquests with Tristan, but they forgot to mention the intoxication he churned. The mouth on my nipples, the fingers swiping over my clit, the cock pushing me into a shuddering orgasm, I could escape none of those things. And I would certainly never escape Tristan. The rivalry between us had turned into something sick and unhealthy, reminding me of the words we had exchanged.

Go to Hell, Tristan.

Only if I can take you with me.

At this moment, I ascertained that Tristan would take me to Hell with him rather than go down alone. Lives would be ruined if we were found out, but we were now in this together because as his cock repeatedly plunged into me until I saw stars, I could no longer deny the truth in his proclamation.

I liked fucking my brother.

My breathing labored at the dirty thought, and my clit throbbed with the next graze of his fingers, and I exploded. Tristan drove into me over and over while I lost myself to an entirely parallel universe. Wave after wave of pleasure hit me so hard that my body wouldn't stop trembling long after he shoved his come deep inside me.

My heart thundered from the depleted orgasm, but the sensation was trumped by Tris' subsequent confession.

"I love you, Angel."

I winced as he pulled out his thick length. For minutes, I couldn't form a word, absolutely stunned. Meanwhile, Tristan kept stroking my cheek as if he had informed me of his dinner selection for the night.

Three simple words.

I love you.

When we were young, Mom forced us to say those three words after our fights. Later, it became our norm to say 'I love you' every time we made up.

We had exchanged those words millions of times throughout our lifetime. I never realized until now that Tristan never said it to anyone else, not even his own mother.

I stared at him blankly, trying to digest. "W-What! How?" I had never interrogated him about his feelings, I realized.

"I'm a man, Sara. A man who isn't related to you by blood. I spent years watching you, falling for you. You did the same. Did you not think I'd notice how closely you watched me day and night? Even at that fundraiser, you were watching *me* instead of your date."

I searched his face, trying to find any truth to his words. "I watched you because we were rivals, and I wanted to anticipate your next move."

"You watched me because you couldn't look away. You played pranks on me to get my attention, the same reason I did it. You wanted me to notice you."

He rolled off me before gathering me in his arms. It was odd to be in a post-coitus cuddle after our heated exchange from moments ago, but whiplash was the one thing that felt familiar between us.

"Did you always feel this way?" I asked suddenly.

Tris scoffed, matting my hair down. "No. I remember a time when I only saw you as my bratty sister and the exact moment those brotherly feelings died off."

"When did it start?"

"My feelings for you?"

I nodded. "When did you start feeling this way?"

"A little while ago, Angel," he said with a self-deprecating smile. "Before it was appropriate for me to look at you in that way."

"It's still inappropriate for you to notice me," I pointed out. When he remained evasive, I urged, "Tell me."

"Why do you want to know?"

"Because I-I want to understand."

Tris shook his head. "You were too young for the kind of attention and desire I had developed. It was sick; I knew it. I tried to stay away, but... I just couldn't do it anymore."

"Please tell me." Because I really needed to understand this fucked up thing brewing between us.

He gave in with a resigned sigh, pulling me to his chest.

CHAPTER 26

Tristan

Four Years Ago

Glowering at the luxurious home in the heart of Georgetown, I yawned with my arms outstretched. It had been two long years since I last visited. I should have come home for Christmas or over the summer. However, the last two years of law school had been a real bitch, and the eight-hour drive was hardly a breeze.

My parents visited me twice in that time and had been holding a grudge over my extended absence. I was about to receive the admonishment of the century. I'd much rather sneak inside to avoid the encounter altogether and faceplant on my bed instead.

The only folly in my carefully laid out scheme was a sight in the distance. When I caught the movement through the corner of my eyes, my gaze snapped in the direction of our porch.

An unknown figure was gracing this undeserving earth with her divine presence, taunting the already limited skills I possessed of denying myself instant gratification.

Who in the hell?

My mother, a self-proclaimed matchmaker, loved to set me up with a plethora of her friends' daughters. She was on the warpath to secure me a match before my first ballot at the elections. This was most likely another one of Mary's attempts to find the 'love of my life.'

Usually, Mom's matchmaking habits irritated me to all hell. This time, it merely gave me pause.

The seductive wet dream had her elbows propped against the ledge of our porch, the tight globe of an ass jutting out. Oversized sunglasses sat over the rim of her nose, so I couldn't make out her face, only her body.

An erotic little body.

She wore cut-off jean shorts with a white t-shirt. Her thick thighs were on display, and I could only see the side profile from my angle. Her hair was spun into a high bun, highlighting a long neck and a delicate collarbone. The sun shining behind her head wrapped her into a halo effect, distorting her skin color. My best guess was olive complexion with dark hair.

Running through my mental inventory, I tried to recall the daughters of Mary's friends to match the description.

None that I could think of, I mused.

I wanted to go up to her and demand her identity. However, there was something so serene about her that I stayed put to watch her for a few more uninterrupted minutes. This was hardly the welcome home I had envisioned, but I wasn't complaining.

Unable to look away, my stance remained frozen like a predator studying their unsuspecting prey. The girl was unaware of her surroundings, engrossed in watching the sunset and the music she was listening to on her air pods. Her perfect ass jiggled when she moved, my cock jerking to the rhythm.

Seriously! What in the hell?! Since when did I have such immediate reactions to a woman? I hadn't even had to approach girls in years as they generally came up to me willy-nilly.

I mentally willed her to look my way. She only had to see my pretty face once, and she'd come running like the rest.

As if on cue, the temptress finally glanced over. Just as I had predicted, our gazes locked. She grabbed the edge of her sunglasses and pulled them over the crown of her head.

Crystal-gray eyes.

Complexion, the color of honey mixed with beige.

Voice so unique that when she uttered my name, I recognized it even from a distance.

My shock subsided at long last. "You little shit," I found myself murmuring. No doubt my voice was barely audible.

What in the holy fuck?

Before I could process or admit that I had just fully salivated after my little sister, Sara ran toward me at full speed (bare feet, might I add) and threw her arms around my neck.

The scent of jasmine clouded my judgment, stuffing down my horror from seconds ago. Instead of focusing on the mortifying thought, I was forced to admit that while I didn't feel at home standing in front of my childhood home, I did experience the sentiment in Sara's warm embrace.

"What's wrong, Angel?" Sara seemed emotional in my arms, twisting my heart.

"I missed you," she spoke in her raspy voice.

No one in this world got so emotional over my absence. Sure, women pledged their lives to me. They begged me for my body or blubbered for only one more night or one more fuck. But they were never real emotions.

My stone-cold heart underwent an unaccustomed warmth. Sara's affections were generally my kryptonite.

We detangled so my attention could divert to the woman staring back. The last time I saw her, she was a skinny fourteen-year-old rebel with dirt under her nail and a gap tooth. Since then, Sara had undergone a massive transformation into womanhood.

It pained me to notice her matured body. I tried to dismiss the feel of her breasts pressing against my chest or her undeniable peach of an ass. My hand gently rested on the small of her back, inadvertently sensing the feminine curves under the thin scrap of her top. I froze when the material shifted, and I made contact with her bare skin.

I held my breath, aware of the heat coursing through me.

Holy fuck.

"God, Tris. I know you hate speaking to other humans, but can you at least say hello?" she asked sardonically.

She assumed I was quiet per usual, but my taciturnity wasn't from a lack of motivation to speak. I was trying to contain the sudden lecherous thoughts escalating around my sixteen-year-old sister.

This was utterly atrocious.

I didn't know it was Sara since I only saw her side profile, and she had transformed out of her previous fourteen-year-old body. Now that I realized it was my sister, I simply needed to snap out of it. That's all.

I shook my head, hoping the thoughts would go away if I shook hard enough. "I'm just surprised by the theatrics," I teased, pinching her cheeks in the way I used to when she was younger.

Our eyes clashed, my fingers lingering over her heated skin that felt like molten lava under my touch. I was suddenly aware that although we had detangled, neither of us had taken a step back, nor did I want to.

Instead, I voluntarily drowned in her sea of crystal orbs glistening with unshed tears. My fingers hovered over her fiery hot skin. Sara's curious pupils moved to the corner of her eye to follow the circular motion made by the pad of my thumb.

Abruptly, I dropped my hand, turning my head sideways to cough. Dismissing the stubborn thoughts in my brain, I took a step back.

"I wasn't expecting to see you," I commented. It's the other reason I hadn't expected the 'unknown girl' to be Sara. It was a school day.

"I'm full of surprises."

"Hmm. How come you aren't in school?"

"It's senior skip-day, dufus."

"You're not a senior," I pointed out.

"And you are supposed to visit more than once every two years."

"Touché." I smiled at my worthy opponent. For two years, our pranks had to be limited to mail and long-distance efforts—prank calls, fake letter notices, etc. We had a plethora of real-life tricks to catch up on. "Where are the parents?"

"Inside. Come!" she sang, dragging me by the hand.

As we entered through the large wooden doors of our not-so-humble abode, Sara talked my ears off with the new developments I had missed. When I noticed the gentle sway of her hips, I hastily averted my eyes until we walked into the main foyer. By that time, I had learned of all the girls Mom had planned on setting me up with (Lilith was the front runner), the colleges Sara had visited, and everything there was to know about the Kardashians.

"Tristan!" Ragu and Mary called out in unison from the top of the staircases.

"Mom. Ragu," I politely greeted the duo.

"Oh, honey. I can't believe it. You are home," Mom gushed, her voice cracking from emotion. She sprinted down the steps and charged toward me.

Raguel remained on top of the staircases. His eyes darted to my fingers that were entwined with Sara's. It was innocent enough, so perhaps I was subconsciously conjuring up a disapproving look. All the same, I retracted my hand, though Sara remained blissfully oblivious.

Mom engulfed me in a hug. "It's so good to have you home."

"How are you, Mom?" I asked, patting her twice on the back.

"I'm good, baby."

"Welcome home, son," Ragu added, joining us downstairs to shake my hand. "I can't believe the whole family is back together," he added pointedly.

Rubbing the back of my neck with a hand, I said, "Guess it's been a while."

I finished with the last of my law school classes this week. Now, all I had to do was follow the blueprint laid out by Dad. The plan had been to attend law school in South Carolina so I'd get the residency status needed to run for that state's Congress. My campaign rested on the next generation and moral fortitude. For too long, politics had been ruled by old men who were out of touch. They were constantly involved in scandals and preaching what they didn't practice.

I wanted to represent something new—a young candidate with an impeccable reputation representing the interests of the upcoming generation.

I didn't come home for two years because I lived, breathed, and ate that motto. I had worked on every do-gooder project to build a base with the younger demographic of South Carolina and was practically a shoo-in for Congress.

However, I also had a small network in the DC and Virginia areas. Mom and Ragu wanted me to campaign here to become a congressman for Virginia. If I heeded their advice, I'd have to wait to first maintain residency in Virginia and build rapport, all of which would take more time. Not to mention, Virginia was much too competitive for a first-time congressional ballot.

"Tris, did you decide about congress?" Mom asked.

"Yeah."

"So? Where do you want to run, South Carolina or Virginia?" She held her breath.

My choices were laid forth for me.

Return to South Carolina after this short visit and win the upcoming election in a landslide. The downfall? Continue living eight hours away.

Alternately, I could move back home and get a place of residency in Virginia. Start from scratch in a near-impossible state to win for a first-timer but be less than an hour away from... everyone.

I glanced at Sara, then at the makeup smudge she had left on my shirt when she hugged me. It was an easy choice. "Virginia. I'm moving back home."

CHAPTER 27

Sara

"But why?"

"Because I'm starving, and it's dinner time." Tris pulled out of the parking lot without giving me the chance to reconsider.

Tris showed up at the shelter unannounced, insistent on taking me to dinner. No matter my refusal, he was adamant. Perhaps I could have fought him more, but I gave in, unable to stop thinking about his confession from last night.

Four years.

Tristan said he had been harboring these feelings for four years. Though the subsequent deed was terrible, at least it shed light on how Tris got to that point even while hating his actions.

I tried to assess how it might feel to want someone for years without the ability to do anything about it.

Frustrating, I bet.

I harbored a crush on Tobias and couldn't even wait four weeks to take him to bed. Of everything that had gone down, I was most grateful for never having gone through with it. I could now ascertain that Tobias wasn't the man for me, and sleeping with him would have only led him on.

I had woken up early to check on Tobias. He was fine, sans some bruises. Tris was an idiot for beating up a cop and was lucky Tobias opted not to press charges.

The sorrow I had felt over that kindhearted man confirmed my belief that the best thing I could do was to keep him far away from my family drama. This time, I firmly communicated that there was nothing more I could offer Tobias. Not even a friendship.

If that's how Tristan reacted when Tobias came by to check on me, I couldn't imagine his actions if we pursued an actual friendship.

"Why do you want to have dinner?"

"Because I want to discuss the shelter."

"What about it?"

"Steve researched the developers who purchased the plot. Apparently, that company works under an umbrella corporation by the name of CARP."

My brows pinched together. "CARP?" The name sounded oddly familiar. Where had I heard it before? "Doesn't Lilith represent CARP?"

Lilith worked as a no-nonsense lobbyist, and if I remembered correctly, CARP was the largest organization whose interest she represented.

My heart sank to the bottom of the ocean. Lilith constantly guaranteed Tristan the necessary donations to fund his campaigns. Without the backup from Lilith or her counterparts, Tristan might as well say goodbye to his political dreams, which meant he planned to shut down the shelter to play ball with CARP.

"That's correct. I'll ask Lilith to set up a meeting with you and the developers. Perhaps we can come to a compromise that works for both parties."

Color me stumped. "W-What? Meeting with me?"

"Of course. You have been working at this shelter since you were fifteen and know the place inside and out. Who better to put together a presentation about the benefits of keeping it open?"

Presentation? "I don't understand. They already bought this piece of land and all the surrounding lots too. What reason would they have to meet with me or to keep this shelter open?"

Tristan shrugged. "Tax write-off, good publicity, social responsibility. The public has been against the developers since they bought the plot. The PR reasons alone should convince them into meeting with you. If you put together a presentation to help them realize it's infinitely better to keep the shelter open instead of kicking helpless children out on the street, what reason would they have *not* to agree?"

It was a good plan, I grudgingly admitted. A great one, in fact.

Sometimes Tris' strategies reminded me of the need for diplomatic leaders in office. He wasn't emotional but came up with achievable goals to placate both sides.

Hope bloomed once more, but I tried not to get ahead of myself. Whenever Tris had a strategy, the family got together to play devil's advocate. It was done in preparation for his debates so we could identify any holes in the plan before the opposition could.

I pursed my lips tightly. "These people are backing you. Wouldn't it hurt your campaign if you set up a meeting to stop them from something they want? I mean, Lilith represents CARP's interest, and you need their endorsement to win."

This shelter didn't fit the developers' agenda for gentrification. If we stopped them from tearing it down, all the surrounding properties they purchased would become a dud. Once they found out that Tristan's sister was the one leading their downfall, they'd surely prefer him to rectify the situation on their behalf to offset the business loss.

"Don't worry about me, Angel. I'll be fine."

"And what if they don't agree and still want to tear the building down?"

"Then I'll ask them to cut their losses and sell all the plots to me instead of further sinking their reputation."

Did I hear him right?

The lot for the shelter alone was in millions. If Tris bought all the surrounding plots, we were looking at tens of millions of dollars.

Tris was rich. Filthy rich. But transactions in the upwards of millions could only be sanctioned by the lawyers who maintained the Marcolf family trust. This wasn't the run-of-the-mill favor. Tris would have to bend over backward to make this happen.

I couldn't refuse his offer to set up a meeting. Not when so many families would still have a place to call home. But I was aware of the sacrifice he was making to help them. Tris was risking his career and a war with the same people who funded him.

For the first time in so long, I didn't find myself filled with reproach. If anything, my heart pitter-pattered at his selflessness, chest burning at the act of generosity. Despite what he did to Tobias and me, I was overcome with emotions. My lips parted, unable to find the right words to express my gratitude. "Thank you, Tris. That's very generous."

"And I also want to take over the costs for the shelter." He glanced at me. "The place obviously needs more upkeep and extra staff. We should also renovate the basement to add more apartments. That should ease the overcrowding."

I didn't know how to react. Tristan had changed his tune immensely after threatening to run the place to the ground.

"We can discuss the remaining details at length over dinner."

I hesitantly glanced at my interlaced hands, suddenly wondering if his atrocious crime could truly have been a mistake. An awful mistake. If so, I couldn't deny Tristan was going to immense lengths to make things right.

I further faltered when his Aston Martin came to a halt in front of a familiar Italian restaurant, infamously known to be equal parts fancy and romantic. I had once mentioned it'd be the perfect date night spot. The words had passed my lips so long ago that I forgot about it, and yet, *he remembered.*

Before I could get my bearings, Tristan parked his car and rounded it to hold open the passenger side door for me.

What the hell?

Tristan didn't open doors, nor did he cater to women. The seemingly minute act was one he had never performed, not even for his own mother.

I managed to step out of the car unruffled but jumped when he unprecedentedly grabbed my hand. "Are you insane? Do you have any idea what people will say if they see us holding hands?" I turned around to inspect our surroundings. Although thinly-veiled—owed to the mere fact that we were at too romantic of a restaurant for a platonic rendezvous—appearances had to be kept up for the outside world.

"They'll say we look good together," he replied simply.

Tris pushed me forward with a hand on the small of my back. We didn't walk through the front doors of the restaurant but rather through a side entrance and were promptly greeted by a young hostess awaiting our arrival.

She gasped upon catching sight of Tristan. I would have camouflaged what's between us in the off chance the hostess recognized a congressman or knew a reporter, but I needn't bother. I was the least of her concerns as she swooned over Tris while he addressed her in perfect Italian.

She professionally wised up and motioned for us to follow, the dreamy gaze persisting. I absentmindedly studied the interiors and modern decorations as she led us to a private room that screamed romance with its soft lighting and the soothing sounds of a water fountain. Tristan guided me to the table set for two in the center, just as the hostess placed our menus in front.

I blinked when he pulled out a chair for me.

The distinct gestures—a private room at a fancy restaurant paired with chivalry—carried significant weight. Tris didn't indulge women, and I had no idea how to process these romantic indications.

The sudden shift baffled me, but the stranger in the room prevented any further interrogations. After Tris slid my chair forward, I pretended to intently study the menu for our hostess' benefit. It was the classic sign that her presence was no longer required, and we needed a minute.

She merely hovered, too distracted with salivating over Tristan to catch my drift.

She is so damn obvious, I mentally griped.

By now, I should have been desensitized to the reaction Tristan brought forth in women. I had no idea why I was exceedingly bothered by it today when this had supposedly been normalized throughout my life.

Perhaps the leering and the blatant disregard for my presence proved offensive for my taste. For all she knew, I was his date, not his sister. But she had decided that someone like me couldn't possibly be with a demi-god like Tristan.

Tris took the seat across, gaze shifting between the hostess and me. "Everything okay, Angel?"

"Fine," I muttered sulkily. *Why won't she leave? Make her leave.*

Noticing my unease, Tristan took matters into his hands. "That'll be all, Isabela," he announced without sparing her a second glance. "We'll let you know if we need anything else."

Something resembling victory surged when Tristan repeated the word, *we*. The hostess' continued denial of my existence had rushed a wish to humble her. The way Tristan, the sex god, solidified his interest in me satisfied that carnal desire, followed by an abrupt queasiness in my stomach.

A horrifying realization dawned on me at the same time the hostess disappeared. The man was sex on a platter with offers in the plentiful, and though he might be discreet, I doubted he lived the life of a monk... and *that* was the man who had unprotected sex with me. Twice.

I had been so consumed with misery that it had slipped my mind. "Condom." Cold panic clawed my insides. "You didn't use protection either time... when..."

I couldn't get myself to finish the sentence.

Tristan rose, the legs of his chair screeching on the wooden floor as he pushed it back. He grabbed my hand to pull me to standing. Two calloused hands caressed my face. "Breathe before you start hyperventilating," he instructed softly. "I have always used protection other than with you. And in any case, I haven't had sex with anyone else in a long time."

How's that possible? Women walked around with the female version of a hard-on for that man.

"I'm clean," he reiterated to subdue my panic.

"But what if I am... pregnant?" I asked choppily.

That day, before Tristan had stunned me with his presence in my room, I had visited my gynecologist and got on the birth control shot. She had warned that it could take up to ten days for the shot to be effective. If I had unprotected sex between that time frame, pregnancy was a possibility. So, I had bought condoms in preparation for having sex with Tobias.

Instead, it was Tristan who showed up. He didn't use a condom, and he came inside me.

How could I have been so stupid as to forget? It was Biology 101.

One man + One woman = One baby (or multiple, depending on your luck).

Liquid ice ran a cold shiver down my spine.

"It's unlikely that you're pregnant from only a couple of times," he pacified.

How could he sound so callous? Tristan didn't seem freaked out, not even a little. If anything, he was entirely unaffected.

"In any case, it's difficult to confirm right now... unless your cycle's about to start."

I shook my head. My last period was two days before... the incident. "Maybe you can send Steve to pick up a pregnancy test—"

"Drugstore tests don't generally give you accurate results this quickly after the fact. A blood test would be more accurate. Let's schedule one before jumping to conclusions, okay? But we might have to wait for a little while to find an appropriate doctor. You do remember what happened to Susie, don't you?"

Last year, a senator's daughter, Susie Crony, fell victim to teenage pregnancy. When the opposition party got a hold of this information, they spread the news as part of their negative propaganda. It was popularly believed that someone at her doctor's office 'anonymously' blabbed about the results.

In our circle, it was one thing to call on a gynecologist for birth control; it was entirely another for an unwed woman to even visit a local drugstore to purchase a pregnancy test. With the elections around the corner, Tris' opponent was searching for any excuse to tarnish the Marcolf name. Our family was being watched, and unless in the confinement of our own home, we kept to our best behavior while in the public eye. It'd only take one person to ruin us. Only one person to further drag my already questionable reputation through the mud.

Oh, God. On top of worrying about a potential pregnancy, I now had to wait until Tris' staff had vetted a discreet doctor's office.

"What happens if the test comes back positive?" I asked shakily.

"If it turns out that you're pregnant, we'll adjust. You love kids—"

"We can't give anything to a child between us other than a scandal," I whisper-screamed. What the hell was wrong with him? We both bore the last name Marcolf, and Tris' name was widespread. Unless we opted for a life in hiding by changing our identities, we'd doom any child we brought into this world. Even our parents would refuse to acknowledge a child between us.

"I'll find us a way, Angel."

He continued to pacify me with soft kisses on the forehead while I took in jagged breaths to calm my racing heart. I felt terrified of going through this ordeal alone and felt suddenly relieved for Tristan's quiet assurances that he'd find a way. We stayed in the semi-intimate huddle in silent camaraderie.

With his expression neutral, he pulled me close until my head met with his chest. He glanced where I had left a wet stain on his shirt but didn't admonish me for ruining his expensive brand-name clothing. Nor had he checked out his hair on any surface with a reflection thus far. He hadn't even said anything stupid like, *you look less ugly tonight.*

His focus had solely been on me, and I realized that due to our emotionally charged exchanges thus far, I hadn't pressed him about the most basic question every woman asked herself when graced by Tristan's attention.

Why me?

"Why are you being so nice?" I inquired, voice hoarse even days after our battle.

He laughed softly. "I can't be nice?"

"Be real. Why are you doing all of this?" I glanced around the spacious room. It must have cost a small fortune to secure a private room at such a fancy restaurant.

"Isn't it obvious?"

"Not to me."

He peered down with a penetrating gaze, sending unexplainable jolts down my spine. "I told you how I felt last night, and I meant it. Even after all this time, how can you not understand my feelings?" The rare tenderness laced in his tone shocked me to my core. Gone was his arrogance and vanity as he simply said, "It's impossible to be around the most beautiful woman on earth without falling in love."

A mindboggling part of me launched a somersault inside my chest. Did the God of beauty call *me* the most beautiful woman on earth? Tristan had called me many names before (from ugly to horse face), but the word *beautiful* was never part of the vocabulary.

I stopped breathing, unsure how to respond.

He tried to appear irritated over my prolonged silence. In reality, his emotion was something else entirely.

A thirst for me.

Blood rushed to my head like vertigo. Quietening my heart, I reminded myself that Tristan wouldn't bring me to dinner if his intentions were nefarious. Yet, the intensity in his eyes was impossible to ignore. I squirmed uncomfortably under the gaze heating my skin, and when his eyelids drooped, his intentions became crystal clear.

"Tris," I protested softly, pushing against his chest. "What are you doing?" I glanced around the empty room. Surely, he realized that his career would be ruined if we were caught in the act.

I tried to move away, but his hands locked onto my hips. The warmth of the bare touch grazed through my thin dress-shirt and almost lit the skin underneath on fire. My heart thumped loudly against my chest, and I wondered if he could hear it.

"I want you to kiss me," he whispered, licking his bottom lip. My gaze landed on the generous flesh, feeling lost from all the emotional turmoil surrounding the same man.

He had gone from being my brother to a man who hurt me deeply.

Tonight, he had been a savior, seeking redemption through acts of kindness. All the while, he wanted to be my lover, who was currently adamant that I make the first move.

"If anyone catches us—"

"I've secured privacy for this dinner. No cameras, not even for security."

"Tris, I don't think it's smart—"

"Please, Sara."

I was rendered speechless for several moments, dumbfounded by the simple word, *please*. Tristan Marcolf bowed to no man, nor did he plead. Not even for his precious career.

With one humble word, he had practically changed his persona.

Who was this man staring back at me?

My heart was at my throat, an odd form of anticipation rising by the minute. Tristan barely noticed my inner conflict, body shaking with need. He leaned against me, trapping me between him and the table. One warm hand landed on my cheek, the other wrapped around my waist. His lips were a hair's breadth away, the rise and fall of his chest apparent against mine.

He had set up the scene, and I only had to take the last leap. With my mind scattered and the word *please* ringing in my ears, I conceded and leaned forward.

Two firm lips moved against my mouth with an urgency I had never known. His tongue probed for entry, and then it was moving against mine, firmly at first, then gently, like he was savoring every taste.

"I'll happily risk everything for you, Sara," he murmured between kisses. "All I ask in return is that you give me a chance."

The words were so tender; his eyes filled with pain and hope. I felt like we were mourners at the same grave, trying to rebuild a precious item we had lost—the bond we used to share. It was sad. Heartbreaking, in fact.

With great effort, I managed to reclaim my previous seat as Tristan called on the server to take our dinner order.

I watched, first with slight disbelief and then with exasperated annoyance, as the waiter's lingering gaze perused Tristan. I doubted that our server's sexual orientation dampened his curiosity over Tris or the eyes of the rarest of colors.

Did Tristan find these hollow adorations exhausting, especially at such moments when he was emotionally drained from the week's trials? I couldn't help but wonder if his looks were as much a curse as they were a gift.

CHAPTER 28

Sara

"And why would we do that, Ms. Marcolf?" The tall, older gentleman in the perfectly pressed suit asked me. Christopher Jones was the head of Public Relations for CARP. He wasn't in a particularly good mood, exhausted from the long and drawn-out PR nightmare.

"Presumably because you can't afford the continuous bad press," I countered just as sharply.

As promised, Tristan had delivered this meeting by twisting Lilith's arm. Upon her insistence, the developers agreed to send over two representatives—Taylor Sorenson and Christopher Jones.

My job was to show them the upsides of keeping the place open for one more year and evoke their sympathy with a tour of the place. If they met with the residents and learned about the good this place did for them, hopefully, CARP wouldn't be so quick to turn their backs.

Lilith, Tristan, Jen, and the two men filled the shelter's small, shabby conference room. The round wooden desk was only large enough to accommodate four. I sat at the desk with the two gentlemen. There was also a couch off to the side. Upon arrival, Tris had claimed the sofa, so obviously, both women had flocked to sit next to him. I already had to remind Jen twice about her husband.

"Our umbrella corporation has been backing Mr. Marcolf's campaign." Taylor Sorenson, the other perfect suit from CARP, nodded his head toward Tristan. "If we are his ally for your brother's election, surely, you can find it in your heart to pave the way and end this bad PR for us." Mr. Sorenson (or Taylor as he insisted that I called him upon arrival) was the younger and more pleasant of the two gentlemen, but make no mistake; he was a shark at the end of the day.

"I assure you that my brother's campaign donations hold no significance in this room."

"That's not what I meant, Ms. Marcolf."

"No matter. I'm happy to pave the way with the press, but only if you agree to keep this building open for one more year," I responded, feeling exasperated. My presentation about the perks of keeping this shelter open had long commenced, but Q & A was still at large.

"That's not possible, Sara," Lilith chimed in. "Surely, we can come up with something else, such as relocation. CARP is willing to pay the moving fees."

"We already looked into relocation," Jen protested. "It's not a viable option in such a short period of time."

"Moving this many families without disrupting their lives is impossible," I explained.

Tris held up his hands in surrender to calm the escalating tension in the room. "Let's all take a breather. The bottom line is that DC law sides with renters. If this shelter decides to hold its own, it'll cost CARP more in legal fees and bad publicity. In retrospect, one year isn't so bad. Wouldn't you much rather try to find a middle ground?"

Once again, I remembered why Tristan made for such a good leader.

He knew when to speak to diffuse the situation. Otherwise, silence was his power.

And because he spoke infrequently, everyone listened when he voiced an opinion. The room finally fell quiet to contemplate his words.

I had attained that the only option was to ask for more time. Finding suitable accommodation within the same price point of rent as this building required a lot more time. If they gave us another year, it might be possible.

So far, they had only agreed to one more month. I needed to stay sharp to make them see it my way. However, it was distracting as all hell to watch Jen and Lilith's subtle moves to gain Tris' attention, which had been starkly focused on me throughout the meeting. Every so often, his gaze would wander to the curves of my white wrap dress and then to my legs, bared from the thigh down.

It convoluted my already unfocused mind.

Tris' undivided attention scared me at times. All the same, no longer could I deny that I wanted him, too. If I was being candid, it felt good to be touched without the guilt I otherwise carried. Specifically, it felt good to be touched by *him*. What we did together left me transcended every time, and I was always itching to experience it again.

Though Tris hadn't found me a vetted doctor yet for a pregnancy test, my birth control shot was now fully effective. We had spent the last few days cocooned in my room while he whispered all sorts of degrading, dirty things into my ears—things a well-respecting woman from my society would never ask to hear—and it had ignited a fire inside me, one I had never let another person witness.

The years of perversion I hid under this angelic façade had come out to play. The sexual energy I harbored to keep everyone at bay while dying a little inside each time I denied myself was now bared for him to see.

And God, I wanted more.

We spent hours and hours between the sheets, and I only ripped myself away long enough to create this presentation. Yet still, I wanted more. I wanted the dirty sex, wanted it to feel good, wanted what he gave me. His touch. His hands. His tongue.

I visibly shivered, closing my eyes.

"Are you okay, Angel?" Tris rose from his seat.

"You look a little flushed," Jen chimed in with a frown.

I cleared my throat and took a small sip of the water, turning my attention back on the men here to meet with us.

Focus, Sara, focus.

"Sara?" Tris sounded concerned, but the way his heated eyes grazed my skin, he knew exactly what I was thinking about. He had become attuned to my needs and knew damn well that my mind was no longer on this meeting.

Fuck. What the hell was wrong with me?

This shelter meant everything to me. The kids and the families saved me when I needed salvation. Now, I had to save them, but I couldn't get my head in the game.

I couldn't focus. I couldn't speak. I couldn't manage unless I got another hit of what he gave me.

This was insanity. The repressed sexual feelings from over the years had bubbled to the top of the surface, and my mind refused to focus on anything else. It's like we were addicts. No. Like we were slaves to our desires. All I heard were the swarming around my ears with this voice saying, *Give in, give in, give in.* And I swore that Tris could hear the same call.

"Let's take a break," he announced abruptly to the room, probably a little sharper than intended. "Why don't we do the tour portion of the presentation now? It'll give us time to stretch our legs and think things over."

It wasn't a hoax. Jen had, in fact, mapped out a forty-five-minute tour of this place under Tristan's careful guidance. She was to show CARP the residents who needed the most help, demonstrating the importance of keeping this place open. Plus, we had been trapped in this small office because of the presentation, followed by all the tiresome back and forth between the six of us.

A break was rational, but the way Tris was vibrating, we both knew he wanted much more than just a 'break.'

"That's a great idea!" Lilith exclaimed. I rolled my eyes when she leaned forward to give Tris a view of her cleavage.

Like always, he ignored her and addressed the room in general. "Gentlemen, Jen has planned a wonderful tour for you to see the inner workings of this place."

Jen sprang to her feet without missing a cue, ready to do Tris' bidding.

"After you," the nicer of the two men, Taylor, motioned for me. Despite being resolute in his stance, he had been cutting me glances upon arrival. I could tell it was a little nicer than need be for a professional setting. And if I could tell, then so could Tris.

"No!" Tris barked.

Taylor jumped but promptly camouflaged his stunned expression.

With only my eyes, I tried to communicate with Tris not to ruin this meeting with his stupid jealousy.

Tris caught my drift. With his politician smile firmly tucked back in place, he changed gears. "My apologies, gentlemen. My sister and I are unable to join the tour. We must stay behind and discuss some of the many good points you have made thus far to see if we can come up with a resolution."

Jen didn't bother hiding her disappointment. "You're not coming on the tour then?"

"I'm afraid not." His gaze was solely on me. It was not how a brother should glance at his sister. You had to be blind or an idiot not to catch the drift, and Lilith was neither of those.

She looked between the two of us. "Perhaps I should stay behind as well to help come up with a resolution—"

"No," Tristan cut her off before remembering himself. "Lilith, you need to accompany Mr. Sorenson and Mr. Jones on the tour. I'd hate for CARP to think their best lobbyist is working against them." He plastered the most charming smile on his face, the one I knew was fake but could floor women all the same. Only the slight tapping of his finger against his thigh gave him away. He was about to come unleashed.

I clenched my thighs together, willing everyone else to leave. God, we might start ripping each other's clothes off even while they were in the room. Ridiculous. It hadn't even been eight hours since he was inside me.

Luckily, Lilith conceded. "Very well then. After you." She motioned at the two men as Jen opened my office door.

We were staring at each other like manic animals, waiting.

1 Mississippi... 2 Mississippi.

They had barely stepped into the hallway, the soft commotion of their footsteps still audible outside these doors, when I charged to the door and locked it. I hadn't even turned the knob when Tris was on me, impatient hands turning me around and slamming my back against the door. Then his lips were on mine, frantic, insatiable, hungry. His tongue probed for entry, two large hands squeezing my breasts and pressing me further into the door.

I could hear the shuffling of feet in the hallway, but Tris didn't seem to notice with only one thing on his mind. And God, why was that so fucking hot?

It was so wrong to want this right now, but I couldn't stop myself from grinding against the fingers that were now rubbing against my sex.

Tristan shuffled me back to the desk and bent me over the table. He hiked my dress up to my hips, dragging my underwear down to graze my bare pussy. My naked ass and throbbing cunt met with the cool air-conditioned breeze, making me shiver. I panted, squirming against the fingers rubbing my clit. His hand covered my mouth, but it failed to muffle my moans once his fingers moved between the wet folds of my cunt.

"Oh, God," I said behind his hand.

"Shh," Tris cooed. "I don't want anyone else hearing you come except for me."

There was no way those five people missed how we looked at each other. Only one thought was on our minds, as we had manically kicked everyone out. The impatience. The desire. The lust.

Surely they'd question their senatorial candidate for staying locked in this office with his sister. They didn't have to hear us or witness this explicit act to draw their own conclusions. With the elections around the corner, a scandalous photo in this position would ruin our lives, not just his chances at the polls.

So, why couldn't we find it in us to care?

All I could think about was Tris' strong right leg parting my thighs until I was spread wide open for him. When I heard his zipper, my heart thundered, threatening to break out of my ribcage. His hot, rigid erection rubbed against the delicate skin of my cunt, and I moaned louder this time.

"Quiet," he warned again, nipping at my ear.

I gasped when the head of his thick cock probed against my opening. Without a moment to spare, he plunged so deep inside me that it sent me flying, face smashed into the desk. He didn't give me the chance to acclimate and started fucking me with punishingly rough and selfish strokes while the harsh material of his slacks rubbed painfully against the back of my thighs. With a hand banded around my chest to keep me firmly in place, he mercilessly took what he wanted until I groaned.

"Oh, fuck. Oh, fuck." The hand clamped over my lips loosened from his attack while I moaned over and over.

A loud strike landed on my ass, a strict warning to be quiet. I still failed to follow suit.

"I'm starting to think you *want* them to hear you."

I tried to say no, but no words came as he ground his hard cock between my thighs, fingers swiping at my clit repeatedly.

"That's it, isn't it?" he hissed. "You want them to hear you. You want every woman to know that I can't even finish one meeting without wanting to sink my cock inside you. I should punish you for making me feel this way."

He smacked my ass again before his hand moved to my chest to part the fabric of my white dress down the middle and pull my bra down. My exposed nipples met with the cool wood of the desk.

"What would they think if they knew you loved spreading wide over this desk like a little whore," he breathed. "What would they say if they knew how much you liked being fucked by your brother?"

My pussy clenched around his cock, eyes rolling to the back of my head.

I had no idea why I loved the dirty talk that tethered on perversion. I wouldn't like it outside of these perimeters, but Tris and I have always had a fucked-up way of pushing each other's buttons in private while keeping up a respectful front. Perhaps this was the way to keep our old dynamic alive while things between us had otherwise evolved. Perversion in private and the respect he showed for my cause in public. Or maybe it was simply thrilling to see Tristan unleashed when he was normally so diplomatic and collected.

Whatever the reason might be, the words drove me to scream my head off. His hand slapped over my mouth in another failed attempt to silence me, although he never stopped thrusting into me. With my hips pinned against the edge of the desk, he slammed into me over and over. He fucked me until I was floating out of my very body and into a separate universe entirely.

His body shuddered as the same ecstasy met him. Fingers dug into my hips painfully when he shoved into me for a final time, murmuring the words, “I love you,” before his seed spread inside me.

Hearing those words sounded fresh with new meaning, yet familiar, all the same. Everything had a different connotation between us now.

His weight slugged against my back, face dropping against my cheek. I caught sight of his dark hair when I tilted my face. His drooping eyelids were resigned with lethargy, lips hovering over my cheeks for soft kisses.

With a self-satisfied lazy grin, he detangled. He cleaned me up and rearranged my clothes with such tender aftercare that I wouldn’t have believed it was the same man who bent me over this desk and fucked me punishingly with vile words on his lips.

His eyes darkened when I managed to stand. Apparently, the disarrayed sight of me was a hard-on for Tristan. His cock, which was glistening and on full display between his unbuttoned slacks, stirred.

“No,” I said preemptively. My eyes nodded toward the door. “Not again. That was already too risky.”

With a lopsided smile that stopped my heart, he challenged, “It’ll take them forty-five minutes to see this place top to bottom. And it’s only been twenty minutes.”

Then he stalked toward me again and made me scream until I forgot to voice any more objections.

CHAPTER 29

Tristan

It was difficult to look away from Sara's disheveled state. The white, wrap dress contrasted with her honey skin, showing off her narrow waist as she tried to smooth it down. And when she turned around to fix the haphazard desk, her perfect globe of an ass made me groan aloud.

I had practically kicked everyone out of the room to have my way with her and felt zero remorse. That irritating human, Taylor Sorenson, ignited the madness I preferred to conceal under the public's watchful eyes. The cold-blooded male in me needed to mark Sara after spending an hour watching that sorry excuse of a man leer at her.

I should have received a medal for the restraint I had exercised. The things one must do for love. Sara admonished me for snapping at the man, but I would have preferred to gouge his eyes with kabob skewers.

Instead, I settled with taking it out on her pussy.

We managed to straighten ourselves out, along with the office, before both representatives from CARP returned from the tour. The moment they returned, I immediately wanted to kick those worthless people out for a second time. Since the first abrupt interruption had already swirled enough doubt, I managed to keep it in my pants.

Nonetheless, I couldn't help the distaste in my mouth as the clan settled for Round-2 of the negotiations. It was a stark reminder of how similar these men were to me—only concerned with the bottom line.

The thought gave me pause over my life choices.

Jones dove in, "I hope you had some time to think things through, Ms. Marcolf." His eyes roved over Sara as if examining for leftover hints of our tryst. I had to admit. There was a sick thrill in getting away with fucking my sister right under their noses.

"And I hope you had the chance to see what is it that we do here, Mr. Jones," she countered politely. "Did you visit Mrs. Alberta in Unit 204? Surely, you don't wish for her to be left without options?"

I had advised Jen to map out the specifics of the tour. Mrs. Alberta had a broken arm, leg, and a face almost unrecognizable from bruises. The sight had been so daunting that it evoked my sympathy, and I was a hell of a lot more coldhearted than these bastards. I hated using that woman as emotional bait, but it demonstrated the need for this place.

"Yes, I did," he replied, rubbing his chin. "And while I sympathize for her cause, it simply isn't reason enough to keep open a place that's depleting our funds by the day."

Lies. This place wasn't worth a fraction of CARP's profits. Steve had done the research. CARP could easily keep this place open for another year, which was the reason why I had suggested the timeframe to Sara.

The hard truth? Both men were promised significant bonuses if they wrapped this up within months instead. I thought they'd change their tune after interacting with the families seeking refuge and the children with limited options. Who relished in turning children onto the streets?

Damn. These fuckers were colder than me.

I shuddered.

Were they merely poor replicas of me? Unless Sara forced me to do the right thing, I was also only concerned with the bottom line, finding a solution, or attaining what I desired by any means necessary. I had never concerned myself with the journey itself or the methods to reach the end.

Like a revelation coming to life, I realized that my life required changes. I suddenly wanted to be a better man than Taylor Sorenson or Christopher Jones. Someone worthy of Sara.

She was better than this lot, and she deserved more from them. God, she deserved more from *me.*

It was insane. She was younger than me by a lot. We were almost eleven years apart, yet... I aspired to be her.

I couldn't stop watching as she argued with Jones over his utter disregard for human life. And when he asked her for a cup of coffee from the espresso machine in the conference room, an irritated Sara made him a cup, then 'accidentally' spilled it on his lap.

She was magnificent.

All the while Sara spoke to them, I tried to catch her eyes for small reassurances. To let her know that I was somehow different from this lot, though it had become abundantly clear I was the same.

"Can we count on your support, Mr. Marcolf?"

Five expectant faces looked my way. I had long tuned them out, busy staring at Sara. Could the other four pairs of eyes tell that I had no interest in them because the shade of their eyes wasn't gray?

"Sorry, I missed that last part." Count on my support? That's generally my line.

"We asked if we could count on your support?" Sorenson repeated. "As much as we'd like to help, the longest we can afford to keep this place open is three months. Can we count on your support to have your sister smooth things over with the press?"

I glanced at Sara. Was this where the negotiations had stalled?

Three measly months? Three fucking months? Going through the DC legalities would get her more time.

I almost threatened them with the information Steve had gathered. Jones kept a mistress on the side, and Sorenson was developing a cocaine habit. Usually, I didn't care if someone was a garbage person, so long as their checks cleared. But suddenly, I felt embarrassed for Lilith, Sorenson, Jones, and by extension, for myself because we were all cut from the same cloth.

What kind of a person did that make me?

Not someone deserving of Sara.

These were the kinds of people I associated myself with in my pursuit of more sponsorship checks, more power, and more shallow nothingness. However, as I glanced at Lilith with her expectant eyes, hoping I'd take the deal so she could return to CARP and boast of her achievements, I felt queasy. Lilith was the picture of beauty, and yet, her beautiful face made me physically ill. Why had I considered her an ally? I didn't like her, or Jones, or Sorenson. They were greedy money-mongers, entitled, and self-absorbed.

It suddenly became crystal clear that not only did I dislike these people, but I also disliked my life while around them.

There was a road map, and I had followed it blindly. I chased after power and gorged on the superficial feel of it. It had sucked everything out of me until I was hollow and empty, and God, I didn't want this life at all. I had never given myself the room to consider doing the right thing to get to the end. A journey that might make me proud. That might make Sara proud, too.

I stared down at the garbage people, and my first impulse was to threaten them with all the awful things Steve had discovered. But then, where did that leave me? I'd be a garbage person, too, because two wrongs didn't make a right.

Instead, I said the only thing that I could. "No." I was beyond feeling reproach and pity. Instead, I only wanted these people out of my life.

"Excuse me?" Jones squinted his eyes.

Lilith laughed nervously. "Oh, I think he misunderstood—"

"I said," I gritted out, "No. I will not be smoothing anything over with the press. Instead, I'm going to help my sister file a lawsuit against you." I crossed my arms across my chest and leaned against the wall. "I was a lawyer before I was ever a politician. I know of the DC tenant laws you've broken and will slap you with every one of those indictments. I'll pile up so much paperwork for you that instead of one year, it'll take you multiple years to claw your way out."

The stunned expressions in the room finally ended with Jones' words. He glanced at Lilith. "Is this a joke?" he exploded. "We pay for Marcolf's campaign, so he can fuck us over when we need him to do his job?"

"Mr. Jones, if you'd just let us have a word in private."

Lilith rushed to my corner of the room.

She dropped her voice so only I could hear her. "Have you lost it, Tristan? CARP is the biggest sponsor for my lobby group. The checks I donate to your campaign all come from them. They funded more than seventy percent of your last election. These developers work for CARP. The moment word gets back to the umbrella corporation that you jilted them, you'll never see a dime again. But that's not even the biggest problem. All the big names that have endorsed you so far will all pull out. Your political career will be over."

"Get. Out." I chewed out to no one in particular.

The words were said with such malice that Lilith gasped. Wisely, she didn't argue. Neither did the two men. They quickly packed up their things, made some threat about how I'd never see another check or get an endorsement, and exited. An awkward Jen lingered for a few minutes before following suit.

"Get your stuff together. We're leaving," I informed Sara harshly, my hands shaking from anger. I wasn't angry at her. I was angry at myself. I had become a politician they could keep in their pocket by buying my loyalty. And I had let it happen for years.

She simply watched me as the door shut after Jen. Sara hadn't exhibited a modicum of shock or emotion throughout the drama.

"Why did you do that?" she finally asked in a whisper. "That was political suicide."

I shrugged easily. "So be it."

Baffled, she argued weakly, "But this... it's your dream."

I mulled the words over with my brows drawn together. Yes. Despite my cold, unfeeling ways, I had hoped to leave a better world behind. I had campaigned endlessly, keeping the interests of the next generation in mind. It was a shame that I'd never get to see my work come to fruition, but if it meant not working with scum bags, then I was okay with my decision.

I stopped, the realization slapping me in the face.

It turned out that I couldn't sell my soul for the sake of my desires.

"It *was* my dream," I said after an elongated pause. "Dreams change."

"Don't be ridiculous. This is what you've wanted ever since I have known you. I'm not letting you quit. Despite our differences, I know one thing for sure. You were born to be a leader, Tris. And if you don't have the support of those people, it's going to be near impossible to win the election. It's not just the money but the endorsements, too."

"I know," I agreed. "That's why I'm going to drop out of the race." Why hadn't I thought to do so before? There wasn't so much press covering my every move as a congressman. If I became a senator, my life would be under a microscope. Sara and I were generally limited to the confines of her room in fear of getting caught. It'd only worsen.

"What!" she exclaimed, her emotions rising. "You can't. The elections are in less than a month. You shouldn't even be here right now. You should be going door-to-door campaigning like our parents are currently doing on *your* behalf. After everything you have given up getting to this point, why would you suggest dropping out?"

"Because it's turning me into a shit person," I retorted.

"Then let's find a way to do things differently. If you don't want to be in the pockets of those corporations, then let's find another way. But I'm not letting you sacrifice your lifelong dream—"

"You're not making me sacrifice anything. This is *my* choice because what you're doing here is a hell of a lot better than even one thing I have done in years."

She glanced at me with glossy eyes. "Tris..." she trailed off in a whisper.

"And that's not the only problem. No matter how we dice it, keeping your day job as a reputable senator is impossible when you're fucking your sister. And I'd really like to keep fucking my sister," I added with a smirk. Now that I was thinking of it, it wasn't a bad idea. Perhaps I could fuck her one more time before Jen returned with her incipient adoration.

Sara stared at me like I had grown three heads. "This isn't funny."

"I wasn't joking."

Sara shook her head. "No, Tris. The shelter will find another way. Maybe we can talk to them—"

"Stop. It's done with."

But it wouldn't be Sara if she knew how to stop. "No. I don't accept that," she announced, crossing her arms over her chest. "If you don't want those people's money or support, fine. But you don't get to drop out or give up on something you have worked toward for your entire life. Not without a good reason."

I opened my mouth to argue, but Sara swiftly cut me off.

"Please, Tris. I believe in you from the bottom of my heart. You were meant for greater things. Please don't drop out. Just promise me that you won't drop out until we have exhausted every resource. You can fund your own campaign. And fuck it. We'll do this together without endorsements."

Did she really believe in me to this extent?

I always assumed Sara blindly supported me because we were predestined to be a political family. But did she actually believe in my cause, my ideas, the things I had set out to achieve?

Here she was, asking me to indulge her again by not dropping out of an election that had just turned nearly impossible to win. I should say no because no one could win the Senate without significant donations or endorsements.

Instead, I watched her as Sara yapped away with more ways of keeping the campaign alive.

God, I had never met anyone who liked to talk as much as her. She talked SO DAMN MUCH, and why did that little fact have me so mesmerized? I loved to hear her blabbering like it was music to my ears. And by the time she was done, I had somehow agreed to continue without proper backing or funds.

Only one thought now remained on my mind. The possessive glint in my eyes made her swallow her next rant. The way my body was vibrating let her know that the time for conversations was over. The only thing I wanted now was to feel the warmth of her arms around me.

Somehow, she understood my nonverbal need.

She stopped speaking and slowly peeled off her dress as I watched. I turned the lock to the office door and stalked toward her. But before I could grab for her, Sara held up a hand.

"Wait! I want to try something different."

"What, Angel?" My eyes roamed her naked skin, impatience thrumming through my veins.

"You said... the other day you said that's how our first time should have been. I want to recreate our first time by doing something I have never done."

I stared at her, perplexed.

"Anal. I want *that* to be our first time."

Sara

"Anal. I want *that* to be our first time."

The hunger of raw appetite flickered in Tris' eyes. "Angel—"

"I want this with you," I announced.

"You don't have to convince me, baby. But anal sex requires... certain preparation. For one, there is no lube here. Why don't we go home—"

"No. Right here, right now." I didn't know why it was so important, but I needed this instant gratification. We had to seal the deal.

Something had suddenly shifted in our relationship. This man had held me tenderly and soothed away my panic over a pregnancy scare. He spoke reassuring words of helping the needy, and now he had delivered with a sacrifice I never expected. He had offered to give up the most essential part of himself, not only for me but for everyone at this shelter.

I had to give him something, too, and this was all I had left. I wanted to rewrite our history by giving him all of me. By letting him be my first, the way it should have been.

The only thing to remain between us was this fear of what had happened in Tristan's room. I had never returned there, and Tris never pushed for it. My room had become our sanctuary as of late, but I was tired of hiding in fear of an unknown manifestation lurking in the shadows.

"There is baby oil." I nodded toward my small desk on the other side of the room. Occasionally, I used baby oil on my legs for extra sparkle. Who knew it'd come in handy at such a moment?

With a sly smile, Tristan moved toward the drawer, practically ripping his dress shirt open en route and ridding himself of his slacks and boxers.

Slowly, I started clearing the rest of the items off the table, making space. Tristan returned with the bottle of baby oil in hand and groaned when he saw my body already bent over the table.

"Shit. What are you doing to me?"

Within seconds, his hands were all over me, running them over the curve of my back, down my ass. He uncapped the baby oil, then knelt behind, taking the bottle along. I felt his hands trembling as he grabbed my ass cheeks to spread them wide. Without warning, his tongue probed against my asshole.

"Fuck," I hissed, spreading my legs wider to give him more access.

He swirled his tongue around my puckered hole, and then I felt the heated drops of lubrication. He started to work a finger doused in baby oil inside me.

"Oh, God." My nerve endings flared at the sensation. "Oh. My. God. Tris."

"Fuck, you're so tight and hot inside here," he said harshly, the same earnestness getting to him.

I peered over my shoulders to find him rising from his knees, keeping the finger firmly lodged inside. He poured a bit more oil down my crack before adding a second finger. We had done this before where he had given me two fingers while fucking me into the pillow. But it burned when he tried to work in a third finger.

"Fuck!" I hissed, rising to my tippy toes to adjust.

"Want me to stop?"

"Don't you dare!"

With a slight chuckle, he grazed my shoulders appreciatively and kept working the fingers inside me, though, for a moment, I didn't think it'd be possible. He kept on adding more of the oil, layer by layer, until he finally forced another finger inside me.

"Holy fuck," I cried out. Painful tears leaked out of the corner of my eyes, but it had become vital to experience this more than anything else in this world.

When I looked over my shoulders again, I found Tristan slathering his cock with oil before fisting it in his hand.

"We are going to do this slow, baby," his voice vibrated in anticipation of claiming another part of my body. He rubbed his lubricated cock against my sex. He withdrew the fingers and pressed the head of his cock in their stead.

I braced myself against the edge of the table, my breath so ragged that I could hardly recognize it. When his cock pressed deeper, I instinctively tightened.

"Relax, baby," he breathed.

I tried to open for him, to spread myself wider, until I had started welcoming him inside me little by little. His dick pushed inside and past the initial resistance.

"God!" he bit out, head dropping between my shoulder blades, pausing. "Holy shit, baby. Holy shit."

I was entirely breathless but could hear his attempts to steady his heart, which was beating as loudly as mine. Tris was slow in his movements, setting a pace that drove me positively insane. He listened to my breaths, plunging forward when the pain had subsided. Then he massaged my clit over and over until I melted into him before surging forward to sink all the way home.

"Oh, fuck," I gasped.

He took an equally bated breath without moving for several moments... waiting, inhaling me, caressing me, dropping sweet kisses, until I was shaking, trembling, and once more, on the edge of a cliff.

Droplets of sweat covered both of us as his fingers on my clit sped up, and he started moving inside me.

He pivoted his hips back and surged forward. "You like that I'm ruining you back here?" he asked in a voice devilishly low.

"Yes!" I moaned, throwing my head back right as he bit my neck. "God, yes."

With a hand between my shoulders, he pressed square against the table while he stood behind me, fucking me. The fingers on my drenched clit had me so close while my nerve endings back there were flaring in every way.

"You're so wet, baby. So very wet. You like it dirty, don't you? Do you like me fucking you in the ass?"

"Yes. Yes."

He gripped my hips, going rougher now, slamming into me as I screamed. He chased his own release while the fingers on my clit sped up to match his ecstasy. Everything felt so slick behind me, but it didn't lessen the building pressure. There was a feeling threatening to implode, unlike never before. I writhed against his fingers, body tightening beyond belief. My knuckles were turning white by the way I was gripping the edge of the table. And all the while, he was stretching my virgin asshole.

The thought sent me spiraling.

"Fuck." I came with slow waves of pleasure, rolling my hips at the same time Tris pulled himself out and his warm seed landed on my ass cheeks and legs.

His weight fell on top of me, keeping me trapped on the table. With the slick mess between us, I was surrounded by him, consumed by him. His scent, his taste, his gentle kisses, and the way he nuzzled my neck.

And most of all, his sacrifice.

The thought made me happier than I had ever been. I was ready to live my life alone. Suddenly, I had *him*, and now there was hope that we could change the world together.

With my cheek resting against the desk, I reopened the fantasies inside my head. There were so many hopes and dreams, followed by an alarming reality.

The damn curse.

Initially, I slept with Tristan to somehow hurt him. In the snap of a finger, he had killed his lifelong dreams. My heart lurched for the sacrifice he made here today. I hadn't wanted it that way. I didn't want him to choose this shelter because I believed he was meant for bigger things. It was improbable he'd win without the support of bloodsucking corporations. Yet, he didn't even bat an eye.

Tris had finally become the man he was meant to be.

For the last few days, I hadn't been able to keep my hands off him because he evoked something in me that I had repressed for years. Now, Tris had made a different place for himself... in my heart.

Which meant that the fear of the damned curse had returned. Tristan told me that he was invincible. After days of insatiable sex, he hadn't been injured, but that didn't mean the threat had dwindled.

Just the mere idea of it sprung tears to my eyes.

"Hey!" He lifted and turned me around.

Grabbing a Kleenex off the dispenser on the table, Tris cleaned me up before carrying me to the sofa. He kept me cradled on his lap as he took a seat.

"What's wrong, Angel?"

I wrapped both hands around his arms. "I'm so happy that I feel sad."

He chuckled warmly. "You might have to help me out here."

I lifted my head to peer at him. "I'm so happy right now that it hurts, but I'm sad because happiness doesn't last for me. I know that you don't believe me, but if we keep this up, you'll get hurt sooner or later."

Tristan rolled his eyes. "Not this damn curse thing again. I have fucked you so many times this week that according to your theory, I should be dead."

I cracked a smile. "Please don't dismiss this. If you get taken away..." I couldn't finish the sentence. If he got taken away, everything in life would turn desolate.

He stroked my hair. "No one's taking me away."

"Our parents are coming home next week. We both know that I have zero capability of lying. They only have to ask me once before I crumble. Most likely, I'll offer up the information willy-nilly." Yeah, that's how terrible of a liar I was. I couldn't look at a person and fib. "Then what? Dad will bring out his gun and murder you for real. Bam. Curse proved real."

The bastard seemed amused by my internal struggles. "Let's tell them about us before they find out."

"What? You can't." We had a significant age difference, and he was supposedly my brother. Dad would never accept what was between us.

"We had to tell them someday."

"But Dad's going to—"

He kissed my forehead. "Leave it to me, Angel. I promise I'll find a way. No one's taking you from me."

I shook my head. He didn't understand the whole predicament of our situation. "I know you don't believe me, Tris," I said quietly. "But as long as you're with me, you're not safe—"

"I know where this is going, and I'll stop you right there," he warned, his voice suddenly serious. "Everyone out there is against us." He pointed an accusatory finger toward the office door, voice shaking. "But in here, when it's just the two of us, I don't want to hear one single thing that'll keep us apart. Is that understood?"

"If something happens to you—"

"Don't," he cut me off sharply. "I don't want to hear more protests about why we can't be together. So, don't!"

The sternness in his voice made me swallow my next objection. Instead, I wrapped my arms around his neck, hoping, praying, for the millionth time that this curse was only inside my head because I had only just found the man he had become, and I'd be lost without *this* man.

"I won't voice any more objections, but you have to promise me something in exchange."

"Anything."

"Please don't break my heart again." I leaned back to search his eyes, silently pleading. "If you hurt anyone else..." I couldn't finish the thought but hoped he understood its meaning.

I was choosing to forgive him for what happened between us and for hurting Tobias. In exchange, all I asked was for him to be *this* man. A good man. We were rebuilding the trust between us, and I wouldn't survive it if he broke it again.

Somehow, he understood everything I was communicating with only my eyes. "Never," he promised just as meaningfully.

CHAPTER 30

Tristan

"How are things with Sara?"

"Good. Her twentieth birthday is coming up in a few weeks. So, planning a few things for the occasion."

"Hmm. You seem happy."

I tried to hide the grin by extending my index finger over my lips. It was ridiculous to have this big of a smile stretching over my face, but when I tried to subdue it, I felt it expand.

Yes, I was happy, sans a tiny complaint. I was losing my taste buds.

Fucking weird. I couldn't taste salt anymore. It started a few nights ago when Sara and I ordered takeout. I had winced at the bland taste. Meanwhile, Sara complained that it was too salty.

I had paused midway of sprinkling more of the condiment out of a disposable salt packet that came with the takeout. My vanity hadn't entirely vanished and wouldn't allow me to admit the loss of taste. I had grudgingly dug into the flavorless food.

Since then, everything I ate tasted bland.

Besides the troubling early onset of losing my taste buds, life was good. In fact, it was great.

Our parents' extended travels had granted me unrestrained access to Sara. During the day, I worked tirelessly on my campaign, which I was now funding on my own. I spent my nights rolling around with Sara between the pink sheets of her bed. Any free time, I helped her at the shelter with repair projects, distributing new clothes, painting the walls, even listening to her raspy voice while she told fairytales to keep the kids entertained. Shockingly, my efforts at the shelter were getting me immense press as a politician of the people, but that's not the reason for my actions.

Of all the women I have had, all the money I had accrued, the power I had gained as a politician, none of it gave me one-tenth of what helping Sara had provided for me.

Serenity.

Only, our serene time together was due to come to an end. Our parents were coming home, as I had run out of excuses to keep them away.

That grudgingly brought me back to Michael's doorstep. He might be a pest, but Sara would have never returned my affections if I didn't follow his advice. I needed his advice once more.

"By your smile, I assume things are going well between you two."

"Yes, it is. I'm happy." I long stopped pretending that Sara and I were nothing more than a dream. It was easier if Michael knew, as he always seemed to hit the hammer on the nail. His advice thus far had worked like a charm, and it was so simple.

Sacrifice.

Our biggest obstacle still remained at large. I had put off the appointment for a pregnancy test under the guise of finding a vetted doctor. With an impatient Sara ready to march into a drug store to purchase a test, I finally conceded. She was due to see the doctor tomorrow. If she was pregnant and we were to have a family of our own, she'd want to show off our children proudly instead of subjecting them to a life of secrecy. Sara hated deceit, so we had to come clean to our family. Possibly to everyone.

But how could I give her something that was out of my control?

Legally, a marriage between us wouldn't be recognized. The world had known us as siblings for far too long. Society would turn our relationship into a laughingstock, and our children would forever be ridiculed.

Hope had filled my heart that perhaps Michael had one more trick up his sleeve to find me a way. One where she'd be mine forever, and society would have no choice but to accept it.

"That's great to hear, Tristan. So, what would you like to discuss today?"

"The ending to your story."

Michael smirked. "That's twice in a row you have asked about my story."

"Color me curious. You've been telling me this story for fifteen years. Is it ever going to end? Does Asmodeus get the girl?"

"How could he? He couldn't touch her, and they were never destined to meet."

I frowned. "Then why wouldn't Asmodeus let Sarah be happy with someone else, given they had no future?" As soon as I asked the question, I heard the truth resonating within the words.

A slow, victorious smile spread on Michael's face.

If he thought this was a breakthrough, he was in for a rude awakening. I had known of my selfish desires for years. I just didn't care.

"That's the dilemma, isn't it? If the demon could never touch her or be with her, should he let her be happy with another? Or should he make her equally miserable?"

I had asked myself the same question and already knew what I'd do —anything to not walk this earth alone. So long as she was at by my side, it didn't matter whether Sara was miserable or happy.

Well, perhaps it mattered a little.

Sara smiling while I painted the walls of the basement. Sara giggling when I tickled her under the sheets. Sara staring at me when she thought I wasn't looking.

Yes. I preferred a happy Sara for sure.

It just didn't change the outcome, even if she wasn't. There'd still be no alternatives for her other than me.

"So, what did Asmodeus choose to do in the end?" I asked, feigning the answer didn't matter one way or another.

Michael smiled. This time, the smile was kind, while his eyes were filled with pity.

Sarah stared out the window of her room with trepidation.

With shaky legs, she took her first step toward meeting her ultimate demise. She could no longer live in a world where she was responsible for the death of another innocent. Although she was about to commit a grave sin by taking her own life, what happened to those innocents was no less of a sin. And had it not been God who said, an eye for an eye?

Seven men had loved her, and all suffered the wrath of an unknown manifestation. Now, she had fallen for a man whom she loved more than herself. She couldn't bear the thought of Tobias' still body, dead at the clutches of an ominous threat, all because he made the grave mistake of loving her.

No. She had to protect Tobias even at the cost of herself.

With one forlorn look backward, Sarah jumped out of her window.

But before her body was met with the demise from the concrete below, a warm light shone from above the ground. She found herself levitating in the air instead of meeting with her untimely death.

An amber-like glow lifted her, carrying her back into the safety of her room. Even though he couldn't physically touch her, Asmodeus used his levitation powers to save Sarah and gently placed her on the bed. He grated his jaw in anger at her attempt to release herself, for she was his. Even her life wasn't hers to part with and only his to take.

He stared desperately at the woman he loved, inept in erasing her fear and unable to wrap her into a comforting hold. "Please, my heart," he whispered with a tenderness he had never shown another, "please do not take your life from me. I need you."

Sarah opened her eyes in shock, unable to understand why she couldn't take her own life. She thought it was nothing short of a miracle that she had been spared, never knowing the hand Asmodeus' had played.

Convinced that it was God's doing and he wanted her to live, hope finally blossomed in Sarah's chest. Given God's miracle, she was convinced that the curse had been lifted.

Rushing to her table, Sarah wrote a note for her beloved, Tobias. She informed him of the happy news and agreed to marry him if he'd still have her.

Asmodeus froze.

He realized that if he harmed Tobias, Sarah would attempt to rid herself of her mortal body once more. Tobias was her last ray of hope. If he died, so would she.

Asmodeus' rotten heart constricted against his chest, unable to comfort the woman he loved and too inadequate to let her go or be with another.

But what choice did he have?

With a heavy heart, the demon decided to let Sarah live a life with Tobias.

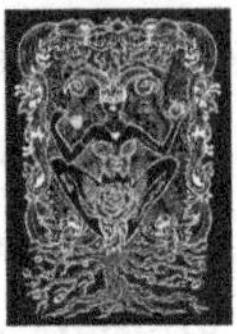

I wondered if Michael had a death wish.

Did he suggest that the woman I loved was suicidal, or did he suggest that I let Sara go to be with another?

Either way, self-preservation wasn't this man's forte.

"Thank you for that story. You've known me for a long time, Michael. Tell me, what do you think I'll do to you if any of those things were to come true?" I raised my brows.

To my annoyance, the fucker smiled. "For your sake, I hope none of those things come true."

"Then why did you tell me that story?"

"Because that's what happened."

"Enough of this ridiculous parallel you keep drawing between me and this demon," I snapped.

It was one thing to joke and make up stories to teach me a lesson. It was entirely another to threaten Sara (potentially the mother of my child) with morbid premonitions.

"You've been doing this shit for years, and I let it go because..." Why the hell had I let it go on for so long? I paid this man four hundred dollars an hour to call me a sex-crazed demon on a weekly basis. In the end, I couldn't think of a valid reason and instead said, "No more make-believe stories to show me the light. I only came here to discuss how to handle Raguel once we told him the truth about us—"

"Raguel is quite an uncommon name," he said absentmindedly. It took me several seconds to process Michael's random shift in gear. Did he do drugs before this session? "The only other time I have known that name is from my story. One that you now refuse to hear."

I scoffed. "Of course, there's a Raguel in your story. Let me guess. He plays Sarah's doting father."

Michael nodded humorlessly.

I shook my head. "What did I just tell you about drawing a parallel between my life and these stories?"

Michael brushed back some of his long, honey-colored hair. "Humor me one last time." His blue eyes gleamed so purposefully that I felt taken aback. What the hell was going on? "You've come so far, and as you said, it's been years. Don't you want to hear how the story ends?"

"You just told me how it ends."

"I didn't tell you how it ended for Asmodeus."

Damnit.

I did want to know because I was hoping somewhere along the line laid the answers on how to win Raguel's approval. I reminded myself that I paid Michael all this money because his advice had proven effective. I had almost everything I wanted in life. I was so close to the finish line that I could practically taste it.

I closed my eyes with a heavy, conceding sigh.

As the years went by, Asmodeus watched Sarah and Tobias live their lives in peace, have children, and grow old.

The demon would still find Sarah alone in those same gardens and watch her for uninterrupted moments. Sarah felt the same pull toward the unknown manifestation she'd never been able to explain to another. And every day she found herself in the gardens waiting for... she didn't know what she was waiting for, but she answered the call all the same.

This went on for years until the day Sarah died a mortal death.

A pain like no other gripped Asmodeus's heart because now that Sarah had died, she'd ascend to Heaven, and he'd never see her again. Broken-hearted, Asmodeus reclaimed his throne as one of the Seven Princes of Hell. He cursed God for sending Sarah to Heaven and spent eons in pursuit of the corruption of men to taunt God's children.

Asmodeus rarely showed his form and instead could only be heard in a murmured whisper. With a depraved smile, he spoke in the ears of men, tempting them to give in to their wicked desires. He made them long for what one must not ought, so they could be led astray from Heaven and straight into the pits of Hell.

He refused to suffer alone for eternity.

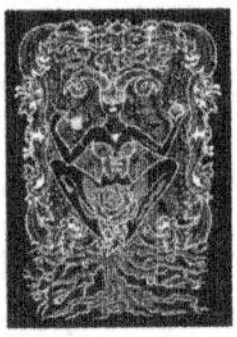

For several moments, neither of us spoke. I was no longer angry.

"Tell me, Tristan. Did you never find it odd that a name like Raguel could exist in this day and age?"

Michael was all over the place today. Why was he dragging Sara's father into this again during such a pivotal moment?

It was out of sheer curiosity that I played along. "Not that uncommon. Raguel's family has a long-standing tradition of passing down first names. Sara was named after an ancestor, as was Raguel."

"Hmm." Michael looked thoroughly bored as if expecting the answer. "After their wedding, Sarah and Tobias also started a similar tradition of naming their children after their parents."

I rolled my eyes. Michael really needed to work on his originality. "I'm shocked. Didn't see that one coming at all."

"Tobias was of the Nineveh family. For them, it was a time-honored tradition. Sarah adopted the practice, and names like Sarah, Raguel, Edna, and Tobit, were passed down generation after generation."

My eyes slightly widened. Before Sara and Ragu changed their surname to Marcolf, their last name was also Nineveh.

Had I ever disclosed that information to Michael?

My blood ran cold, irritation spiking. "Well, I'm sure the whole lot of them were very pleased with their secondhand names and lived a happy life."

"Unfortunately, they didn't." Michael shook his head. "Asmodeus was always known to be more mischievous than cruel, tempting humanity with desires. However, after Sarah's death, the broken-hearted demon turned into... an Anti-Cupid of sorts. He toyed with humanity with the first sins to plague them." Michael looked at me meaningfully. "Do you know who became his favorite pastime toys?"

I didn't respond because it was rhetorical.

"Sarah and Tobias' kin," Michael answered his own question. "Although Sarah and Tobias lived a happy life, Asmodeus tormented their descendants. He was hell-bent on proving they'd succumb to superficial pleasures and that only his love for Sarah was real."

"But, why?" I asked before I could stop myself. "They were Sarah's children."

"Nonetheless, they were also Tobias' bloodline. Some speculated it was Asmodeus' pride that wouldn't allow the children of Tobias to find happiness. He'd cultivate plans to torment them, and since Asmodeus was such a fan of theatrics, he'd set up the exact scenario to replay what happened in his own past."

"How so?" I pressed. A suspicion that had lurked in the back of my mind was starting to show.

"Well, Asmodeus knew which two people would fall in love and would predestine it for Sarah and Tobias' descendants, all so it could be ripped away." Michael raised his brows at me meaningfully. "For example, he'll introduce one of their descendants... let's call her Sara for this hypothetical purpose... to a man named Tobias. Then he'll whisper in both of their ears until they find each other irresistible."

Dread coiled inside me.

"Meanwhile, the man Sara truly loves will be plagued with feelings of animosity and envy. Asmodeus will keep whispering in that person's ears, too, until Sara's true love goes astray, thus destroying her hopes. His goal is to force them into the same pain he suffers; a daily heartbreak."

I felt like I couldn't breathe. The air wouldn't reach my lungs. I was choking and swallowed several times. "You can't possibly believe—"

"Sara's biological mother, Maya, was Raguel's first love, was she not? Tell me, Tristan. Did he ever get over her?"

I froze. Raguel might love my mother, but all the same, he grieved Sara's mother on a daily basis.

A daily heartbreak.

All these years, all this time, I thought if there were such a thing as a demon or a fallen angel, that I was their object of desire. That they wanted *my* soul, my pain, my suffering.

But it was never my suffering they wanted. It was Sara's.

I didn't believe in such things past a figment of my imagination, but if there was even a morsel of truth in Michael's words, then Asmodeus knew I'd fall in love with Sara because she challenged me. He knew she'd love me, too.

He didn't give me these gifts because he wanted my soul. He gave me those gifts, so I'd become desperate for something real and start listening to those murmurs in my ear. Until I hurt people. Until I hurt *her*.

I didn't wait for Michael's next words, nor did I interrogate him over his knowledge. Suddenly none of those things mattered other than getting to Sara.

I rushed out of the office without a backward glance.

CHAPTER 31

Sara

I hummed while dumping out the contents of the saltshaker for the tasteless replicas I had ordered online.

This might be my best work to date. Over the last few days, I had been slowly replacing the salt level in Tris' food until he was starting to become convinced that he could no longer taste salt.

That arrogant ass would never admit to losing his taste buds, so it was the ultimate torture. It was especially great when he bought new saltshakers, hoping that he had faulty salt in his home.

Oh, the small joys in life. It was the only thing that brought me back to earth nowadays. Otherwise, I'd be living with my head in the clouds.

Life had turned into a real-life fairytale. All my romanticization had come true through my life with Tristan... except it was exceptionally dirty.

Tris continued to prove that the damned curse was in my head. So, now, there was only one major hurdle. I wanted to tell our parents about us as soon as they returned home.

In the meanwhile, I was living in the Tristan bubble. Things had changed between us. He now held my very heart in his palms.

In the snap of a finger, Tris had become the man he was meant to be. He chose a noble route for his campaign, was living the life of an honest man, and had promised never to hurt another. Even the kids at the shelter looked up to him.

The polls were unfavorable without major supporters backing him. It didn't matter if he won or lost this election; Tris would make a great leader in the future. There was nothing I believed more in this life.

Tris was meant to change the world.

And he had changed my life. It was an inexplicable feeling, but he had become the very air I breathed. I had handed my heart over to him with trepidation, pleading for him to take care of it. Because if he didn't, I'd shatter into so many pieces that I'd never be able to rebuild myself.

It was a petrifying feeling, for he was in possession of my whole life in his hands.

However, that didn't mean I had to stop torturing him.

After dumping out the remaining salt, I proceeded to fill it with the replica I had purchased. There was only one folly in my well-laid-out plan. I had used Tris' laptop to order the salt replicas through his Amazon account because I accidentally left my laptop at the shelter last night. I doubted that he'd check his past orders on Amazon but might notice it if they emailed him a receipt.

I took the stairs two at a time to reach my room and pulled open his laptop that was sitting on my bed. I popped in the password—my birthday—and then searched his email for the order receipt so I could delete it.

God, Tris received way too many emails. I had to filter through them to find an email that resembled an Amazon order receipt.

Odd.

The email was fashioned after one of those Amazon email receipts...

except it wasn't when inspected closely. The memo on the bottom had only two references—initials and a date.

A date that seemed familiar.

That's the date Tristan had shown up at the shelter unannounced and found me with Tobias. That night, Steve had taken Tobias home, then sent a hefty bill for his efforts because those were Steve's initials in the reference section.

It didn't make sense. Steve was part of Tristan's staff. Why would he need to go through these hoops to get paid and make it look like something it wasn't?

There was no incriminatory information on the invoice, but a thought froze my blood. The only reason there'd be such an invoice was because there were too many to keep track of.

I thought what happened with Tobias was a one-off. Was it not? How many of these requests did Steve fulfill, and how often?

I did a quick search in Tristan's email account. There were so many similar invoices... all dating back to four years ago when my supposed bad luck took root.

I had told Tris that I would shatter if he broke my heart again, but I was wrong. I didn't shatter. I was simply numb as I pulled out my phone for my calendar and bank statements, lining every date with an incident that had occurred.

Pages and pages with evidence of Tristan's crimes stared back at me. There'd never been a curse. Instead, Tristan had hurt countless people in unfathomable ways, anyone to come between his obsession for me.

And now, only two people remained in his way. The two people I loved more than myself—Mary and Ragu.

Could Tristan possibly hurt... No, I shook my head only to be countered by a whisper in my ear.

Tris will kill them in a heartbeat. That's what he meant when he said,

"I'll find a way."

I turned around. The room was empty, but I was positive to have heard a voice clear as day. There was another whisper.

He won't stop until they are all out of his way.

Is someone there? I turned again.

You are cursed, Sara.

You ruin everything, and you've ruined Mary's life with your bad luck.

Your father is ashamed of you.

Tristan will never become the man he is meant to be if you keep on breathing.

That voice kept getting louder and louder, and I held two hands over my ears, unable to take it any longer. It called to me from the balcony, tempting me like melody, until I found myself standing at the edge. And now that I was standing here, it didn't seem so bad of an idea to just end it all.

I had never been suicidal. Even now, as I stood on the ledge of this beautiful veranda, my thoughts weren't of desolation. Instead, they were crystal clear.

This was what needed to be done. Almost as if it were my fate, my destiny. Oddly, it made good sense. If I kept on living, it'd only hurt everyone I loved.

After all, I didn't look like a member of my family and only brought them emotional distress. Would they even miss me if I were gone, or would they be relieved?

They'll be relieved, the voice whispered. *It'll solve all of their problems.*

If I kept on living, Tristan would continue hurting people. He couldn't help himself. I was his weakness, and if I was no more, then he'd become the great man he was always meant to be.

That's right, Sara. Take away his weakness. Commit this one mortal sin and join me in purgatory to save him and everyone you love.

Jump, Sara, jump.

CHAPTER 32

Tristan

Four Years Ago

"Can I bum a cigarette?" Curious pair of crystal gray eyes peeked through a thick layer of lashes.

Glancing at the lit cigarette between my fingers, I wondered about my choices in life. What was I doing wrong in life if a teenager could so callously direct such a question my way? Did I come off as a terrible influence on today's youth?

Biting down on a sardonic smile, I leveled the troublemaker. "Do I resemble a cigarette dispenser?"

Sara was in her floor-length debutante dress, no doubt hand-selected by Mary. Her bouncy curly hair was spun in a bun, adding a look of sophistication.

Damnit. She looked older than sixteen tonight, I grudgingly admitted. And really fucking pretty. Damnit. Dammit.

I clenched my jaw, averting her eyes.

Meanwhile, Sara looked me up and down, mulling over my question earnestly. “Maybe,” she drawled.

Shaking my head, I let out a grin. Though I should be disciplining her for the request, Sara had a way of flying under the radar of my anger. Sure, I tormented her, but the jabs were filled with humor, not ire.

“Baby sis, go inside before I call your dad.” I pointed at the double doors to our home, which was currently flooded with guests. It was Sara’s debutante ball. Shouldn’t she be acting all perfect and lady-like?

“Is that a no on the cigarette then?” she asked with a bored yawn.

Sara was intent on making my life hell. Putting my cigarette out on the ashtray, I turned to face her. She looked puny in contrast to my six-foot-three frame, yet she showed no signs of feeling intimidated.

A worthy opponent.

“Since when do you smoke?” I asked with genuine curiosity. Sara was well behaved, a good student, and already turning into a bit of an activist. From what I gathered while I was away, she protested racial equality and women’s rights and had taken up an active role at a shelter our parents sponsored.

Her interest in smoking was unprecedented.

“I don’t smoke, but I decided to take it up,” she stated with utmost sincerity.

“And please elaborate on why your debutante ball is the perfect playground for such groundbreaking undertakings.”

Sara strode closer to the edge of the patio. I loved this space because of its access to the northern wind. It was also easy on the eyes. The antiquated look of the natural stones contrasted with modern pillars and extravagant railings. She hopped onto one of the decorated railings.

"Because you are my older brother," she declared. "And I want to follow in your footsteps. If you insist on smoking, so do I." Without further delay, Sara reached for my cigarette pack.

Before the hellraiser could get any ideas, I swiped the pack to pocket it. "What do you think you are doing?"

"I'm copying you," she replied straightforwardly.

"Enough!" I scolded, pushed to irritation by her antics. "I better not catch you smoking... ever!"

"Why not?"

"Because smoking causes cancer."

"Then why do you smoke?"

"Because I'm an adult."

"So, you are allowed to give yourself cancer?"

"Something like that."

Shrugging her shoulders, the stubborn bane of my existence stayed on the righteous path. "Well, if you get cancer, I want to get cancer with you. If we can't both be alive together, then I refuse to die apart."

I froze, my bated breaths leaving me in spurts.

I narrowed my eyes at the little monster, hoping to set fire to her hair. A part of me was proud that Sara knew how to play her opponent. The other part of me was annoyed that she was doing it to me. Sara was on a mission to make me quit smoking, a habit she had always admonished me for.

My annoyance was tampered down by a variant of other mixed emotions. Although a long shot, my heart exploded at the idea of someone willing to follow me into death. By the same token, if anything happened to my little Sara, my sole connection on this earth would be ripped away.

Drawing my hand back, I chucked the pack of cigarettes into the dark night. The leaves rustled as the object disappeared into the wild bushes.

"Happy?" I sneered, not bothering to look at her. Sara was no doubt smiling broadly.

Without turning, I braced my hand against her shoulders and shoved her off the ledge and into the bushes behind.

That little shit thought she could manipulate me.

Excitement coursed through me as I sauntered back into the house. Sara was no doubt picking leaves off her pretty dress. Any moment now, she'd charge in here to embarrass me or do something equally silly as payback.

To my shock, none of those things happened.

My wandering eyes searched for her livid return. Where was she?

This was ridiculous.

I was to become a congressman, eventually a senator. This event was a fundraiser in the guise of a celebration for Sara. Mary and Ragu threw this grand party in hopes of my imminent success. They quit their jobs, staked their lives, and invested everything into my future because they believed in me. I needed to schmooze instead of anticipating one of my sister's pranks.

Yet, my eyes searched for her.

My parents pulled me in every which way for introductions. I tried to engage in the conversations at hand, a feat that was difficult to accomplish with my eyes in the back of my head.

Sara never came.

My gaze finally landed on two lone figures on the deck. They were standing close and practicing what I recognized as Sara's dance for the ball. And the boy, of eighteen or nineteen, was staring at Sara like a besotted fool.

I froze.

The oddest thought crossed my mind.

For the first time, Sara didn't exact vengeance. She forgot our payback-based ritual, and it was because of that boy. It bothered me more than I cared to admit.

Of course, my sister was bound to get a boyfriend, get married someday, and have a family of her own outside the perimeters of ours. But with the evidence of Sara growing up, the reality of what it meant came crashing down.

I'd lose her once those things happened.

She would have her own life and forget about something stupid, like sparring with me, because her significant other would take precedence. She'd move on, leaving me in the dust.

I stared at the two teens holding hands, practicing their dance, enamored with one another. A strange constriction tightened my chest, almost to the unbecoming point of breathing.

My fingers made a fist, a finite grip that turned my knuckles white. The shallow breaths were probably visible from miles away. More than once, I reminded myself that I couldn't create a scene, and more than once, I almost lost the argument to myself.

All I wanted was to charge outside and tear that boy from limb to limb. To sit with my thumb up my ass was humiliating.

"I'll be right back," I announced, no longer able to participate in the conversations at hand. Those two had been out of sight for far too long. Our parents were so busy pimping out my career that no one was chaperoning the hormone-infested teenagers outside.

"You can't leave now," Mary argued. "You need to meet Mr. Cohn before he leaves. He is a very busy man and is only here for fifteen more minutes." Before I could state my argument, she whispered. "This is your shot, Tristan. It's everything you have worked for."

I hardly paid attention to her blabbering, leaving her to attend to Mr. Cohn. I found myself on the deck, except Sara was nowhere in sight.

The boy, however, stood at the edge of the patio. He was on his cell phone with his back turned to me. The drink he had been nursing rested next to him on the ledge.

It'd be so easy.

A bottle of the sleeping pill from the prescription I had filled earlier rattled inside my jacket pocket. I could squash them with my fingers and throw them in the drink, and no one would be the wiser. A dance would be the least of his concerns, keeping his filthy hands away from my Sara.

A voice whispered in my ear, *Do it before he takes her from you. Do it now. Do it now. No one will know.*

My legs moved forward. I shouldn't. I shouldn't. I shouldn't. I shouldn't touch a hair on some pre-pubescent boy. I shouldn't hurt the youth I was advocating for.

Instead, I saw myself taking those final steps and making an unfathomable mistake. Unbeknownst to me, it'd only be the first of many.

Present

I supposed that was the day to bring me to the brink of this ledge. It was wobbly, and my heart almost gave out every time it creaked under Sara's feet.

She stood on the railing with her eyes on the ground. The jump from the second floor was high. If I were fortunate, she'd land on the grass. But if today were my death day, then Sara would hit the concrete.

"Please, Angel." My voice shook, arms outstretched in a plea.

After leaving Michael's office, I had called Sara endlessly all the way home. She had left my laptop open on her bed, and I saw what she had borne witness to. The evidence of my crimes had left the woman I loved utterly desolate until she stood at this very ledge, heartbroken and shattered.

Somehow, I knew the Devil was speaking in her ears. That's what he did. He waited for your weakest moments and tempted you with instant gratification.

Sara was hurting, and he was giving her the easy way out to get over this pain. If she even took the hour to rethink, she'd be horrified over her actions. A mortal sin that would leave her soul forever in destitution.

But Sara wasn't in her right mind, I knew from the look she sported.

Every time I was at my worst, the demon inside nudged me to give in. It'd be easy to say the 'Devil made me do it.' But did he? Both Michael and Asmodeus' voices were ingrained inside my brain. Yet, when I saw a boy with Sara for the first time, I gave voice to what provided me with immediate gratification.

Where I never did so with my career or other aspects of life, my instincts failed me every time it came to Sara. I *chose* to listen to the most destructive side of me to punish the boy who had touched Sara. I did so again the following year when I caught Alex Bowman trying to grope her. I had scared the jackass in the parking lot before running over his hands. The year after that, her harmless friend from school, Sasha, got a little too close to Sara. I had him shipped off to military school.

On and on, my crimes continued until the day I found two bitchy girls bullying Sara at her college. My fingers had itched, and while they weren't looking, I had shoved them down the stairs from behind.

So yeah. I knew a thing or two about giving in to your first impulse. I was just praying, desperately hoping, that she was stronger than me.

"Please, Angel," I called again. "I need you to step down from there."

"Stay back, or I'll jump," she said with a serenity I had never known her to possess.

I quickly put both hands up in surrender. "Okay, okay. I'm standing right here. Let's just talk for a minute, okay?" Whatever bout of insanity had a hold of Sara, I only had to keep her talking while inching forward to yank her into my arms.

"Do you know why I only like pastels, blues, whites, pinks?" she asked calmly, her voice not her own. "Do you know why I only wear those colors?"

Good. She was talking. I took one breath, two breaths, three breaths. I could do this. I took the smallest step forward, trying to keep her engaged simultaneously.

"Because it's flattering on your skin tone, Angel," I replied evenly, keeping the fear out of my voice.

"Not quite," she announced. "When I was seven, I heard you having a nightmare. I came running to your room, and you picked me up for a hug. You claimed to have seen a demon and needed your little angel. I said nothing and hugged you back. After that, every time you had a bad dream, I wanted to be the angel to save you."

The ground creaked under me when I tried to slide forward again. Fuck. I stopped when she turned her face sideways.

"When we got older," she continued, "you'd look at me whenever you were at a crossroad. It'd be all over your face that you wanted to take the shortcut, and you'd often do exactly that. But there were other times, too, when you'd look at me, then decide to stay the course of a difficult route."

"Yes, Angel," I agreed shakily. "You're the only one who can keep me on the right path." One more small step toward Sara. I didn't have the luxury to freak out right now. I had to keep my head in the game.

Sara turned to face me, and I froze in place, hoping she didn't notice the minuscule distance I had covered during the length of our conversation.

"Those are the colors angels like to wear—pastels, blues, whites, pinks. I dressed like an angel for you. Everything... my whole life... I tried to be *your* angel to chase away *your* demons. To make you choose the right path. I wanted to save you, but you are too far gone, Tris. I've failed."

"No. No, Angel. That's not true. Please, Sara—"

Without looking back, Sara jumped.

I didn't hesitate as I jumped after her. I caught her in mid-air and grabbed her body into a hug, then rotated us to the side. We hit the ground together, and I prayed to my God that I had managed to salvage her by keeping her firmly to my chest, and it was only the side of my body to take the hit.

CHAPTER 33

Tristan

"It's not looking good, Mr. Marcolf."

"Then look harder," I snapped.

Sara and I had been at the hospital since the fall. I tried to shield her, but twelve feet proved to be lethal.

The side of my body hit the ground with a forceful impact. The damages were primarily superficial. My right cheek was destroyed, and my face was so marred with a large scar that no one would dare call me beautiful again.

Otherwise, my recovery was quick.

I was unconscious for less than a day. Other than the bandages covering half my face, minor pain, and a sling around my shoulders, I was back to normal.

Meanwhile, Sara's condition hadn't improved after five days.

It made no sense. The doctors agreed that my body should have protected her from the fall. The internal bleeding was minimum, with no major damages, sans a tiny miracle.

Sara was pregnant.

Despite the birth control shot, my seed had taken root within the early days before it was fully effective. Since she never had the chance to take the pregnancy test, it wasn't until we were brought to this hospital that we found out.

The baby was fine. Superficially, so was Sara. Yet, no one could pinpoint the reason for the lack of recovery.

Almost as if a force was sucking the life out of her.

My throat constricted, suffocating me at the thought of losing her. There had to be a way.

"I don't care what you have to do," I said, my voice escalating with every word. "If anything happens to her—"

"Tristan," Mom whispered with a gentle hand on my shoulder. Her eyes were swollen from crying. Ragu's were none the better. We were in Sara's room in the hospital, surrounding her bed like devoted dwarves waiting for fucking Snow White to awaken. "Stop."

For days, I had been dragging the doctors through the wringer. The more I recovered physically, the more it angered me that Sara hadn't.

Mom knew it too.

"Just stop, Tristan," she said with a head shake.

The doctors took the small window to make their escapes, mumbling an apology as they left. Ragu followed them out. "I'm going to get some coffee," he said over his shoulders.

For days, none of us have slept. Ever since my recovery, I had practically moved into Sara's room. The same held true for Mom and Ragu.

"You need to rest before you tear everyone's heads off," Mom whispered after they had cleared out. "If this continues, all the doctors in this hospital will start refusing care."

Deep down, I was aware that my attitude wasn't helping. Sara was getting the best care money could buy, but there was only so much money could do against God's will. Or perhaps it was the Devil's will.

I closed my eyes. "Why is nothing working?"

"The pregnancy might be complicating things," she replied easily.

Guilt imprinted on my soul. I impregnated Sara to trap her. If that pregnancy now caused her demise, I'd find a way to take myself out of this earth alongside her.

"But they said the baby was fine," I weakly argued.

I wasn't conscious when the doctors mentioned Sara's pregnancy to our parents. Whatever their initial reaction might have been, they seemed to be coping. They were much too distracted with Sara's recovery to focus on the father of the baby.

Although, the suspicious way Mom had been staring at me was a dead giveaway that she knew it was me. Due to the dire circumstances, she hadn't approached the topic... until now. "You mean *your* baby is fine."

I nodded without looking at her. "Does Ragu know?" I managed to whisper, not bothering to deny the truth.

"We both had our suspicions by the way they found you."

They found us entangled, with me embracing Sara against my chest, so the impact landed on my shoulders.

"I don't see a gun in Ragu's hands." If he was livid, he had been doing a great job of hiding it. He hadn't shown an inkling of resentment toward me.

Mom shook her head with a sad smile. "You almost gave your life to save Sara's. Ragu is grateful. In fact, he can't think of a better man for Sara than you. He told me so himself."

My eyes flipped to my mom's in shock. The last time this topic came up, Ragu had pointed a gun in my face.

Mom saw the conflict in my eyes. "You'll understand the first time you hold your baby. Everything else pales in comparison to the possibility of losing your child. If we survive this, do you think for a second that we'd risk losing either of you again?"

Her eyes shone like diamonds with unshed tears. When she stepped forward to take me in a warm embrace, I let her for the first time in my life.

"I love her," I whispered in her arms.

"I know, sweetheart," she whispered back. "We'll find a way."

We had to because there was no life without Sara. I was desperate for a way, and where science had failed, all that remained was divinity.

Stepping out of the hospital room, I retrieved my phone and dialed the last number on it. "Steve, I need you to pull the car around."

It was time to pay Michael a visit.

I slammed open the door to Michael's office. "Give her back to me!" I shouted, cutting right to the chase.

Michael stood from his desk. He didn't ask what this was about and seemed unfazed by the bandages covering one side of my marred face.

"She's lying in a hospital bed, fighting for her life. If you have the ability to help her, then Give. Her. Back. To. Me." I repeated with grit.

No longer did I care if Michael's stories were real or if he thought me to be a crazy person for my allegations. If Sara was a pawn in this game of Hell versus Heaven, then he was the key to saving her.

Even now, the asshole refused to admit how much of his stories were real or if he had a hand to play.

"When you first told me of your dreams, didn't you bargain your soul in exchange for your desires? Now, you have everything you wished for," he said with sorrow in his voice, "and it's because of what happened to Sara."

It turned out that sympathy votes outweighed the influence of big corporations. According to the news, I was the current front runner for the upcoming elections, courtesy of the heroic tales of saving my sister when she 'accidentally' fell off the balcony.

A narrative had been spun, and though news of Sara's pregnancy had gone public, no one would reprimand a girl fighting for her life at the hospital. Our families' reputation remained intact, with only sympathy flowing in every which way. I was leading in the poles and would win this election in a landslide. Hundreds of fan mail and gifts were sent to me daily from women worldwide. Our stocks had gone up in the market, too.

The Devil had delivered on every one of his promises... and I wanted no part of it.

"I don't want any of it. I don't want to give my soul away." I clutched at my heart, which was breaking at the image of Sara on a hospital bed. "Tell me how to stop this. Tell me how to save her."

"You already know how."

My brows furrowed because there was only one word he had repeated over and over. "I had already planned on sacrificing everything for her," I said with my jaw clenched. "I had offered to drop from the race, and image is the last thing on my mind..." I touched my face. "But she's still on that hospital bed. Tell me what else, and I'll do it in a heartbeat."

His eyelids drooped to the ground. "In my story, Asmodeus recreates his own morbid past through reenactments, including the ending."

My step faltered. "No," I said sternly, his suggestion becoming vividly clear.

"If you love something, then let it go. That's what Asmodeus did. He made the ultimate sacrifice."

I wanted to rip Michael's heart out as the ice-cold comprehension settled in. For the ultimate sacrifice had never been my looks, my career, or my money. It was my refusal to walk this earth alone without Sara by my side.

"You know as well as I do that Sara is the only thing you ever truly wanted in life. The rest was fluff."

"Anything but that," I rasped. She was the only one for me. He couldn't take her from me. He couldn't.

"If sacrifice were easy, then everyone would do it," he consoled. "According to the story, she'll survive if you live your life far away from hers."

A life away from her.

I would never see her smile, or the mischief twinkling behind her eyes, or hear the husky way she called me *Tris*.

Michael still wouldn't admit to the existence of divinity, to the validity of his stories, or his association with what's happening in our lives. Yet, I would readily burn in agony forever if there was even a slight chance of Sara living to see another day. With my knees shaking, I clutched at the wall next to me for support.

"Could she truly be happy without me?" How could that thought hurt more than anything else?

"She'll live a good life," he assured.

A good life with Tobias.

I felt as though I couldn't breathe. I glared at Michael, needing a target for the anger I harbored at this cruel and unfair judgment. Death would be a better sentence for my crimes than this pain, but I knew God wouldn't grant me death. He wanted me to roam this earth alone as my atonement for what I had done to Sara. And though I had never admitted to Michael about my crimes, I had an inkling that he somehow knew of them.

"Fuck you, Michael, and your God. How could he make me love her so much only to take her away from me?"

I was ready to rip his tongue out if he said something proverbial like, *God works in mysterious ways*. But not another word passed between us. Michael stood silent, allowing me this pain.

Thoroughly defeated, I left on shaky legs until they carried me to the car and back to the hospital.

I knew what had to be done. *But why, God?* I demanded in my mind. *What cruel reasons could you possibly have to make me love her for all these years only so I could lose her?*

God didn't answer me, and I realized that neither did the Devil for the first time in my life.

God wasn't by my side.

Neither was Sara.

Even the Devil had left me.

I was truly destined to walk this earth alone.

"Her situation has worsened," I overheard one of the doctors on my way to Sara's room.

"I think it's best to let the families know," said another one, twisting the knife inside my heart.

I stepped inside the grey hospital room. If Sara were awake, she'd hate it. She'd complain about the room and demand an outfit change to something white or frilly.

A sardonic smile graced my lips at the thought. I sat next to a quiet Sara, hooked up to machines. The scene didn't fit her, and I wished she'd wake up to complain.

No more doubt resided in my mind. She would die if I stayed next to her.

This fucking hurt more than anything in my life. Not even when she found me out or we fell from the second story did an excruciating pain like this grip my insides. I wanted to rip out my rotten heart to stop the pain. But the image of a dead Sara was one I couldn't sedate even by ripping my heart out.

With a soft kiss on her forehead, I murmured, "I came to say goodbye, my little Angel. I wish you nothing but happiness."

CHAPTER 34

Asmodeus

It had been centuries since her death. All the same, Asmodeus returned to Sarah's grave for his daily visit.

He needn't turn to know that the Archangel Michael had joined him. They were both in human form, and bystanders mistook them for regular mourners at the cemetery. Still, many cast a longing glance at the Prince of Hell because... well, why wouldn't they stare? He was the Demon of Lust, after all.

Michael was a pest. He had been a thorn in Asmodeus' side for too long, always disclosing his plans for the mortals to steer them in the 'right direction.' Whether he was here today in silent camaraderie—as he had done several times before—or to coax Asmodeus into letting the mortals win this round remained unclear.

It turned out to be the latter.

"He gave up everything for her," he whispered. "Let the girl live her life with him. He loves his Sara as much as you love yours."

Michael used the present tense love instead of loved because it was true. He still loves his Sarah with every fiber of his rotten heart. But he could never see her again because she resided in Heaven, the one place he couldn't return to.

Bitterness seeped through Asmodeus as he stared at Sarah's grave. If God had destined for him to live eternity alone, he wanted each of God's children to feel the same pain, especially when they were also Tobias' children. They continued to sacrifice love for hollow temptations. None of them would ever love someone the way he loves his Sarah. So much so that even centuries later, he had her grave maintained to be close to her, though the sight itself caused him irreparable pain.

"Much good it did me," the demon spoke at long last. "I would have never hurt my Sarah the way Tristan hurt his. Yet, God made it so I couldn't even touch her. Despite my devotion, God separated us forever."

"Did God do that?" Michael asked absentmindedly. "You're the Demon of Lust. Mortal women fall at your feet whenever you walk this earth in human form. Think Asmodeus. Has God ever interfered in your choices or theirs?"

Despite his resentment, he had to sullenly grant that God had never interfered with *choice*. It was Asmodeus who murmured in the mortals' ears to coax them, not He.

The words left like hot lava flowing through his broken heart because if God hadn't interfered, what did that mean? Why could he never touch Sarah while she was alive?

"It was never God," Michael spoke softly, a pang of regret laced in his tone. "Don't you see? Deep down, you knew that defying God and sinking into sin would be your downfall. You didn't want your sins to touch Sarah."

Michael placed a hand on his shoulder with a kindness Asmodeus hadn't felt since Sarah. He didn't know how to accept this truth.

"It wasn't God, brother. Instead, you made it so Sarah could never see you, nor could you touch her. Because if she saw your face, she would have fallen in love with you like so many before. But you wanted Sarah to love someone worthy, someone who could join her in Heaven. You protected her even from yourself and with the greatest sacrifice of all. Love."

Asmodeus fell to his knees.

The words Michael spoke were too raw, too honest. He put his hands over his ears, unable to accept the truth.

"Ash, you've refused to see the truth for years, choosing in its place to hurt Sarah and Tobias' lineage. To hurt *all* mortals. The boy has proven the depth of his love with the same sacrifice. Even after all the things you've murmured in his ears, forcing him down the wrong path, he fought the whispers for her sake. And even after he did the worst thing to her, she'd sacrifice herself for him. Come now. Don't take this love away from them."

And suddenly, the Demon of Lust could do nothing more than break down into tears. He wept for his Sarah, whom he protected from himself. And he wept for the two humans, touched by their devotion to one another. How anything could still touch his painfully broken heart was beyond him.

Humbled, broken, shattered, Asmodeus retrieved the heart he had torn out from his chest centuries ago and closed his eyes with a final sigh of defeat.

CHAPTER 35

Tristan

I couldn't have left the damned hospital fast enough. Gulping for oxygen was futile because Sara was the only oxygen I needed to survive. Without her, I was choking like a fish out of water and realized horridly that's how I'd feel for the rest of my life.

I practically sprinted to my car, hoping that my heavy footsteps on the ground would drown out the sorrow budding inside. For more than two hours, I had Steve drive around aimlessly without a city or destination in mind.

I couldn't force myself into selecting a path. The horrifying truth to the matter cut deep gashes inside me in a crisscross fashion. Regret, self-pity, sorrow, and all human feelings that the Devil used to prod me to shed, hit me at the same time.

I was gutted.

I was so broken.

There'd never be a time, not even a millisecond, when I wouldn't be so in love with her that it hurt. I would love her until the end of time.

So, I'd have to carry this pain with me for eternity until my last breath on earth, along with my remaining days in purgatory. I could almost hear the melody of a newly-awakened Sara complaining about the hospital gown. A thought that only made me love her more.

As soon as Steve had driven me far enough from the hospital, I instructed him to call the estate lawyers and transfer my inheritance to Sara. She would do much better with the money than I ever could.

But before he could make the call, my phone vibrated in my pocket. Looking down, I saw Michael's number etched on the caller ID.

Why the hell would he call me now? What else could he take from me?

"What?" I snapped. Could a man not even lament in peace?

"Tristan," he said evenly, ignoring the bite in my voice. "I think you better return to the hospital."

"Excuse me."

"Come back to the hospital," he spoke slowly as if I were a dim child who couldn't understand an easy instruction. "I came by to see Sara."

"Why?" I asked suspiciously.

"I have my reasons," he replied easily. "As it turns out, I witnessed a miracle during my visit... They are calling it God's miracle."

"Sara's awake?" My throat went dry despite the deal I had agreed to. I'd leave, and Sara would magically awaken.

"Yes," came Michael's response. "She woke with only one name on her lips. Yours."

The ground underneath me almost caved, but... "It doesn't matter." The deal was that if I left, she'd wake up.

"But it *does* matter." For once, Michael sounded satisfied with himself. "In my story, an honest sacrifice has the power to break the worst of curses."

"How do you know—" I shook my head.

Why was I still questioning divinity? Michael wouldn't reveal the truth, this much I had ascertained over the years. It was clear that his connection to God was bigger than my grasp on it. And if he was convinced that my presence wouldn't destroy Sara, could it be true?

"What if something bad happens to her again?" I rasped out, hope flailing in my heart.

"Then you'd better figure it out together. God can't save you from yourself, and neither can I." He hung up before I could say another word.

My phone dropped to my side.

"Turn the car around." Without further ado, I forced Steve to speed through the beltway and return to the hospital. My legs tapped restlessly for the entire two-hour drive. Once we arrived at the hospital, I ran all the way to Sara's room.

I froze at the sight of a conscious Sara and watched her for an uninterrupted moment. Ragu was helping her gurgle with mouthwash that she spat into a small portable basin. And it looked like Mary had already helped Sara change into a white summer dress, even though she was still propped up against a pillow on the hospital bed.

Despite myself, I couldn't hold back a smile.

Other than our parents, I expected to see Michael and a plethora of doctors. The sight of both was non-existent.

How could it be? A girl who was unconscious only mere hours ago was suddenly awake and looked like the definition of life itself. There was no proof of what she had gone through other than the scars tarnishing her beautiful beige skin.

It was indeed a miracle.

"Sara," I whispered.

Three pairs of eyes turned to face me, but it was only the gray ones to hold me captive. Sara and I stared at each other, stumped over the course of events. I thought she would look at me with hatred, but her eyes shone with something else entirely.

Relief.

Happiness.

Love.

Our parents exchanged a knowing look. "Ragu and I are going to grab some coffee," Mom said, unprovoked.

Ragu pointedly searched Sara's face in case suspicions of foul play remained in the equation but left once Sara gave him a reassuring nod. He patted me on the shoulder on the way out, which felt like a blessing and a gentle threat.

I remained rooted in place, unable to pay attention to the subtle hint. My gaze was only locked on the girl who held my heart hostage.

The sun rays from the window blinds drew horizontal stripes on her face, caramel skin shimmering. Her hair, which was spun in a bun, now cascaded down to her shoulders. She looked like a bride in her white summer dress rather than a hospital-bound patient.

No. Not a bride.

She looked like an angel that had reclaimed her throne in Heaven.

"I asked for you earlier," she said huskily. "No one could find you. Where did you go?"

"Not far, Angel," I replied, cautiously moving closer.

I had already come so close to losing her that I was worried it'd take one rushed movement for her to disappear forever. Dipping my knee into the hospital bed, I sat with my body turned to her. "Thought I had lost you forever," I added lamely.

"Yeah," she tutted. "I'm not dying until I make you pay. I have already come up with five things, and they are all so awful that I'll even give you hints." She started counting things off with her fingers. "First of all, I'd be very careful about your morning coffee from now on—"

My lips smashed against hers, my heart bursting with bright light. I had kissed her so many times before but never like this. Like we had infused into one.

She leaned back from the kiss; all traces of previous humor were now gone. "Tris, if you ever hurt anyone again—"

"Never again." I went back to her lips for more, kissing her over and over. "I swear it on you. I swear it on our baby. Tell me that you believe me."

Sara searched my eyes to find the truth in them. With some reluctance, she nodded slowly, before talking my ears off about how she planned to make me pay for my past mistakes.

Apparently, after she woke, Sara found out about the pregnancy, something that made her as happy as it had made me. She also remembered that I had jumped to save her. She was filled with confusion over her actions. Sara wasn't the type to consider such things as ending her life, but I knew the call of temptation a little too well to press on the matter.

The sequence of events after she woke up was followed by a conversation with Michael, giving Sara a new lease on life. The optimism she lost had returned, though she wouldn't disclose what she and Michael had discussed.

I was okay with it as long as she forgave me.

Her suspicion was warranted after everything I had done, but I hoped she could see the sincerity in my eyes. I had turned over a new leaf because of Sara. She was my strength. She had been all along.

I kissed her again and again with those promises, hoping to instill them in her. Though it was odd kissing her with half my face camouflaged with gauze. When Sara touched the tape covering my cheek, I winced.

"Does it hurt?"

I shook my head. "No, Angel."

I had removed the gauze only once to find half my face nearly unrecognizable. The gash in my cheek was too deep for plastic surgery.

My eyelids drooped from nerve damage, and the stitches were sure to leave scars for years.

When the doctors peeled off the bandages, and I saw my new face, I had been too distracted by Sara's recovery to care. No longer was I worried about my image or concerned with vanity. I had simply covered up the wounds with gauze and medical tape.

But now that Sara was awake and peeling the tape off, I realized that the one thing I had to offer her—my looks—was gone. What reason did she have to love me now?

I gently grabbed her hands. "I've to warn you. It's not the face of the man you remember."

"I want to see," she insisted, removing the last of the gauze.

I held my breath while she inspected my face for what seemed like an eternity.

If she lied and said it wasn't so bad, I'd know. She was a shit liar.

If she turned away in disgust, it'd break me in half.

If she showed me pity, it would gut me.

There was only one correct response that would tell me this wasn't a deal-breaker. And by God, she was the perfect woman because that's how Sara reacted. With the perfect response.

"Uff, that's rough," she said, tilting her head to study the scar better. "Does this mean that I'm finally hotter than you?"

My lips quirked.

Her fingers wiggled over my right cheek. "Perhaps we can cover it up with some makeup. Or we'll just put a bag over your face. And if you expect me to have sex with that face, you'll definitely have to go down on me a hell lot more, ahhh—"

She squealed as I grabbed her ankles and dragged her down until she lay flat on the bed. In an instant, I loomed over her body. "Really. I didn't know you had complaints in the bedroom. Should I start by fixing that?"

I nipped at her ear, making her giggle. I went back for her mouth, kissing her while one arm wrapped around her, the other still in a sling. My body shook at the possibility of this being snatched away, and I could only force myself to stop for clarity.

"You really don't care what I look like?" How could she not?

She looked at me with clear eyes, honesty shining in them. "If anything, I prefer you this way. Scars are kind of sexy on a man, and you were a little too pretty before."

My lips were on every part of her skin, kissing her repeatedly with gratitude and relief. With her hands locked around my neck, she kissed me back with absorption until I was convinced that my looks didn't matter. It never had for her.

The confirmation that something ugly only brought us closer made me simultaneously believe in Heaven and Hell. I could barely detangle our lips to murmur the biggest truth of my life, "I love you, Sara."

There was no hesitancy as she murmured back, "I love you too, Tris."

EPILOGUE

Coming abruptly to a stop, Asmodeus watched the couple on the bench. They didn't notice him lurking in the shadows of the large trees, engrossed in their conversation.

The man bore a large scar on the side of his face, which seemed to be the result of an unfortunate incident. It had mended fairly well, though distinct. The girl wore an ivory dress, holding a cup of Mocha Latte in one hand, the other interlaced with the man's fingers.

They were quite a scandalous duo. Supposedly, he had once won the senatorial race by a landslide but resigned the very first week. Instead, he took on a large corporation and fought them to keep a small shelter open. He was successful in his efforts, and the place continues to thrive to this day.

Later, the man moved his entire family to Australia, including his parents and adopted sister, who transferred to Macquarie University in Sydney.

Though an official reason was never provided to those back home, gossip spread that he had impregnated his adopted sister. It was speculated that Australia was the furthest they could move in order to live as husband-wife while avoiding the judgment of their former associates. Apparently, they married in a church without filing official paperwork.

Rumor had it that the girl sitting next to him was, in fact, his sister. Then again, this was all hearsay.

Asmodeus kept his distance from the couple and knew little of their new lives other than 'stumbling' upon them on his daily route at this very park.

From the conversations he had overheard, the boy had opened various youth centers around the city, shaping the minds of the next generation. He sounded passionate about his work and was in the process of becoming an Australian citizen so he could get involved in politics.

As for the girl, she was finishing her last year of college, all the while frustrated by the ways of life. Every week, a new injustice irritated her, though her husband never tired of hearing about it.

In the beginning, her incessant talking annoyed Asmodeus. But now, Asmodeus found himself wondering, *What is bothering you today?*

"This is total bullshit. That professor only favors male students because he thinks girls can't do math. He is practically pushing for all the female students to drop out and stick to cooking or painting."

"Angel, you hate math, and you love painting."

She gasped as if he had struck her. "That sexist pig doesn't know that. He shouldn't be encouraging me to drop his class because it's too *difficult* for my puny brain." She used air quotations around the word *difficult.*

"But, baby, hadn't you planned on dropping his class anyways to focus more on your freelance artwork?"

“Over my dead body. I’ll never give him the satisfaction.”

The man bit his bottom lip in an effort to subdue his laughter, all the while pacifying his passionate wife. “Let me get this straight. You want to stay in a class that makes you miserable instead of pursuing something that you actually want... And all to stop your professor from getting what he *might* want out of the deal.”

Her hands turned into fists. “Stop being so rational about this.”

“My mistake, baby,” he responded dryly.

“It’s the principle of the matter. And whose side are you on, anyway?”

“Yours, Angel. Always.” He dismissed any remanent amusement. “I just hate to think that you’re willing to be miserable and all to stick it to a man you hate.”

She stared at him incredulously. “It’s like you don’t know me at all.”

The man couldn’t do it anymore, breaking out in hysterical laughter. Even Asmodeus found himself smirking from behind the trees.

“It’s so unfair.” She threw her hands up in the air, frustrated by her husband’s lackluster reactions. “He’s making the girls in his classroom unwelcome because of his archaic views, and there isn’t a thing I can do to help.” She pouted, though there were now traces of the real sadness she harbored. She looked over at their daughter, playing with her building blocks in the nearby playpen. “I can’t imagine any of her opportunities getting taken away.”

The man with the large scar looked from his young wife to his daughter. The tiny human with mounds of curly hair raised her hand to wave to her doting parents, who smiled brightly in turn. They had named her Sarah Ash Marcolf based on a tradition the girl’s family followed. Sometimes, Asmodeus liked to imagine that the middle name was a namesake to him, a reminder of their past.

It was unlikely.

They never truly believed in Asmodeus' presence in their lives. After the entire ordeal the couple had supposedly endured, no one could confirm what actually happened to them. If he had to guess, the couple didn't understand it, either. Everything that happened was based on hearsay and a gut feeling. A murmur in their ear.

Asmodeus might have learned to tolerate them, but they were puny mortals, after all. Their hearts weren't open enough to accept such possibilities without physical evidence, and they had accepted their past as an unexplainable phenomenon of life.

The man took his wife's hand and kissed her knuckles. "What if we drive by this professor's place tonight and TP his house?"

Mischief twinkled in the girl's eyes. She squealed before taking her husband into a hug, glad that he had finally seen the light.

Asmodeus wondered if he should also pay this professor a visit and toy with him. He had become protective of this duo and felt annoyed by this development that troubled them.

The man happily embraced his wife, eyes closed as if fearful this warmth might get taken away from him. It appeared that even after all these years, she managed to leave him utterly breathless.

This was generally how their arguments ended.

As the years went by, Asmodeus spent his time between his kingdom and roaming the mortal realm. Every day, he returned to this park and watched the man with the large scar and the girl with the crystal eyes for an uninterrupted moment. Asmodeus liked to imagine that, unbeknownst to them, they felt the same pull toward an unknown manifestation. That's why they returned daily, to give him glimpses of hope and humanity and happiness.

Eternity might be a long time, but it was suddenly not so unbearable when you had a family to watch over.

A review for an author is like leaving a tip for your server. If you enjoyed Sara and Tristan's story, consider leaving me a review on Goodreads or Amazon. For your copy of the extended epilogue, be sure to join my Newsletter at drethianis.com

AFTERWORD

Thank you for giving me a chance by reading this book. Remember to join my Newsletter drethianis.com or my Facebook group for an extended epilogue on the duo. If you enjoyed Sara and Tristan's story, consider leaving me a review on Goodreads or Amazon. as your word of mouth helps me grow.

ABOUT THE AUTHOR

Drethi Anis is a dark, contemporary author and prefers to write anti-heroes. Drethi's stories will always have angst, obsession, and a dark twist. Though toxic love and darkness are major players in her books, romance is still a priority.

Stay tuned for future releases by signing up for her Newsletter. Connect with the author directly on her Facebook Group, Instagram, or Linktree.

Made in the USA
Monee, IL
13 November 2024

70051592R00177